QUEEN OF
DARKNESS

Blood & ... ce)

A Soulbound ...cers Novel

Riley Storm

Queen of Darkness

Copyright© 2021 Riley Storm

Edited by Olivia Kalb – https://www.oliviakalbediting.com/

Cover Designs by Jacqueline Sweet Covers

TABLE OF CONTENTS

CHAPTER ONE

"Look out!"

At my shouted warning, Aaron ducked, dropping his shoulder and rolling underneath the tentacle-like arm of our Plant-Fae attacker. The green leaves twisting off the ends of the long appendage narrowly missed the master vampire, but its millions of tiny barbs left the barest of scratches down the back of his suit, shredding his fine Italian silk with ease.

I knew he'd be sour about that.

"How do we stop this thing?" he called back, dodging to the side as another leafy attack came whistling at him.

"Working on it," I muttered as the Plant-Fae whirled on me and lashed out with two of its "arms."

I flung myself away, anticipating the strike. The sentient tree-trunk-like Fae was dangerous, but it had a habit of giving away its attacks. Its four yellow, oval eyes blinked angrily at me from where they sat about eight feet up the trunk, and it tried to strike me again.

I grunted as the vine slammed into my stomach, knocking the wind from me while flinging me across the street.

"Ow," I wheezed, getting to my feet as fast as I could.

I wasn't fast enough. The vine snaked around my feet and up my calves, its barbs tearing at my skin, opening a million tiny cuts as it slowly tightened.

I reached around frantically for something, *anything*, to use, and my fingers closed around the slatted grates of the storm drain sewers at the edge of the curb. I gripped tightly as the Plant-Fae tried to haul me in closer, to where its shorter vine-tentacles could grasp me. I didn't know what the whirling mass of them hid, but I doubted I wanted to find out either.

"A little help here!" I shouted at Aaron, wishing the vampire would hurry up and do something to distract our attacker.

"Working on it," came his reply, uttered word for word like my earlier response.

"Very funny, but work faster! This thing seems rather determined to collect my stupid Blood Letter! I'd rather it didn't."

My fingers squeezed tighter around the sewer

grate as the Plant-Fae hauled back, trying to pull me toward it.

"I don't think so," I growled, staring at it. "My life is my own."

Although it was by far the weirdest thing to come after me in the past two weeks, it certainly wasn't the first. A Blood Letter had been put on my head, and all manner of bounty hunters were out there trying to collect the reward for killing me and bringing proof of it to the Bounty Hunter's Guild.

At least I didn't warrant a huge bounty, thanks to being a relative unknown in the paranormal world. That meant I didn't have to fear any of the truly scary bounty hunters. It simply wasn't worth their time.

But this one seems particularly persistent, I observed.

Something heavy came flying out from the far side of the street, slamming into the Plant-Fae and causing it to loosen its grip on me. While it recovered from the attack of the flying landscaping stone courtesy of Aaron, I yanked on the sewer grate, lifting it. Then I scrambled a few feet away from the Plant-Fae.

"Take *this!*" I screamed, just as the creature started to tighten its hold on my legs again, and slammed the grate closed with every ounce of strength my mutant vampire-shifter heritage granted me.

The metal whipped down, slicing *through* the vine-like arms as it *clanged* back down.

The Fae went berserk, whipping vine-arms around everywhere, while tree-sap-like blood leaked from its severed arms, splattering everything and everyone.

"Ew!" Aaron exclaimed as he came to my side, trying to flick the sticky droplets off him. "That is *not* going to wash out."

"Your suit is destroyed anyway. Stop bitching," I said, untangling the dead ends of the vines from my legs and getting to my feet as blood dripped down my bare legs.

Thankfully, my own blood didn't spur any reaction from my vampire heritage, or I would have been in a tough spot just then.

"How do we stop this thing?" I asked as the Plant-Fae recovered and turned toward us.

"Same way you deal with any weed," Aaron said, brandishing a pair of hedge clippers he must have found alongside one of the abandoned houses in this section of my hometown of Seguin.

"I'm not sure that weed killer from the hardware store is going to be strong enough for this," I said as we split apart, a vine whipping through the space between us.

Aaron became a blur as he moved, and the hedge clippers sliced down like oversized scissors, severing the vine.

"No need," he said before breaking the locking pin that held the two pieces together and handing me one. "We'll cut it out."

I snagged the clipper handle in mid-air, looking at the eight-inch blade and then at the Plant-Fae. Then back at Aaron. "*This* is your grand plan?" I asked, spinning away from another attack even as the Plant-Fae came at us, its remaining six vine-tentacles preparing for an attack.

"You got a better one?" he challenged.

I didn't, so we put the blades to work. Whirling and ducking, we avoided its strikes as best we could and hit back when the opportunity arose. Two more vines fell before the Plant-Fae screeched in alarm and began to retreat, its root-like feet carrying it up and onto the lawn, where they found better purchase, and it moved away faster.

"I think we encouraged it not to come back," I observed.

"Time to make sure it doesn't come back." Hauling back his arm, Aaron held his half of the clippers like a javelin. Taking several steps forward, he flung it with all his considerable might.

The blade wobbled mightily in midair, but it stayed true, burying deep into the trunk of the retreating creature. It shrieked again, slapping at the embedded object with several vines until the clipper arm came free. Then it disappeared into the night, leaving the two of us to recover.

"Well, that was certainly a rush," Aaron said, smiling broadly.

"It's too much," I said tautly, without any humor. "This can't go on. As long as I still have a Blood Letter on my head, they'll keep coming after me. The only one who can stop it is the Vampire Queen."

"Jo …"

I stared at Aaron. "I'm going after her."

CHAPTER TWO

"Jo, we've been over this! Going after Elenia is madness. It's crazy!"

"So is sitting around and letting bounty hunter after bounty hunter come to Seguin and wreak havoc! Eventually, someone strong enough is going to take notice and come for me. What then, Aaron?"

"This is madness," the vampire growled, blue eyes flashing in the dusky light. "You can't just go kill the Vampire Queen, Jo."

"Why not?" I shouted back. "She might be immortal, but that's not the same thing as being invincible. She *can* be killed, and I intend to do just that. This nonsense needs to stop! People are being hurt because of it. I can't keep letting them put themselves in harm's way for me."

Aaron sighed, running a hand through his blond hair. He'd cut it shorter recently, and the gesture was a remnant of when it had been several inches longer.

"You're right about us not staying here," he acknowledged. "We should go. Right now, they know where to find you. We should leave. I can hide you, Jo. I can protect you."

Clenching my hands into fists, I turned away from him. Aaron had a major crush on me. Maybe more than a crush, I didn't know. He wanted to claim me, whatever that meant as a vampire. I didn't know, nor had I asked. I wasn't sure I *wanted* to know. After all, I was still trying to come to terms with the fact that I was a vampire myself.

All my life, I'd thought I was a shifter. As it turned out, my mother had passed on both wolf genes and blood-sucking monster genes. I was the lucky lottery winner of a life full of being a monster who needed blood to survive. Although I couldn't deny that there was something between Aaron and me, romance wasn't particularly high on my "give a shit" list lately.

I had bigger problems to worry about. Like the inner demon in me and the fact that the Vampire Queen had put out a virtual "wanted" poster on me, but without the "or alive" part. She simply wanted me *dead*.

"What is it, Jo?"

"What is it?" I asked, not sure he grasped the incredulity of the question. "Maybe it has something to do with the fact that I'm an immortal vampire-shifter. And also, I'm a woman. Thanks to your queen, that's a combination that results in only one outcome. My gruesome death. A death she's willing to stake a good amount of money on."

"Jo …"

"I can't keep running, Aaron," I told him point-blank, letting him look into my jade eyes and see my resolve, my determination. Letting him see that I meant business. "Not anymore."

"Going after her is insane."

I shook my head. "Two weeks ago, I let you talk me out of going after her. That was what was insane. This could all be over now."

"Or you could be dead," he pointed out. "Which, I might add, is a far more likely outcome right now."

"Thanks for your support." I glared at him.

"If there were any hope of success, I'd be the first one to go," he said hotly, angered by my insinuation that he wouldn't be there for me. "But we already snuck into her palace once. Well, you did to rescue me, but the point still stands. She thought she was unassailable behind the walls. That she couldn't be reached. Now you've shown her otherwise. She's going to have pulled back her elites. The palace will be infested with them. Can't you see that?"

"I can see that," I said, nodding. "But I also

know that I can't just sit around, Aaron. I have to actually *do* something, and I need you to see that."

"I'm saying we do something. We leave. Find somewhere she won't find us. Hell, if Fenrir could hide for hundreds of years, so can we."

"No," I said firmly. "I have to stop it. I have to find a way. If I start running and hiding now, then I'm going to have to run for my entire life. This stupid Blood Letter will be hanging over my head for decades, centuries even, like the Sword of Damocles. Nowhere will be safe for me. Or anyone around me."

"So, what, you'd rather go and die just to do something? Is that it?" Aaron asked, his temper quite visibly fraying. "You'd rather just leave me?"

I frowned at him. "Is *that* what this is all about? You think I'm doing this because I don't want to be with you? That I don't want to go off with you?"

"It certainly feels that way."

"*Argh!*" I shouted, clenching my fists so tightly that my fingernails started to jab into my palms. "You arrogant, idiotic *moron!* I can't let myself *be* with you if I'm always going to be looking over my shoulder, fearing that someone will come after me. How am I supposed to let down my guard if I have to always watch out for an attack that I can't see coming?"

Aaron didn't have a response to that.

"Three bounty hunters have come after us in the last two weeks, ever since Bianca died," I said.

Bianca, a mage imbued with considerable power from an elder god, had been the first hunter to come after me. She'd only been stopped through a lot of luck and the sacrifice of more good shifters than I cared to think about. The funerals had only finished two days ago.

"And we dealt with both of them," Aaron pointed out. "The two of us."

"Yes, we did. But we won't always," I said, quietly but firmly putting my foot down. I was done arguing. "Eventually, someone will come for us that we *can't* deal with, Aaron. That's why I have to go to her. That's why I have to find a way to end this now, while I still can. Even if that means she has to die."

"Jo–" he started to protest, but I shook my head, short hair bouncing everywhere.

"No, Aaron," I said, my voice dull, flat. Devoid of emotion. "I'm going after the queen. I'm putting an end to this. If you can't support that, then you'll just have to stay here."

I didn't wait for a response. I turned on my heel and walked away. Before I left, I would have to pay my respects to the Alpha and let him know I was departing. His town, and my pack, would be safe now. No more attacks would come their way.

As I walked, I pulled up my memories of Queen Elenia's throne room from my first visit to Madrigal, the city of vampires. I pictured her sitting there, tall and lithe, her dull reddish hair falling down her back, black eyes alert and aware.

I'm coming for you, I snarled at the memory. *And I won't stop until one of us is dead.*

CHAPTER THREE

My anger began fading as I approached Aldridge Manor, the home of our pack leader and the pack's central hub. Replacing it was a burning sense of purpose. I finally had something to direct my energy and anger toward, something that could actually result in some good coming into the world.

Good that would combat the negative of what I'd become. A monster who had to feed for all eternity. My fingers played with one of the vials of blood I kept on me at all times to ensure that I wouldn't cede control to the Hunger and go off the rails.

Aaron has been doing this for who knows how long. The rest of his team has been doing it for centuries as well. If they can do it, so can I.

Maybe. But that didn't mean I liked it.

The three-story manor house sitting at the top of a slow-rising driveway from the road was no longer the dark, imposing thing it had been under our former Alpha. Now, it was bright and almost welcoming. Lights were on everywhere, and some people even wandered the grounds talking quietly amongst themselves.

Johnathan really has come into his own, I observed, my lips quirking upward. I certainly hadn't expected it of him, but when his father was killed and the torch passed to him, Johnathan had well and truly stepped up to the plate.

I exchanged nods with a pair of guards making their rounds and headed up the wide stone steps to the front door, letting myself in. Turning left, I strode down the hallway, the thick runner rug covering up the rich hardwood underneath, dulling the sounds of my boots.

"Is he still working?" I asked a shifter while I passed his desk.

"Hey, Jo. Um, yes, he's in there."

I paused. Something in the speaker's tone rang like a warning bell. "What is it, Kyler?"

The other wolf shifter sighed, biting his lip before looking up at me. I nearly gasped at how *young* he looked. We were the same age, but his face was full of a youth and exuberance that I didn't see when I looked in the mirror.

And innocence. This one hasn't seen what you've seen, journeyed where you've been. He hasn't felt death like you have.

19

Good. I hoped he wouldn't have to. I didn't wish what I'd been through on anyone. Nobody deserved to find out they were a monster.

"There's something you should know," the young-looking shifter said at last, having made up his mind. "But you didn't hear it from me. I know Johnathan was going to tell you himself."

"What is it?" I growled, growing impatient with waiting. Whatever it was, it was bad news, and drawing out the delivery would only make it worse. Just rip the bandage off and be done with it.

"We lost two more," Kyler said quietly. "That plant thing ripped through a house on its way in."

I didn't react.

Two more of my pack. Dead. All because they'd been at home. Where it should have been safe. And that *thing* had just killed them while trying to get to me. I was the real target, but they had paid the price.

"Get me their names, please," I said softly.

If Kyler replied, I didn't hear it. I was already moving down the hallway again, lost in a fog of self-hatred. Why did *others* have to pay the price for what I was? Too many had already laid their lives down for me. The pack was paying a horrific price, and all that blood landed on my hands and my hands alone.

"Come in," came a strong, masculine voice when I knocked on the door at the end of the hall.

I pushed open the heavy wooden door and entered the Alpha's office. Johnathan sat at his big L-shaped desk across the room, situated in front of a giant bay window that ran from floor to ceiling. Curtains were pulled over the windows, but I knew the view was amazing, showcasing the forest behind Aldridge manor. The sunsets certainly made it worthy of a working office.

"There were more," I said bluntly, coming to a stop a respectful distance from the edge of the desk. "I heard."

"Yes," Johnathan said with a sigh, looking up from the paperwork. His eyes were a deep, regal blue, unlike Aaron's bright sparks of sapphire. Normally they were strong and determined, but right now, they looked tired.

"All because of me."

The Alpha didn't look away, but he didn't deny it either.

"I want to thank you for coming to my aid," I said slowly. "When the mage attacked here, Aaron and I, we would be dead if it weren't for you and the pack. I owe you my life."

"*I* would do it again," Johnathan said.

The emphasis on the word could not be missed by even the most oblivious. He had chosen that word on purpose. I. Not "we."

"But not the others?" I asked quietly, starting to wonder if this conversation was going in a different direction than I'd intended.

"I won't ask them to," he said. "The pack has already sacrificed so much. We were already weakened by what my father did to us. When he and his enforcers died, our strongest were ripped from us. They'd been the ones in power, the ones who knew all the secrets. Then when the mage attacked, we lost many more to her and the vampires."

I nodded, not sure of what else to say. Johnathan spoke only the truth. The pack had suffered much, with little to show for it.

"Asking them to shoulder any more responsibility would make me a bad Alpha," he said. "Though, I swear to you, if you need me, I will be there for you."

"Thank you," I said quietly, though I hoped fervently never to have to take him up on that offer.

"I will also ensure your mother and father are protected. They will have guards until this is all sorted out."

A heavy sigh slipped through my lips as a tiny bit of the weight on my shoulders lifted. "Thank you," I repeated. "I appreciate that."

"They are part of the pack, and we protect our own," Johnathan growled, demonstrating yet again that he was the right choice for Alpha. "You needn't fear for them anymore."

I nodded slowly as we finally came to the point of the entire conversation. The undertones had been there from the very start, but we'd addressed everything else. There was nothing more to do but put it out in the open.

"You want me to leave." It wasn't a question.

Johnathan looked away, and for the first time, I could sense his shame for even desiring such a thing.

"I will not ask it of you," he stated emphatically, finally meeting my eyes. "I will not banish you from your pack. From your hometown."

He might not cast me out, but it was clear in his eyes that he hoped I would go of my own accord. Johnathan was too proud to ask because I was part of the clan. We were only a few years apart in age, and he had once dated my best friend in the entire world. That accounted for something, but it was obvious to both of us that this was beyond the pack.

"I understand," I said softly, swallowing back the quiver in my voice.

The first domino was falling. I was being asked to leave to keep the pack safe. Johnathan made it clear that it was only temporary. That was why he'd said he would protect my parents "until it was all sorted out." Once I was no longer a danger to the pack, then they would welcome me back.

But in the meantime, I needed to go.

I'd already been planning on it, but choosing to leave versus being told you're no longer welcome are two different things. If I needed a place to stay or to lay low, I couldn't return.

Not until the Vampire Queen was dead. Or I was.

I'm going to need to find my own way now.

That wasn't going to be easy. Word was getting around now about who I was. The Blood Letter was an open call for bounty hunters to come after me. I would have to start over. Make a new identity and find a place to hide.

And there was only one person I knew who could do that for me.

CHAPTER FOUR

"Hey, Mom," I whispered, sitting down gently in the ancient white chair next to her bed.

My mother lay under the covers, staring at the ceiling, unseeing. I often wondered what was going on in her brain all this time. Did she hear and understand the outside world but couldn't respond? Or did her drugs prevent her from having any coherent thoughts?

No, she must have some idea. Some cognitive awareness. Otherwise, how would she have managed to come down the stairs and start yelling at Aaron when he first came to the house.

'First came to the house.' That made it sound like it had been forever and a day ago, but in reality, it had been a little over a month, nothing more. It felt like so much longer. Everything that I'd seen and done, crammed into these past few weeks, had aged me years, decades even. To step back and think about it seemed impossible.

Sighing, I returned my focus to the woman on the bed. She didn't look frail; her shifter heritage kept her looking healthy and normal, despite the vacant look in her eyes. Her hair was cut short to help my dad manage it better, and she was dressed in a plain white nightgown, as always.

"I have to go now," I continued, talking to her like she could understand me. "I can't stay here. I can't just try to hide and do nothing. I have to try to *stop* this. To keep you safe."

There was no response, but I hadn't expected one either.

"You're going to be free of this," I whispered. "I'm going to kill her, Mom, and then, I'm going to take her place. I'm going to prevent anyone from coming after you. We'll learn how to deal with our demons *together*. No more pills. You'll be you again."

I smiled at her. "I can't wait to meet you. The real you."

To my shock, my mother's head turned slowly toward me. She stopped partway, unable to complete the move, but for an instant, just an instant, our eyes locked.

"Mom?" I gasped, realizing that we were making eye contact, and she *knew* it.

She blinked. Twice.

It wasn't much. It was practically nothing. But

it was also everything in the world to me. She *knew* me. She understood what I was saying.

The awareness faded, replaced once more by the distant stare, but it didn't matter. The woman I wanted to meet, the one my father had fallen in love with, was still in there. She was just trapped by the effects of the drugs. Drugs she'd made my father swear never to take her off of. He hadn't known why at the time, but we did now.

And I was going to ensure he could break that promise.

"I'll see you soon, Mom," I said, leaning over to kiss her on the forehead before getting up and heading for the door, where I paused to look back at her. "You and I have a lot to catch up on."

Then, I left, pulling the door closed behind me and heading down the stairs to say my most difficult goodbye.

My father was waiting, and he swept me up into his arms without preamble.

"Are you sure you have to go?"

I stepped back from the embrace. "Yes, Dad. I can't stay here. It's too dangerous for everyone. Especially you and Mom. One bounty hunter already got to you guys, and I nearly lost you. I can't let that happen again. I just can't."

My dad looked unconvinced. "We're your parents, Jo."

"I know." My eyes flicked up the stairs in the

direction of my mother's room, where she lay in an almost comatose state due to the drugs she took.

Drugs that prevented her from shifting during the Wild Moon, keeping the darkness inside her at bay. A darkness that had been born into me and that had found its freedom three weeks ago. My vampire heritage was now loose on the world, making me a threat to everyone.

Especially Elenia, queen of all vampires. There was a rule in the vampire world that only females could sit upon the throne. A matriarchal society, which in theory sounded like a good idea. Except when a psychotic killer rises to power and begins killing off anyone who could ever become a rival to her throne.

It was now a royal decree that any female vampires must be killed. On sight. That was why my life was in danger, and my mother's would be, too, if she ever stopped taking her pills while Elenia was on the throne.

Which is why the queen has to die. For me, but also for my father, who has been deprived of his mate for twenty-two years and stuck caring for her, keeping her in that comatose state as per her last coherent wish. He deserves to be able to see her again.

And selfish as it might be, I wanted to meet my mom. I knew my mother, but I'd never met my *mom*, the person behind my mother. I wanted to know what she was like.

And I would.

"It'll be for the better this way, Dad, trust me."

"I do trust you, my dear Jo-Jo. I trust you completely. I just don't *like* it. This is your home. I'm your father. I should be able to keep you safe."

"And you did," I said with a sad smile, blinking back tears. "You kept me safe for twenty-two years. You protected me and taught me to be the woman I am today, Dad. All that I am is because of *you*."

Wordlessly, my father embraced me again. I let him.

"I wish I could do more for you."

"You've done so much for me already," I said, squeezing him tight. "But if you insist on doing more, then you can *believe* in me, Dad. I'm spreading my wings and making my own life. That comes with choices and decisions. Sure, maybe we both don't *like* them. But that doesn't mean I'm not doing it."

My dad loosened his grip but still held me by the shoulders so he could look at me. "I want you to know, Joanna Alustria, that no matter what you do, no matter what decision you make, I am proud of you and who you've become. I am proud of the strength you've shown through this trial. Most importantly, I want you to know that I love you. I'll always love you, no matter what you become."

Now it was my turn to hug him again as I furiously tried to stop the tears from falling down my cheeks.

"Even if I become the queen of the vampires?"

"Ha!" he boomed in his trademark laughter. "*Especially* then. Why, I'll basically be royalty at that point. Maybe they'll finally give me a discount down at the pub."

I groaned.

"Can you knight me? Is that a thing?"

"You're not actually a vampire, Dad. Be grateful for that," I pointed out, but I couldn't help my smile.

Trust my dad to find a way to lighten the mood when it grew overly dark. He was great at that.

"I know. But still. Gotta try."

We hugged again, and this time I took a step back, glancing around the interior of our little farmhouse where I'd grown up.

"Where's Aaron, by the way?" Dad asked, looking past me at the door. "He's not waiting outside, is he? He knows he's welcome."

I chewed on my lip. "No, Dad, he's not here. He and I ... I need to do this on my own. This is my problem to deal with."

My dad's eyebrows lowered in a frown. "You two get in a fight?"

I shrugged. "He thinks this is madness."

"Is he wrong?"

"No," I said. "I agree. But that doesn't mean I don't have to do it. This has to end. I've got to find a way to stop her. He'll come around. I hope."

My dad nodded slowly. "Bit of a lunkhead, that one."

I giggled.

"But smart," he added more seriously. "He'll come to understand eventually."

"I hope so." I sighed. "I should get going, though. I've already hung around later than expected."

"Okay. But first, one more hug."

I obliged and then headed for the door. "Take care of her, Dad. And of yourself."

"I will, dear," he said, following me, pausing in the open doorway as I made my way down the porch steps. "You take care of yourself as well. Come back safe."

I only nodded, not trusting myself to say anything more. That was one thing I couldn't promise. Not with the task that lay ahead of me.

Walking down the laneway to the road, I looked back over my shoulder and waved. A wave of cold descended over me as I took in the farmhouse and my father standing on the porch. The chill descended down my spine like a foreboding promise.

As if I would never see this place again.

CHAPTER FIVE

I stared across the cobblestone road from where I hid in the shadows, watching the front door of the nondescript house very carefully. Nobody had gone in or out of the aging brown bungalow for quite some time. Nor could I pick up any signs of movement from around the house itself.

It seemed as empty and abandoned as it had every other time I'd visited. Of course, I knew better because I knew what was beyond that front door. Magic was at work here, and it kept everything contained within.

Still, caution is warranted. Best not to leave any-thing to chance.

My prior visit to the Duke of Hamelin, better known simply as "The Broker," had been a rather abrupt and pointed meeting. I had entered and effectively bullied my way into a meeting with him. Although he hadn't said anything at the time, I knew that another such entrance would not be forgiven.

For all I know, he's put out word that I'm no longer welcome.

It was that fear that kept me crouching in the shadows, looking across the road. I wanted to see if anyone was waiting to ambush me. I was on my own now, and I had to be cautious. I couldn't be seen as weak, but neither could I simply waltz into a place as widely used as the Broker's without surveying it first.

My legs began to ache from staying immobile for so long. I knew I had to get going. The longer I sat there, the more time I gave those trying to track me down. I needed to get in there and try to finagle a meeting with the Broker. With his help, I could disappear and begin to formulate a way to eliminate Elenia.

Eliminate. Such an uncaring way of talking about killing someone. Cold and sterile, like an assassin.

I shook my head. That wasn't me. Was it? If the opportunity came for me to pull the trigger and end her threat forever from a distance, would I turn it down just because it wasn't a fair fight? Did that actually matter to me?

Probably not.

"You're stalling," I whispered to myself, getting up from my crouch.

Giving my legs a moment to resume proper blood flow, I took one last look around, making sure nothing had changed. Then, I crossed the road and slipped inside.

The instant I crossed the threshold, my senses were assailed by an abrupt change. The light inside was bright and vibrant, the long, slim hallway lit by numerous fluorescent bulbs in the ceiling. On top of that, music pulsed rhythmically, courtesy of the invisible band farther inside. That was probably the coolest use of magic I'd ever seen, and each time I came, I enjoyed it again.

I approached the end of the hallway. Already, I could see the top of the silver ball that floated high above the bar at the center of the circular room. Lights bounced off its surface as it spun slowly on top of a waterfall cascading down the sides of a display.

A smile creased my face. This place was starting to feel almost homey to me. I'd been here so often, it seemed, and I was now beginning to know what to expect from it. Some of the fear of the unknown was fading.

"You shouldn't be here."

I started, coming to a sharp halt as a tall, human-looking male swept around the corner, a silky white cloak billowing out behind him.

"Hello, Decan," I said warily, greeting the personal steward and bodyguard of the Broker with an abundance of caution.

I'd learned the hard way during my last visit that though he may *look* human, he certainly wasn't. Not entirely, at least.

"Joanna." He doffed his top hat and bowed slightly, giving me a polite greeting. "You should go."

For a moment, I found myself wishing that Aaron was with me. I needed someone to steady me, to keep me even at this unexpected turn of events. While I hadn't been planning for the red carpet to be rolled out, I certainly wasn't expecting to be *banished* before I'd barely entered.

Aaron would also be able to use his clout. He'd spent centuries building up his reputation, and people were reluctant to turn him away for any reason. I could certainly use some of that right now.

"Sorry, Decan, I can't do that," I said, forcing myself to stand up to him.

Decan hesitated.

If nobody else were there to do it for me, I would have to do it on my own. After all, I'd left Aaron behind. That meant I was going to need my *own* clout now. My own reputation. I was no weakling. He wasn't about to push me around. It was time I demanded some respect.

Just don't push it. You don't want to come off as a mouthy asshole, either. Just confident.

"I'm afraid I must insist," Decan said, his eyes darting around, refusing to stay on me for long as if simply *knowing* I was there was enough to burn him.

"Are you going to toss me out?" I asked.

Decan chewed on his lip, decidedly unhappy that I refused to leave. Considering that he hadn't tried to use force, I had to wonder if he'd stop me if I pushed past him.

Only one way to find out.

Steeling myself, I moved to the side and eased past Decan. I wasn't going to bother pausing at the railing. I knew what was down there. The circular bar at the center of the bottom floor would be packed with all sorts of people, as would the standing and sitting tables nearby. Even the second level with its tables overlooking the floor below would be full.

There was never any empty space at the Broker's. It was a place to see and be seen. It didn't operate on any set hours, as far as I was aware. It was simply always open. There was always the dull roar of numerous background conversations. It gave the sense of being *alive*.

That sense was missing now. I paused to scan the bar, trying to find what was missing. People were everywhere as always. The instruments still played themselves, their tune as lively as ever. I couldn't pick anything out as wrong.

Yet something *was* off.

I continued along, keeping the railing to my left as I slowly walked the circular balcony of the top floor. My senses were on high alert, and I was ready for anything, from someone jumping me to attacking me at a distance and everything in between. My hackles were up, and my wolf sensed it, too.

Danger.

Making it to one of the stairwells, I followed the spiral steps down, placing each foot with care.

"Don't go out there."

I paused as I reached the ground floor. The stairwell spit me out near the end of a hallway. To my left was the bar floor. To the right were other doors that I figured were offices.

"What's going on, Decan?" I asked, crossing the hallway before turning, keeping a firm wall at my back. "I'm here in peace. I want to make a deal, that's all."

"You should go," he said. "Now."

Shaking my head, I walked down the hallway away from the bar. "I can't do that, Decan. I've come to bargain. A good bargain, just like he'll want. You know he likes to deal."

"Please, Miss Alustria," Decan said, the first word a barely audible whisper. "Go. Now."

I paused and regarded Decan. "That's not an

order. You're not throwing me out."

Decan pushed past me, walking farther down the hallway to a random door. He glanced at it forcefully as I slowly followed him, moving farther away from the activity behind us. "Take this exit. Trust me."

Exit? I'd thought the ground floor held only offices. Not doors to different places. What separated the floors, I wondered? And where did this door go?

Despite my curiosity, I couldn't let myself give in to temptation. What I *needed* to do was figure out why the heck Decan was trying to get me to leave. His methods were unusual, given his more *forceful* nature. If he were anyone else, I'd have said he was trying to help me.

Had I pissed off the Broker somehow, and Decan was trying to help me avoid his wrath? Was that it? Yet he'd arrived quite swiftly to block my path after I'd entered. Almost like he'd known I was outside and had been waiting for me to come inside finally.

"What the hell is going on here, Decan?" I asked. "Something is wrong. What is it? Why do you want me to go so badly?"

Decan stiffened.

"Because," a cold voice said from behind me, "he doesn't want to get in trouble for helping you."

CHAPTER SIX

Recognizing the voice, I spun, hackles rising.

She was walking down the hallway with steps so smooth that it looked like she was floating. A wave of cold preceded her, and goosebumps rose on my arms.

My teeth bared in challenge, and my wolf and I growled a warning at the tall, lithe woman, her height forcing us to look up ever so slightly. She played the psychological advantage to the max, drawing herself up to her full height as she came to a stop. After nearly eight hundred years as the ruler of all vampires, Queen Elenia had certainly learned how to project her status to those around her.

"Relax," she said, taking in my hostile stance, waving her right hand at me dismissively, as if I were no more than one of her subjects to be commanded. "This is neutral ground."

Her casual arrogance and air of expectation astounded me. My jaw dropped open, and I simply stared. Did she really expect me just to face her and have a civil conversation? This was the woman who had put a *death warrant* on my head!

"Well, come now, pull yourself together, woman. Stop staring at me like you're some sort of imbecile. Honestly, child, it's embarrassing for the both of us." She *tsked* at me like an irritated mother.

I tensed, ready to go for her throat, but a hand on my shoulder stilled me.

"This is not the place for that," Decan said, the warning clear.

"Relax," Queen Elenia commanded once more. "I will not partake in any violence here. I do not wish to offend the Broker. Much as I want this one dead, his long-term favor is more important."

"If only you had that level of caring for, oh, I don't know, *anyone* else," I snapped.

The queen glared at me, her eyes darkening with fury at my impudence. I didn't care. She needed to know that not everyone would grovel before her.

"I wouldn't worry about it," she said with false sweetness. "It won't be long before you're dead and of even less consequence to anyone."

"A grape is of little consequence until you

choke on it," I pointed out, wondering if it was a smart idea to make her more aware of me than necessary.

In the end, it probably didn't matter. The queen was already on alert after I'd raided her palace with Jaxton and the rest of Aaron's team. By stealing him *and* Fenrir from her clutches, she had to be well aware of who I was. Not to mention, she knew that I was also a vampire, having undergone my shift and my first feeding.

I was a rival to her throne, and she didn't like that. Not one bit. How long, I wondered, had it been since she had to contend with someone who aspired to take her down? I doubted she was used to that idea.

"This place might be off-limits," the queen finally replied, her supple red lips curving upward in a wicked smile, "but once you leave ..."

"You really aren't that good at making threats, are you?" I challenged, finding a burst of confidence as I realized she had to be *worried* about me if she'd signed a Blood Letter, of all things. She could have just dispatched some of her goons to kill me, but instead, she'd gone further than that.

It almost screamed of desperation. How ... *interesting.*

"Oh, I'm very good at it," she spat back, her eyes flashing with fury.

"Then I guess nobody told you that spoiling

the ambush is a terrible way to ensure I walk into it. They're supposed to be a *surprise*."

Veins popped in her neck as Elenia fought to restrain herself. "Oh, don't worry, it will be far less obvious than you expect."

I turned to look at Decan. "She really doesn't get it, does she?"

Decan looked on impassively, refusing to comment or participate in the confrontation, staying only to step in if any violence broke out. Complete neutrality, nothing more, was all I could expect from him.

"Don't bother turning to him for help," Elenia gloated. "He won't be able to assist you. Will you, Decan, darling?"

I saw a tiny tremor make its way down Decan's spine. Was that from fear? Fury? Or something else? Judging by the slight narrowing of his eyes, I thought it was more likely fury. Elenia certainly had a way with people.

"I asked you a *question*," Elenia hissed into the silence that followed.

A wave of frost spread out from her, stiffening the fabric of my clothing and causing my hair to stand on end. Fighting back a shiver, I glared at her, wishing yet again that I could rip her throat out where she stood, putting an end to all this.

"The deal is done," Decan ground out through clenched teeth.

Definitely fury. He hates her as much as I do, it seems.

"Good. Then, as per the terms of our agreement, neither you nor your boss is to provide her with any assistance. Is that understood?"

Decan's face turned dark with anger. "I do not take orders from you," he rumbled ominously. "Do not presume you can command me."

I prepared to step aside, not wanting to be in the path of Decan's visibly mounting fury. He'd hit me once before and knocked me flat to the ground with ease. I didn't wish to get on his bad side. However, if Elenia wanted a go at him, she was more than welcome. I would gladly watch that.

"You signed an agreement," Elenia growled. "You are bound by it."

Decan stepped forward. "I am bound by my oath to my liege," he snarled. "*Not* to you. If you so much as *speak* to me again, I will have you thrown from here. In pieces."

Along the hallway, doors opened as men stepped out in near unison. They stared at the vampire queen with dark expressions. Although they looked human, I knew better. They were operating under faery glamours to disguise their appearances.

I kept my eyes on Elenia's face. It was quite enjoyable to watch her quiver with rage. I doubted she was used to being dismissed like that. Even peers of the other realms usually had more respect for her than what Decan had just shown.

Elenia recognized the danger, and yet, she still hesitated.

"If you attack me," Decan warned, breaking into a wide smile at complete odds with his words, "that is the same as attacking the duke. Do you really want to do that?"

"*Hmph*," the queen said with an aristocratic sniff before turning on her heel and striding away without another word.

Decan gestured at the men in the hallway, and as one, they stepped back through their respective doors, letting her pass.

"God, I hate dealing with her," Decan grumbled as she turned the corner and disappeared.

"You and me both," I said, glancing up at him. "But what's this deal she's talking about?"

Decan's face hardened. "Come. I will take you to the Duke. I suspect he will want to see you now."

He stepped past me without another word, his long legs forcing me to hurry to keep up with him. As we walked, I thought furiously about everything I'd just learned. I was getting what I wanted. A meeting with the Broker. That was a good thing, wasn't it?

So why did I suddenly have a very bad feeling

about my plan?

CHAPTER SEVEN

Decan ushered me into Duke Hamelin's office.

"I'll go find him," he said once he observed the empty, black-stained desk against the wall to my left. "Have a seat. This shouldn't take long."

I nodded but didn't sit down. At that point, I was too antsy to be still. The queen had come here and made a deal with the Broker about me. A deal she'd gotten Duke Hamelin to sign, stating that he would not aid me in any way? I grimaced. She had anticipated me, it seemed. How, I couldn't know, but she'd known that I would come here, seeking help, and she'd sought to cut me off from it.

All that remained now was to find out just how good a job she'd done. After all, I knew Duke Hamelin loved a good bargain. He was a stickler for following the letter of the law. Not so much the spirit of it. If I could find a way around that, then perhaps I could still extract some help from him.

While I waited for either Decan to return or the Broker, I looked around the office, though my eye repeatedly returned to the glass case sitting on a shelf behind the desk. Sitting on a plush cushion inside was some sort of old-fashioned instrumental pipe. It was old and carved from simple wood. I had my suspicions about what it signified about the Duke of Hamelin, but I didn't dare ask.

The rest of the office was rather plain. There were two filing cabinets to the left of the pipe's shelf, while the right side was empty space. I knew there was a secret door worked into that wall, but I couldn't discern its outline. I didn't dare inspect it, lest I run the risk of being right in front when the duke emerged.

Several framed paintings of various landscape scenes covered the rest of the walls. The office was plain but functional. Nothing more. It provided no further insights into who the duke was or what he liked. The man was a mystery.

The main door swung open, and the Broker entered, forced to duck his head low below the door frame. Most people I encountered were taller than me. Some even loomed over me. But the Duke was one of the few who truly *towered* over me. Closer to eight feet than seven, his thin form was all legs and arms.

"Miss Alustria," he rumbled as he settled behind his desk, the pure black ovals of his eyes resting on me, the lack of an iris unsettling as always.

"Duke Hamelin," I replied politely, bowing my head slightly in respect, noting where he'd entered.

I wondered at that. Why had he come from there and not whatever secret rooms were hidden behind the door in the wall? What did that mean? The previous times I'd met with him, the Duke had already been seated or had entered from behind the wall. Just what had he been doing when Decan found him?

"Thank you for seeing me," I said before he could speak more. "I would first like to apologize for the brusqueness of my prior visit."

The Duke waved one hand at me, his creepily long fingers much too big for the size of his hands or even his body. "All is forgiven. However, I do not believe I can do any further business with you. In fact, all I can offer is to see you safely out. After that ..."

"I'm already aware that she'll be waiting for me," I said, acknowledging his unspoken point.

"Indeed. There are only a few exits available to you," the Duke said. "And she will know them."

That was another interesting piece of information. I couldn't just use any old exit, it seemed. Was that part of his deal or because of some other reason? Perhaps due to the exit locations? I simply didn't know.

"So, why did you agree to her deal? Did she threaten you into not helping me?"

For one moment, the Duke was something I'd never seen before. Speechless. He stared at me with such incredulity that he didn't know how to respond. I braced myself, half expecting him to come over the desk and attack me for even suggesting such a thing.

Instead, he flung his head back and laughed. His entire body shook as the room filled with his laughter.

"Absolutely *not*," he said forcefully once he recovered, his customary neutral expression returning. "She is neither so brash nor so stupid. Not when there is a more natural solution to her problem."

"Natural solution?"

The duke spread his hands wide. "She paid me not to help you, of course. It was an offer I could not refuse."

"Well, shit," I muttered. "So, you can't help me with a new identity or somewhere to hide that's off-grid?"

He shook his head. "No. I am not to interfere."

I nodded slowly, considering his words. "Did she specify what exactly would constitute interfering?"

"She did." Duke Hamelin's face twitched ever so briefly as he realized where I was going. If his eyes were capable of conveying emotion, they probably would have indicated some amused humor, but as pure black as they were, I couldn't get a read at all.

"What did she say? Or can you not tell me?"

The duke appeared to think for a moment before a sly grin broke out, curving upward on his long, thin face. If I didn't know him better, I'd have been deeply unsettled by the look. However, having dealt with him before, I knew that Duke Hamelin was enjoying himself immensely.

As I said, he obeyed the letter, not the spirit.

"No, as a matter of fact, she did not. However, I am afraid it will do little to help you. She said to offer you no aid if you were to come asking for help."

"Were those her exact words?" I asked before he could continue.

Duke Hamelin paused just long enough to replay a memory in his head before he nodded. "Yes. She said, 'You will not offer her any aid if she comes asking for help. You will not provide her shelter or assistance in hiding or any items that can be used to harm me.' In this instance, 'me' is Queen Elenia and 'her' is, well, you, Miss Alustria. As you can see, it was quite specific."

I slowly smiled as he finished repeating the queen's orders back to me.

"So," I said slowly, "if I come to you, say, looking to *buy* information, you would be able to provide it? After all, I'm not *asking* for help. I'm offering to *pay* for information."

The Broker considered my words. "I cannot see why that would be an issue. Nothing is being provided for free. Nor did you ask for help. As long as you do not ask for information about where to hide or where to find items that could harm Queen Elenia, then you should be okay. A simple transaction is not off the table."

"I'm glad to hear that you're open for business as usual," I said, halting a broad grin from filling my face.

"What is it you wish to know?" he asked without preamble.

I had to restrain myself from leaning forward. "I want to know if anyone has ever successfully rid themselves of a Blood Letter without dying, and if so, how? Keep in mind, I'm talking about people who've done so without the originator of the letter taking it back. I want a loophole, a back door. That's the type of answer I want."

The duke grimaced at my clarifications. I knew he hated such specificity, but I didn't care. I wasn't going to waste my time or his. Not with Elenia butting in.

"That," he said after some thought, leaning back in his chair, steepling his fingers under his chin, "is *very* expensive information indeed. It would take an equally expensive payment."

I wondered just what it was he had in mind as payment. Would I even be able to come up with it?

"Are you sure you want to pay?" he asked when I didn't initially respond.

My stomach sank. He was clearly warning me that I would not like what he was asking for in return. Not that I was forced to pay. I could always choose not to hear his answer.

No, I can't. He has me trapped, and he knows it. I need to be rid of this stupid death warrant so that I can focus on Elenia and not have to watch out for random bounty hunters getting in the way of things. I don't have a choice.

"What is it going to cost me?" I asked, deflated.

A wicked smile came over his face, curdling my blood and nearly forcing me to take a step back at its dark promise. It was a stark reminder that while he might dislike Queen Elenia, he was definitely *not* my friend. I'd forgotten that at some point, but now it felt like I was getting a harsh reminder.

Slowly pulling one hand out from under his

chin, he pointed one pale, creepily long finger at my arm, where the bands were clasped around my biceps.

"Those."

CHAPTER EIGHT

"These?" I fingered the rings nervously.

Could I even give them away? The Rings of Kline were the relic of an ancient, long-dead shifter god. I didn't know much about Kline, the god of mind and body, but his rings had been all that stood between me and death on multiple occasions. To part with them would be … bad.

Are they even yours to give away? Vir gave those to you. They belonged to his brother. He was really just loaning them to you, wasn't he?

"A bargain must be made," Duke Hamelin said, prodding me in the face of my indecision. "I cannot accept less than what the information is worth."

"I doubt these are of equal value," I pointed out.

"Value is what someone assigns to something," the Duke replied. "To others, you might be correct. However, I suspect that to you, the information I can give will be just as important as these. If I'm wrong, however …"

I grimaced. He was right. I didn't have much of a choice. Without knowing how to get rid of my Blood Letter, I couldn't follow through with my plan of killing the queen. If she were dead, she couldn't cancel it. Meaning, for the rest of my life–which could be forever now that I was effectively an immortal vampire—I would be forced to defend myself from the threat of a bounty hunter.

I did not want, or need, that stress. The letter had to go.

"Very well," I said, my throat tight as I slid the first ring off my arm and placed it on his desk.

Vir would have to be okay with this trade. After all, he had told me to use them as I needed. If this were what I *truly* needed, then he would support that. Wouldn't he?

I didn't know. I could only hope.

I slid the other one off, placing it on the Broker's desk next to its twin, and a tremor wracked my body. I was really doing it. I was giving up one of my most powerful advantages.

Regret blossomed, and I lifted a hand, ready to reach out to take them back. Maybe I was making a mistake. Perhaps I should keep them and find another way.

Then how will I deal with the Blood Letter? I don't know anyone else who can help me with it.

"There," I said sharply, putting my hand back down, forcing myself past the indecision. I had to move forward, to start fixing my life, so that I could kill Elenia and take her throne.

Only then could my mother and I finally live in peace.

The Broker reached out and collected the rings, placing them with some care into a drawer in his desk. Once they were out of sight, he leaned forward. Due to his height and my lack of it, we were still nearly at eye level of one another.

"There is a loophole, as you say," he began. "Did you read the contract of the Blood Letter when you issued your own?"

"No," I said. I hadn't realized there *was* one. Mr. Orrin, the shadowy contact with the Bounty Hunters Guild, hadn't said anything about a contract. Only what I had to do to put out a Blood Letter.

Idiot! Of course, there has to be a contract. Something more to it. If you'd been thinking, you could have asked him and read it yourself.

I wondered if the Broker would go back on our deal now and give me the rings back. Unlikely, since he'd already revealed where I needed to look. If anything, he'd get angry at my attempt to renege.

"The fine print states that the bounty is collectible via body or blood."

"Blood?" I asked, the question popping out before my brain could catch up with my mouth.

"Well, of course. It is called a *Blood* Letter for a reason." The Broker grinned.

"That makes an annoying amount of sense," I hissed through clenched teeth.

He nodded. "The spirit—" He paused to cringe at the idea. "The *spirit* of the letter is that it must be paid via death, or the body of the person named."

"But that's not the only way, is it?" I asked eagerly, leaning forward.

At last, some positive news!

"No," Duke Hamelin agreed. "One may also pay by offering the required amount of their own blood. They must, of course, survive having that much blood drawn. They also must deliver it in person to the Guild less than twenty-four hours after the first drop is drawn. If they can do this, then the Guild will consider the letter canceled."

I burned that information into my mind. There was a way out. A way for me to get past the letter.

"Of course," the Duke continued, "Elenia will still want you dead. She will not stop just because you thwarted that one attempt on your life. I would expect her to increase her attempts to kill you after that. Assuming you survive."

"I know," I said. "But now I won't have to worry about any *other* unknowns appearing and trying to knock me dead."

"Your first worry should be surviving," he said ominously. "Everything else will be moot if you die during the attempt."

I eyed him warily. "Just how much blood are we talking here?"

"It varies by creature."

"And for someone like me?"

"A human is forty percent. A shifter is forty-five. There is no amount for one such as you, but I would go with fifty, just to be certain."

I goggled at him. Fifty percent of my blood?

"Over two liters," he confirmed to my wordless stare. "It will kill you."

"Unless," I said slowly, staring at the top of his desk and the drawers beyond, "you have a way to survive something like that. A way to bring yourself back to health."

My eyes were looking past the solid wood desktop to the contents of the drawer. Where the Rings of Kline, and their healing powers, now rested in the Broker's possession.

"Such a way would be beneficial indeed," he agreed, never once following my gaze or reaching for the drawer.

He knew what he'd done. Yet again, I was confronted by the fact that the Broker was *not* on my side. He was neutral. But that didn't mean he was oblivious. His demand had been on purpose.

"You tricked me," I accused, though I was angrier at myself for being so easily duped than anything else. I should have seen something like that coming.

The Duke of Hamelin stood abruptly, his black eyes hammering into me with the weight of all his power. I staggered backward a step before catching myself.

"I do *not* trick anyone," he said, his voice hard. "The bargain was made fair and square. You *chose* to accept it, and that is your prerogative. I did not force you to do anything."

I stood perfectly still. Never had I seen the Broker so pissed. I'd offended him with my comment.

"However," he said, leaning forward, "given your ... *extenuating* circumstances and, perhaps, my own personal desire to see you succeed, I will overlook it."

If you wanted me to succeed, why did you demand the rings as payment? You could have asked for anything else.

I had to remind myself that him wanting me to succeed didn't mean he would let himself be taken advantage of. The equality of the bargain.

"That being said," he continued, "this is the last of the hospitality I will extend you, especially after your previous visit to my place of business. It is time for you to leave, Miss Alustria."

I grimaced, but what choice did I have?

"Always a pleasure doing business with you," I said, nodding my head before showing myself out.

Decan was waiting in the hallway, but I ignored him for a moment as I tried to fight the sensation of walls closing in. I'd gotten an answer, but everywhere I went, I seemed to find myself banished.

What was I going to do next? I needed help. I just didn't know where I would find any.

CHAPTER NINE

"**C**ome, Miss Alustria," Decan urged after giving me a moment to absorb everything.

"Where are you taking me?" I asked warily, following him down the hallway, alert for a trap. My eyes darted to each door we passed. Would someone jump through and grab me? One of the queen's agents, perhaps?

"Simply showing you out. I wish I could do more to help you," he said apologetically.

"Thanks, Decan," I muttered. As we came to a stop at the end of the hallway, I surveyed the crowd of people in the bar, keeping solid walls on either side of me. I wasn't ready to venture out there among all the Broker's denizens. At least one of them had to be an agent for Queen Elenia.

"I do like you," he said. "You have come far since you first set foot in here, and for that, I commend you. It is unfortunate that I, too, must obey my liege and give you no further aid."

"Yeah, tell me about it. Seems to be the story of my life lately. 'We'd like to help, but we can't.'"

That wasn't fair, of course. Johnathan had said he would help me if he could. But he couldn't ask more of the pack in good conscience as the Alpha. How could I ask them to either? So many had already died for me. Pouting like I was then did nothing more than tarnish their memories. It was what it was, and I had to deal with that and move on, not sit around whining about it like a child.

It's time to grow up. So start acting like it.

"All of us serve a master other than ourselves," Decan said. "Whether we know it or not."

"Don't worry about it," I said, figuring he was apologizing again. "It's fine, seriously. I'm still allowed to stay here, aren't I?"

"Of *course*," Decan said, waving his arm at the bar in front of us. "You are not banished. Anyone in here that isn't employed by the Duke might be willing to help you. They are not bound by any contract."

"No," I said. "But odds are that some well-placed rumors about *why* she was here accompanied her presence. I bet everyone out there knows who I am and that I'm hands off."

"It does seem likely," Decan admitted.

"Yeah. I suppose I'll have to go. Just have to

find a way past her ambush first. Then, I'm home free."

There was only one place left for me to go, and I really did *not* want to go there. Dani and Vir would welcome me to their realm, the Direen, which was the ancient abode of the shifter gods, but I didn't want to intrude. My presence there would bring others to them, and with Dani being pregnant with the child of a god, I wasn't going to overstay my welcome.

But I needed to go *somewhere*.

Beside me, Decan visibly restrained himself from ... something.

"Everything okay?" I asked, glancing over my shoulder to ensure that it wasn't trouble.

"Of course. I simply thought that perhaps you might enjoy the drinks on the second floor better."

I glanced at him.

"It is merely a suggestion, of course," he said.

"The bartender there is pretty good at making drinks?"

Decan smiled. "Oh, yes. I think you might find the atmosphere to be more to your liking as well."

"Thanks," I said.

"Do not thank me," he said. "I did not do anything for you. I simply made a suggestion."

"Of course. As any reasonable host would do," I replied, keeping my face calm.

Decan bowed his head. "I must return to my liege now."

"Be well, Decan," I said, wondering if I'd ever see him again.

The Broker's right-hand man retreated down the hallway, leaving me to contemplate the bar. Neutral territory. The queen herself had said she wasn't going to make a move on me here. That she would wait for me to leave to attack.

So, how the hell do I turn that information to my advantage?

Starting with whatever was on the second floor that Decan wanted me to find seemed like the best option. I took a deep breath and stepped out into the bar, letting the full effect of the noise wash over me. I stuck to the edges, seeking the nearest set of stairs that would take me up a level.

"What is it that you wanted me to see?" I said to myself as I climbed the stairs, conscious of the number of eyes on me.

I could *feel* it. The entire bar knew who I was. Knew that I was untouchable. Conversations dulled or stopped entirely as I passed. Full tables of people glanced at me over the rim of their drinks, trying to be surreptitious and failing. All I needed now was a spotlight on me to complete the feeling of being center stage.

Reaching the second floor, I endured more of the same. Some openly stared at me, while others quickly looked away if they caught my eye. Purses and bags filled empty chairs at tables, indicating that I wasn't welcome at any of them. I'd been thoroughly ostracized.

Will this be my life from now on? I wondered as I started up the steps to the second floor, trying to seek out what Decan's hint meant. Was the queen's agent up here? Or maybe there was a secret exit she wasn't monitoring?

I glanced over the balcony railing to the main floor. Numerous eyes were averted, returning to their drinks or conversation partners. Rolling my eyes, I hung back from the edge, deciding to stick to the shadows.

What the hell had Decan been trying to tell me by saying the second-floor drinks were better? My eyes scanned the room as I walked, but I didn't note anything out of place. Everything seemed normal, and–

Hello, what do we have here?

A solitary figure ahead caught my eye. Hunched over, with a hood on, they sat at a table against the outer wall of the circular floor. Keeping very much to themselves. *Not* the ordinary for an establishment like this.

I refrained from making a beeline to them.

Instead, I continued on, trying to act like they didn't draw my attention. I stepped up to the bar, catching the bartender's attention, and ordered a water, which drew a sour look. Using the bar as a backrest, I swept my gaze across the room, not paying anyone special attention.

As if sensing my gaze, he looked up slightly.

I nearly gasped at the familiar taut face, brown eyes, and nose that had been broken at least once before without quite healing properly.

Steeling myself, I walked over to them and sat down.

"*Fred?*" I hissed under my breath. "What the hell are you doing here?"

"Hello, Jo," came the baritone. "How are you?"

"Um, been better," I said with a tense laugh. "But you know how it goes sometimes."

"I do." He looked at me, concern in his eyes. "I wasn't expecting to see you here. Alone."

The reference was pointed. He wanted to know where Aaron was.

"Didn't have much choice," I explained. "My options are slightly limited right now."

"That can happen," he says.

"What about you? How are you? Is everything okay? I haven't seen you in weeks. Not since you ran off in the Underworld, pursued by those hell-hounds or whatever."

Fred shrugged. "I told you I'd have to lay low for a bit until things calmed down."

"So, things are calm?"

"They were," he said, smiling to take the sting off his next words, "until you sat down."

"Sorry," I said. "I wasn't thinking."

"Don't worry about it."

"At least now I can thank you. For what you did, helping Aaron and me find Fenrir."

"You found him?"

"Eventually. It's a bit of a long story. We had to break him out of the queen's clutches. Turns out I'm like him. A hybrid. So, now the queen wants me dead."

"I heard about the Blood Letter."

"Yeah," I said. Fred wasn't being very chatty. "Do you want me to leave?"

"No, it's fine."

"All right. Well, I still owe you a thanks. Can I get you another drink?"

Fred waved it off. "I was just doing my job."

I frowned at him. "That wasn't a job. You volunteered to be chased by those things."

He shrugged. "Sure, it was. It's in my contract to Aaron."

"You people and your contracts," I said, wondering why they were so obsessed with the things. "What's so important about them? Aaron is always going on about them, too."

Saying his name brought flashes of pain to my stomach. I missed him. His solid presence and his awareness of this new world I was slowly discovering. A world that did not like what I was.

"Where is he?" Fred asked, ignoring my question.

"Seguin," I said. "We, um, had a bit of a fight. A disagreement, really."

Fred perked up slightly, worry filling his normally flat eyes. "Over what?"

I opened my mouth to say but hesitated as I was reminded of all the other patrons. "There are probably too many ears here for that," I said instead.

Following my train of thought, Fred nodded. "Okay, then, let's go back to Seguin and talk about it. It should be safe to move now."

I shook my head. "I can't. I need to lay low somewhere else for a bit. Figure some things out."

Fred grinned. "Well, how about that. Sounds like you came to the right person."

"Maybe," I said, wincing. "But there's one problem."

"Which is?"

"Elenia won't let me leave here alive. She has the exits watched, and the ones I can take are apparently well-guarded."

"She can't have them all guarded," Fred said. "Together, we can take more exits than you could survive alone."

"There'll still be someone watching for her," I pointed out, wondering how Fred's presence would open more doors.

Fred's face creased into a frown. "Good point. We need to convince her we've gone elsewhere. Which means finding her watchers here and dealing with them. I've already marked one. We just need to find the second."

I nodded, my spirits feeling buoyed. Maybe I wasn't as alone as I thought.

"So," I asked, hunching over the table, "what do we do?"

CHAPTER TEN

Simply walking up to Elenia's lookouts and breaking their necks was out of the equation. Even for Fred. Since we couldn't enlist the Broker's help—

"Wait a minute," I said, holding up a hand. "I might have an idea."

"You do?"

I nodded slowly, a smile playing over my face. "How's your relationship with the Broker?"

"Neutral, I think," Fred said slowly. "I've never met him. He stays out of my way; I stay out of his. Usually, I stay out here with the rest of the team when we've all come together. Why?"

"Well, Elenia told the Broker he's not allowed to help me out in any way. She paid him off."

"Damn," Fred whispered. "That's cold."

I shrugged. "I'm getting used to my avenues of help being cut off. I'll manage. That's not my point, though. She paid to ensure the Broker didn't help *me*. There's no reason *you* can't go ask him for help."

"He's not going to kill her reps for us," Fred said. "That's not his style."

"No, you're right," I said, biting back a grin. "But I bet he'd have no problem *identifying* them for us. So we can be sure that when we hit them, however we do it, we know we got them all."

Fred nodded. "I'll be right back, then. Good idea."

He slipped from his seat, hood pulled down low, and went up to the bartender. He ordered a drink and said something else to him. While the man behind the counter started fixing the drink, Fred waited patiently. Others came and went. Someone walked up and also ordered a drink. After a quick scan to assess their threat level, Fred didn't bother acknowledging them.

His drink made, he came back to the table and sat down.

"So, will he help us?" I asked.

"There are three inside," Fred said under his breath as he took a sip. "One per floor. Whoever she has posted on the main floor won't be an issue. He can't see us leave. Which means we just have to deal with two of them."

I stared at him, unable to hide my shock. "You already knew that? Why didn't you just say so?"

Fred frowned. "What? No. I just found out.

Asked the bartender. He relayed word about what info I wanted. Then, the other guy passed it to me."

"What other guy?"

"The one who came for a drink," Fred said. "You didn't see?"

I shook my head. "I saw him, sure. I didn't see any signs of communication."

"That was the point."

There was a lot I still had to learn, about the Broker, about Fred, about this entire world. Everyone seemed to know things I didn't, and if I didn't start picking up on it soon, I would end up in a bad way.

"That was all so fast, though."

"My guess is they already had her people marked. They watch everyone who comes in." He upended his drink and finished it in one go. "Come on."

He was up and moving without another word, and I hurried after him, trying to ignore the multitude of eyes that followed us. We made our way nearly halfway around the second-floor bar to the far side, staying far enough back from the edge that those on the first floor couldn't see us. However, there was no doubt in my mind that Elenia's other two goons were tailing us.

"Okay, come on, through here," Fred said, abruptly darting down a side passageway. "Brace yourself. It's a little ... It's going to mess with your brain."

I didn't have time to protest or ask questions before he all but shoved me through a door and into a realm that was full of green as far as I could see. Trees, plants, and long grasses all swayed under a perfect afternoon breeze, though there was no sun in the sky.

"Jo, are you okay?" Fred asked, appearing in front of me suddenly. "Keep it together."

"I'm ... I'm okay," I said, shaking off my daze. "For now. But, Fred—Fred, I know this place. We can't stay here."

Already my body was starting to respond to the realm's magic. And respond in a way I very much did *not* want it to. Fred was an attractive vampire, but it was an idle, appreciative attraction. I might remark on it but would never want to *act* on it.

Until the magic of Faerie messed with me, anyways. I was drawn to look at him in a different way. A way I'd never seen him before.

It's all a trick. You know that. You've experienced it before. Stay strong.

"Come on," Fred said, seemingly unafflicted by the warm, supple influence of the realm.

He took my hand—and his fingers were so long and strong. I grasped them firmly, letting him take me wherever he wanted.

Stop it.

Fred took me around the little grassy meadow where we'd arrived, moving us to the edge until we were staring into the center of it.

"There's nothing here," I whispered serenely while my mind fought with itself, trying to stay in control.

"Not yet," Fred agreed. "But there will be soon. And we need to stop Elenia's man before he leaves here. He won't linger long. Just enough to report that we were here. So when you see him, you *attack* him, okay?"

"Attack?" I said lazily, smiling. "Yeah, sure."

Fred slapped me. Hard.

I hissed and backed away from him, fangs sliding into place as fury came over me.

"You're stronger than this," Fred growled, not even reacting to my challenge. "Start acting like it. You belong to Aaron, not me. You will wait for him."

Aaron.

An image of the vampire, clad in a form-fitting suit with eyes of sapphire and muscles from heaven, flew into my mind. Yes. He was the one I *truly* wanted. The one I would let have my body. My mind.

"Here he comes," Fred hissed.

Fred was right, and he was wrong.

Someone came through the portal. But he was swiftly followed by someone *else.*

The first was of average height. He wore a black jacket, dark brown work pants, and steel-toe construction boots. He had a buzz-cut and a thick goatee. The second man was much taller and wore tight dark blue jeans and a red and black plaid shirt. He also rocked a large lumber-jack beard.

"Shit," I said, my mind momentarily cleared. "They both came."

"You take the smaller one," Fred hissed, pushing me into action as the pair started to turn around, looking everywhere for their quarry.

For us.

I stumbled forward while Fred surged past me, tackling the lumberjack to the ground, rolling over and flinging him even deeper into Faerie, outside the little grassy area around the portal and into a bush. Then, he got up and went after him.

Leaving me and the construction worker to face off. The man looked at me, then over his shoulder to where his friend had gone before making his decision. I expected him to come after me. Instead, he tried to step back into the portal.

Oh, no, you don't.

I launched forward, passing through the back

of the shimmering portal and into the smaller vampire. My stomach heaved as I crossed the magical door, only accessible from one side, and my vision stretched as time slowed. I saw stars and solar systems swing past while the colors swelled into numbers more immense than time itself.

Then, I hit the vampire, and we went down, rolling around. Stunned by my journey through the portal, I was left wide open for his first punch. It hit my jaw, and I fell back against the ground.

Something about being punched, so unlike Fred's slap, snapped me back around, clearing my mind and bringing me back to the present.

The construction worker hauled back one of his boots and slammed it into my side. I groaned, wincing as a rib cracked under the impact. I still managed to grab onto his ankle, and with a grin, I twisted it as hard as I could.

Screaming, the vampire went down, moving with the rotation of my twist. As soon as he was down, I swarmed over him like a damn spider monkey. He managed to duck his head before I could get an arm across his neck.

Angry at being denied, I reared back and delivered an elbow to his head. Then another. Pain shot up my arm, but I hit him again. He tried to toss me, but I hung on tight, a cowgirl with her bucking bronco.

I rained fists down on him as best I could while being shaken around violently. I'd never been in such a close-quarters fight like this before. It was exhausting. Breathing heavily, I wished for my rings back. At least for the moment. I wanted nothing more than to squeeze my legs tighter and snap his spine.

Unfortunately, I wasn't strong enough. Despite his wiry frame, the vampire was much stronger than he looked. I couldn't risk looking around for Fred either. This was my fight, and I had to finish it.

So, I took a cheap shot. When he covered up his face to block my fist, I leaned forward, striking like a snake, grabbing as much of his junk as I could. Then, I squeezed.

The vampire's shriek was unlike anything I'd ever heard. It clawed at my eardrums, provoking a visceral response in me to *stop* what I was doing and let him go. On some instinctual level, a part of me knew no creature deserved that kind of pain.

Then, I twisted.

He bit my arm. I let go, and as the vampire gasped in relief, I plunged a thumb into his eye. More screaming, but it didn't matter. The fight was all but over. Blinded on one side, he cradled his head. I snuck my fingers in under his neck and squeezed with all my vampire-shifter might.

His trachea collapsed in my hand, and he

started gasping for breath. Shortly after, as I disentangled myself from him and stood, he started turning blue, staring up at me with his good eye. His hand grasped at my pants, but I kicked it free just as Fred came up to me.

"Good job," he said.

"Thanks." I shivered as the vampire fell back, weakly writhing as he died. "Now, where to?"

Fred nodded, gesturing to the portal. "Back through there, first, before it starts affecting your mind again."

"And then?" I asked as we left the corpses behind, the grasses already wrapping around them, hauling the dead vampires into its embrace.

"A place Aaron showed me once, a long, long time ago. His home."

CHAPTER ELEVEN

We stepped through a door and onto the creaky wooden floor of a dimly lit hut. Behind us, a fire blazed merrily in the hearth, though it emitted no heat. There was dirt on the floor, a thin layer over the floorboards, and the only light besides the fire came from the solitary window set above a counter that stretched along one wall.

The roof curved inward, rising to a central peak. To my untrained eye, it looked like it was thatched with straw or hay. There was no movement, except for the slow sway of the trees visible through the window, the movement casting crazy shadows across the interior walls.

Wordlessly, Fred motioned me to the single door, gently opening it and leading us out into the darkened wood beyond.

I shivered under the moonlit sky as a cool breeze caused the trees to moan and sag. Leaves swirled across the forest floor while dead trees stretched their branches high above us. Somewhere in the darkness, an owl hooted. Moments later, something small screamed; the cry abruptly cut off as a predator found prey.

Other noises filled the air. The rustling of creatures near and far. A branch snapped as something stepped on it, the sharp crack causing birds to leave their perches, spilling into the sky, a cawing cacophony of protests and warnings to all who trod beneath them.

"Where are we?" I whispered.

"Transylvania," Fred replied in an equally soft voice, swinging his head left and right.

I swallowed, mouth abruptly dry. "Like, *Transylvania,* Transylvania? As in, Dracula? *That* place?"

Fred nodded grimly before pointing to his right and setting off. I hurried to keep pace, looking around wildly as we entered the woods surrounding the empty hut. Glancing over my shoulder through the window, I thought I caught a glimpse of movement inside, but when I looked again, it was gone. Had I imagined it?

My wolf was on guard as we walked, the hairs on my neck standing straight up. Everything about this place had her on edge, and I couldn't blame her. Our night sight didn't seem to penetrate very far at all—as if something were preventing us from seeing into the woods.

Fred had said this was Aaron's home. That this was where he was from.

"But Aaron told me long ago that he *wasn't* Dracula," I hissed as something large growled from off to our left, momentarily silencing the night.

"No," Fred corrected, never taking his eyes off the forest around us. "What he said was that it was Count Drakul who still lives here. That was very much the truth."

"More like a misdirection," I muttered.

"He never confirmed *or* denied it," Fred countered. "I was there, remember?"

I remembered. "Still, he let me believe it meant he wasn't Dracula. Now you're telling me he *is*?"

Fred shrugged, the motion barely visible. "That's his story to tell. Come on. We need to move. We don't want to be wandering out here for very long. There are worse things than old Drakul."

As he spoke, the darkness of the forest seemed to close in on us like some sort of blanket. The wind stilled, and trees sighed as they returned to their natural position, the dead trunks relieved as the pressure faded.

All around us, the noise tapered off. I frowned at that while my wolf rumbled a warning inside my mind. She didn't like it. Something was off about the unnatural silence.

I opened my mouth to ask Fred, but he put a finger to his lips, hushing me before I could make a sound. Noiselessly, we crouched, waiting.

Eventually, the wind picked up again, and the noise returned. I looked around, trying to stay calm.

"What *sorts* of things are out here?" I asked worriedly. "Things for *you* to be afraid of?"

"Things that it would be easier to avoid tangling with," Fred replied. "Especially if we hope to lay low. Come, let's move."

He set off at a brisk pace, forcing me to all but jog to keep up. We followed some trail that only Fred seemed able to see. At one point, we passed through a pocket of darkness so deep I couldn't see more than five feet ahead, thanks to the dense bushes on either side of our trail.

The wind picked up again while a wolf howled at the moon visible overhead somewhere in the distance. I shuddered at the sound. It was *wrong*, somehow. Even my wolf could sense it. She shied away from the sound, wanting nothing to do with it.

"What the hell is this place?" I growled at Fred.

Before he could answer, a branch snapped behind us. *Close* behind us. We both froze, slowly turning our heads, trying to pierce the gloom.

Whatever it was, it came closer. I could feel its footsteps.

"I think we should run," Fred said.

"No argument," I yelped as whatever it was came lunging through the darkness, bushes and tiny trees parting under its bulk.

We spun on our heels and darted off. Fred moved fast through the trees. My legs churned, the duality of my heritage lending me enough speed to keep up on two legs. I knew that on all fours, I could outpace him, but I wasn't going to leave Fred behind. He'd gotten me out of the Broker's, and I owed him for that. Besides, he was a friend.

That didn't prevent me from urging him on faster. We ran up a hill and then down the other side. Behind us, the titanic creature crashed onwards, shouldering aside entire trees in its single-minded pursuit of us.

"I don't think it's giving up," I said as we labored up another steep rise.

A trumpeting roar sounded less than twenty feet behind us. I risked a glance backward, but I still couldn't see the damn thing. Whatever it was, the darkness molded to it, keeping it hidden from my wolf's sight.

"Come on. We're close," Fred said. "See there?"

I looked in front of us as we crested a rise. There, visible on a hill in the distance, were the ruins of what had to have once been a mighty castle.

"That's our destination?" I asked. "Those ruins?"

"Not quite," Fred said. "That's the new castle. The *original* is on the far side of the river at the bottom of the castle's hill. That's where we want."

"Right. Sure."

We raced onward while our pursuer chased, gaining on us bit by bit.

The ruins passed in a blur, and we ran down a nearly vertical embankment and over a road. With giant flying leaps, we crossed the river. I tucked into a ball, coming up out of an awkward roll on the far side. Whatever was after us crashed through the water, spray going everywhere.

"It's gaining!" I shouted. "It must know we're almost there."

"Don't look back! Keep running!"

He led us up a hill and then cut sharply to the left without warning. I nearly wiped out trying to follow him until I came to a skidding stop as we entered a cave.

"Help me with this!" he barked.

I raced to where he struggled with a door hidden against the wall. We pushed on it and, over squealing hinges, flung it shut, the thick latch falling into place moments before whatever chased us slammed into it, shaking the door and the entire cave.

"Great," I said. "Now, we're trapped in here, with that, that *thing* out there."

"It'll give up soon," Fred said, breathing a little heavier. "Other prey will present less of an effort than us ... I hope."

"You *hope?*" I asked, aghast at his lack of conviction.

"The creatures of this wood can sometimes be incredibly stub—"

The beast on the other side shook the door again.

"—born," Fred finished dryly.

There was a third hit, and then, nothing but silence.

"What the hell was that thing?" I asked, staring at the steel door, beyond thankful Fred had known about it.

"A bear ..."

I shook my head, loudly denying his claim. "No way. That thing was bigger and faster than any bear. Wasn't it?"

Fred shook his head, holding a finger to his lips again, urging me to be quiet. "Drakul has a habit of turning things that aren't necessarily sapient."

I was momentarily speechless. But only momentarily. "Are you telling me that *thing* out there is a fucking *vampire bear?!*"

Fred waved his hand sharply at me, trying to silence me, but it was too late.

Behind me, deep in the cave that I didn't realize extended so far, came the sounds of metal scraping on rock.

"Shit," Fred muttered. "He knows we're here."

"This place is *occupied?*" I moaned, though this time, I kept my voice low.

"I told you Count Drakul still haunts the area," Fred said.

"You never said that he haunted this area in particular. Wouldn't it have made sense to go somewhere *else?*"

Fred shrugged. "We're looking for somewhere people won't find you, aren't we? This seemed like the best choice."

"I'd sort of hoped to survive the encounter."

"Who says you won't?"

"You seemed to be a little worried that he knew we were here."

"I'd hoped to announce ourselves and ask for entry," Fred said.

"Instead, we snuck in the back door, and now, he knows we're here. Which, I take it, is a bad thing?"

"I don't know," Fred admitted. "I've never been

inside. Word is, though, Drakul ... doesn't really like visitors."

"Great," I whispered. "Just great. First, a vampire bear. Now, an ancient vampire from history who probably wants to kill us."

"You should *probably* get ready for a fight," Fred said before sliding past me.

Toward the oncoming sound.

CHAPTER TWELVE

"**Y**ou'd rather take him on than a vampire grizzly?" I asked, shaking myself loose, wondering if I dared to shift.

"I'd rather not fight *anyone*," Fred said as we crept down the dark hallway.

I didn't have anything to say to that since I was distracted by my thoughts. My wolf would be infinitely more helpful in a fight. With both Fred and Drakul being vampires, I didn't have to worry about the scent of blood driving me crazy. Vampire blood just didn't have that effect. It was "already" dead, or so Fenrir had told me.

Yet, we were on Earth, and if we *did* run into something, I still wasn't sure I could stop myself. Shifting was a last-ditch choice and not one I was ready to make. There would have to be another way to ensure we survived the coming fight. If indeed it was going to be a fight.

I reached out to run my fingers along the wall. Surprisingly, it felt like carved stones. We weren't in a cave. This had to be a part of the old castle that Fred had told me about, the original.

Torchlight flickered up ahead, revealing that we'd been slowly rounding a long bend in the hallway. I wasn't sure if Fred's vision could penetrate the darkness, but to me, the light was a welcome sight. My wolf's night vision had returned after we left the dark forest, but without any source of light at all, I still hadn't been able to see much.

A low moan echoed from the depths ahead of us, sending a shiver down my spine. Goosebumps rippled across my arms, and the hairs all over my body stood up. Inside, my wolf shifted restlessly, not liking the sound. I could feel her growl. She didn't like this.

"I don't like this," I said quietly, echoing her thoughts.

"Me neither," Fred agreed, saying nothing more.

The metal scraping grew louder. Drakul was getting closer. I still couldn't see any movement, but instinctively, Fred and I slowed. Whatever was going to happen, it would happen soon. No need to rush any quicker to it.

"He's just a vampire?" I said, speaking up to fill the nervous silence. "Right? Like you?"

"Not quite like me," Fred said.

"But, like, a regular vampire, right? We can take him, the two of us."

"That depends on just how true the legends are," Fred whispered back, crouching low as the scraping of metal on stone stopped.

"What legends? The ones that say he's a vampire? We know that."

"No," Fred hissed as his fangs slid down out of his mouth. "The ones that say he has strange powers."

The torchlight went out as flickers of motion flooded the hallway amid the rustle of thousands of wings.

"Bats," I moaned, leaning back against the wall. "He can change into thousands of bats."

Fred didn't reply. I glanced at him, only to see that the bats had coalesced into a shape in front of us.

A tall man stood in front of us. Clad in silver armor, he looked down at us with eyes that burned red. The flickering orange light from the torches was just bright enough for me to see that his hair was a long, brilliant white, pulled back in a half-clasp, the rest falling down his back. Matching facial hair grew thick across his face.

What caught my eye, however, was the longsword he carried casually in one hand, as if not bothered by the weight of the four-foot blade. Its silver steel caught the light and bounced it around. I frowned. Did I see bats in its reflection? There were none in the cave that I could see. Were they *in* the sword?

Drakul spoke in a language I didn't recognize. It sounded vaguely Germanic, which probably meant it wasn't Romanian unless it was some sort of predecessor's tongue. I didn't know.

"Shit," I cursed. "How the hell do we–"

Fred started replying in the same tongue. Drakul's glittery red eyes stared at him like tiny rubies set in his skull.

"What's he saying?" I whispered, watching the sword very carefully.

Neither Fred nor I were armed. If Drakul decided we were hostile, it was the first thing we'd have to deal with.

"He wants to know why we dared disturb him."

"And what did you say?"

Drakul rumbled something, the words tumbling from his mouth like a torrent of water, fast and furious.

Fred shook his head. "I'm having trouble making it out. The dialects are slightly different, and he speaks too fast," he said before saying something else to Drakul.

The creepy vampire barked a single word that did not sound positive.

Gulping, Fred turned his head toward me. "Uh, I think he's saying we have to leave."

"Look out!" I shouted, launching myself past Fred toward Drakul, my hands going for his wrist, trying to stop the downward strike that the Count had launched when Fred's head was turned.

I got there in time to prevent Fred from being opened, stomach to shoulder, but Drakul was stronger than I expected. The blade of his sword pierced Fred's abdomen, pinning him to the wall with a howl of agony.

There was an ear-splitting howl of frustration, then Drakul dissolved into a swirling storm of bats. The resistance I'd been fighting against vanished, and I fell through the bats to land on the floor. Then, Drakul reincorporated in the same spot. He reached out, pulled the sword from Fred's gut, and whirled on me.

I pushed off the ground with all my strength, sending myself sliding down the hallway just before his sword plunged through the stone where I'd been lying. He buried it a full foot into the floor.

"I don't think he's *asking* us to leave!" I shouted as Fred heaved himself away from the wall, leaving a dark spot where the sword had impaled him.

"Yeah, I picked up on that."

Drakul paused in his advance on me, looking over his shoulder at Fred. He ground out some more words in his ancient language. Fred said something back. Drakul hissed and swung his sword at Fred, who dodged wildly.

"Stop making him mad!"

"I'm trying!" Fred shouted back, evading yet another strike. "I told him we're not his enemy. That we're not here to hurt him."

"You know, with the sword and the whole bat thing, I'm not sure he's concerned about us hurting *him*. I think he's more into the idea of hurting us. Or killing us," I said as Drakul abruptly disappeared again. The bats came at me in a sudden rush.

Angry, I reached out and grabbed one, snagging it mid-air thanks to my improved shifter-vampire reaction speed.

When Drakul re-emerged from the cyclone of fluttering wings, he stared at the single one struggling in my hand.

"Stop this," I growled, squeezing tighter. The bat whimpered, a whiny nasally noise.

Okay, that's not fair. It's not a real bat! It's part of Drakul.

Drakul's sword came up; its tip pointed toward my hand. He snarled something.

"He said to let it go."

"Tell him I will if he stops attacking us."

Fred said something in the same harsh tones. Drakul repeated himself.

"He just says to let it go."

"How did Aaron ever put up with this asshole?" I grumped, shaking myself. "Tell him that —oh, shit!"

Tired of waiting, Drakul came toward me, his blade slicing across the hallway, scoring long gouges in the walls as he swung it with almost wild abandon.

"God damn you, Drakul!" I screamed in frustration, backpedaling as fast as I could. "You, Aaron, Alaine, whoever, your entire stupid bloodline! Why can't you just stop and listen for once!"

Drakul paused. He just sort of froze midswing. I blinked but kept easing away, just in case. There was no telling if he would launch another attack without warning.

"What happened?" I hissed as I reached Fred, who stood with one hand clasped over his front, holding his stomach where the sword had gone through.

Before he could answer, Drakul rumbled something. I still had no idea what he was saying, but I did catch one word I recognized.

Alaine.

Fred replied in a rush, and again, I caught the

name used several times.

"He recognizes the name," Fred whispered as he waited for Drakul to reply. "I just told him we're friends of Alaine's."

"Hopefully, that's a good thing," I muttered.

Fred glared at me. "Be positive."

Drakul said something, then turned and, in a flurry of wings, disappeared down the hallway.

"What did he say?"

"I think, if I understood properly, he said 'welcome.'"

"And then just left?"

"Aaron did say he was a bit blunt. I suppose after so many years living alone, you don't develop much of a bedside manner."

"Definitely not used to hosting. Might have something to do with his preoccupation with swinging a sword at anyone who comes near."

"It might," Fred agreed.

"What now?"

"Now," he said, easing past me down the hallway, "we look for some shelter. And you tell me what it is that you couldn't at the Broker's."

CHAPTER
THIRTEEN

It didn't take us long to find where Drakul must spend most of his time. Although the creepy count was nowhere to be seen, the hallway spit us out in a long, rectangular room. Torches guttered in wall sconces lining the sides, and in the center of the room, a rectangular table sat at the foot of an elevated throne.

I expected to see Drakul sitting on his throne, lording over his imaginary subjects, but that, too, was empty. The benches on the table were old but in decent shape. Wistfully, I looked at the empty tabletop, wishing it were covered with food. Now that I was a vampire, I technically only needed blood to sustain me, but food was always welcome.

Don't think about it, and you won't be as hungry.

The words applied to everything.

Fred didn't hesitate. He walked over to the table and plopped down on a bench. "Waiter!" he bellowed wistfully, shaking his head.

"The service just isn't as good as the Broker's, I know," I said, moving to join him. What else was I going to do? "But you have to admit the décor is … also not as good."

"I will admit that," Fred chuckled before subsiding into a waiting silence.

"We had a disagreement," I said, knowing he was waiting for me to elaborate about Aaron and me.

"To the point that he wouldn't come with you?" Fred said. "Must have been one hell of a knockdown fight. Did you tell him his suits make his butt look big or something?"

I snickered, unable to hold back my laughter. "No, but thank you for that bit of ammunition. I'll make good use of that, I promise."

Tapping the table, I shook my head. "The truth is, Fred, it wasn't that he didn't come with me. It's that I left him. Him, Fenrir, everyone. I left them behind in Seguin and came on my own."

I purposefully left out the bit about Johnathan wanting me to leave town for the sake of his pack. It wasn't pertinent to the story, and I didn't want to relive the embarrassment.

"You just left without telling him where you were going?"

"He's not my keeper," I said, perhaps a bit too sharply.

"True," Fred agreed. "But he's done a whole lot for you. He cares about you."

"I know that. But he didn't agree with my decided course of action. I wasn't going to change my mind just because he didn't like it."

"What course of action?"

"Elenia," I said softly, looking up at him, preparing for the same blowback I'd gotten from Aaron. "This won't stop with her on the throne. She'll come after me, my mother, who knows who else. Too many have already suffered and died at her hands, all because I'm something I couldn't control. Well, no more! No more deaths, no more random acts of murder just because a vampire happens to be a woman. That ends, Fred. I'm going after her, and I'm not stopping until I'm sitting on her throne with her dead body at my feet."

I paused, catching myself from getting too worked up, while I held on for Fred's opposing views.

Instead, Fred shot to his feet, slamming a fist on the table hard enough to make it jump. "Fucking *finally!*" he shouted. "Hell, yes! Let's depose that bitch. I am *in!*"

My jaw practically hit the floor as I gaped at him, open-mouthed and wide-eyed.

"Oh, come on," Fred said, sitting back down. "Are you really that surprised?"

"Well, based on how Aaron had the exact *opposite* reaction to you, yes, I am."

"What did he say?"

I sighed. "That it was madness."

Fred tapped his chin. "He's right, you know. It is crazy. Madness. Insane. But I don't care. I'm tired of putting up with her crusty old hag ass on the throne. She's the worst."

"She rejected you, didn't she?" I asked, sensing a bit of his reasoning.

"Hard," Fred said, grinning. "That was before I knew—the point is, I'm okay with her being gone."

"Me, too," I said, wondering what he'd been about to say. Before he knew about what?

"So, when do we do it?" Fred asked, interrupting my thoughts.

"Soon," I said. "First, though, I have to take care of one other thing."

"What? What else needs doing before we kill the bitch? Is it making up with Aaron? I don't want to see trouble in paradise," Fred teased.

I glared at him. "We're not together."

Fred looked doubtful.

"We're not," I insisted. "We're … complicated."

"No, you're in denial," he said. "But whatever,

that's Aaron's job, not mine."

"We're not a thing."

"Then, what are you?" he said. "You're certainly more than friends. You just can't admit it to yourself yet because you're scared."

"Finding out you're some sort of super-vampire wolf thing will do that to you!" I said sharply.

Fred held his hands up in surrender. "Fair point. All I'm saying, Jo, is don't lie to yourself. Lie to me, if you must, but tell yourself the truth at least."

I gave him a steady look, but the old vampire wasn't fazed. He just blinked at me.

"What is this other thing you need to do?" he said, growing bored of my attempt to be irritated with him.

Sighing, I gave up the ghost. "The queen bitch took out a Blood Letter on me."

Fred grimaced as I reminded him. "Right. That complicates things. She must be really scared of you. How are you going to fix *that?* You can't even kill her while it's still there."

I nodded. "I know how to remove one, though," I said, filling him in quickly about what the Broker had told me.

"Your rings!" Fred exclaimed. "They'll help you survive."

I shook my head, pulling up my sleeves to reveal bare biceps. "My payment for the information."

"That slimy sonofabitch," Fred hissed, realizing the Broker had demanded the one thing that could get me through. "He knew exactly what he was doing. That ruthless bastard."

"Yeah."

Fred stroked his chin. "So, how are you going to do this?"

"I don't know," I admitted, fighting back rising hopelessness. It was all just a bit too much for me. "I think … I think I need to talk about it with Aaron."

Fred exhaled strongly. "I'm glad you said that. I was thinking the same thing."

"But how?" I asked.

"I'll go get him. I can sneak around better than you. And bonus, the queen isn't after me. Not with a Blood Letter at least, so it'll be safer for me to go and move around."

"You're going to leave me alone with Count Haunt-ula?" I complained, shivering at the thought of spending time in the creepy castle ruins with the old vampire.

"You'll be fine," Fred promised. "I won't be long. Once Aaron is here, we'll figure out what to do next."

"Just don't get caught by Winnie," I muttered as he rose.

"Winnie?" Fred lifted an eyebrow.

"The bear outside? Never mind," I said, shaking my head. "Thank you."

Fred grunted and then was gone down the hallway. Leaving me alone in an old castle with a mentally unstable vampire who could somehow shift into dozens, or hundreds, of little bats. And didn't speak a lick of the same language as me.

I stared at the wall torches, hoping against hope that they were magical and wouldn't burn out. Despite being a creature of the night, the last thing I wanted was to be left in the dark. Somewhere in another hallway, the sound of metal on stone started up again.

Count Drakul was on the move.

CHAPTER FOURTEEN

Not wanting to be caught out in the open, I surveyed the room again. The double wooden doors at the far end caught my eye. They were open, leading out into what could only be the rest of the castle. Is that where Drakul was?

I moved swiftly to them, pushing the doors closed. They creaked and groaned mightily, giving rise to the fear that Drakul would recognize the sound and come faster. But he didn't, and I got them closed and barred, sliding the thick wooden beam down into place from its vertical resting spot with only minimal extra effort.

"That only leaves ... *four*?" I moaned, "four more entrances."

It seemed likely there was at least one secret entrance as well. The walls were covered in dark tapestries, dirtied by age to the point that they were nearly illegible unless right up close. At least one of them was certain to cover up a passage built into the wall. There was no way I could block them all. Not from someone who had spent centuries haunting the castle.

Accepting the fact that Drakul would get to me if he wanted to, I went back to the main doors and lifted the bracer that kept them closed. It was fun to put my strength to use, lifting something I wouldn't have been able to move just a few weeks ago. With the doors open, I stole out into the castle, eager to explore.

There was a fluttering of wings from behind me, and then all at once, Count Drakul was walking alongside me.

"Jesus!" I yelped. "Where did you come from?"

Not that I expected a reply, of course. I couldn't speak his strange language. Still, it unnerved me that he could move so silently. That gave rise to another thought. Was I allowed in this part of the castle? What if I was trespassing somewhere he didn't want? How would he tell me?

Probably with the pointy end of that giant sword of his.

"So, you and Aaron, I mean Alaine, go way back, do you?" I said conversationally. "Don't suppose you can tell me anything about him, can you? Something I could use to convince him to go after Elenia with me?"

Drakul came to a halt. I turned, readying myself to leap away if he went for his sword, wondering what I'd said wrong. Was the queen's name banned from the castle?

The count worked his jaw, eyes burning red in the back of their sockets.

"Yeah, I didn't think so." I sighed. "What am I doing? I'm talking to a mute."

"Alaine."

I looked sharply at Drakul. "Yes, Alaine. He is my ... friend."

Drakul convulsed slightly while his throat produced a sound equivalent to two boulders grinding together. It took me several moments to realize he was *laughing* of all things. I didn't realize he could do that.

"Alaine ... more."

"What? More what?" I asked, shocked he knew English. Why hadn't he used it earlier?

His eyes burned brighter. "You smell. You smell, Alaine."

"I smell him?" I repeated, frowning. "Wait. You mean you can smell him on me?"

Drakul nodded slowly. "You and Alaine. More friends. You smell, Alaine."

He could smell Aaron on me. Which apparently meant we were more than friends.

"He claim you," Drakul said. "Yes?"

"No," I said, shaking my head. "He *wants* to. But not yet."

Drakul was silent. I waited for him to say more, but he was doing the same to me. Given that he had centuries to practice being silent, I didn't challenge him on it.

"How do you know Alaine?" I asked, speaking slowly as I started walking again. Drakul wasn't going to kill me, so I might as well explore the castle while I waited for Fred to return. It was likely to be some hours, if not longer. For all I knew, Aaron could be long gone from Seguin by now.

"Alaine. Here." Drakul waved his arms wide, encompassing the castle around us.

"Yes, I know he was once here," I said. "Fred told me about that."

Drakul shook his head stiffly, white hair getting all tangled. "That Alaine *return*. Alaine here. *Before*."

I frowned at him. "He was here before that? Is that what you mean?"

Drakul stared at me, considering my words, then slowly nodded.

"Was this where Aaron was born?" I asked, pointing down at the castle floor. "Alaine. Born. Here?"

Drakul nodded. "Born. Die. Born. Here."

Born-die-born? What does that mean? How

are you born a second–

"This is where he was made into a vampire? Where he was turned?"

Drakul nodded slowly.

"Were you here for that?" I asked.

The count shook his head. "Before."

It happened before Drakul came around. Yet Drakul knows of it. He knew Aaron better than I did.

Which wasn't hard. It seemed *everyone* knew Aaron better than I did. Whether as Aaron, Alaine, the Prince of Darkness. Everyone seemed to know his history except for me.

"For someone who wants to claim me, he certainly isn't doing a great job of letting me get to know him first," I said, not expecting any sort of response. "How did he even get the title Prince of Darkness? Why does he call himself Aaron now and not Alaine? I don't get it. Stupid secrets!"

My frustration echoed off the walls. Maybe if I knew more about him, I could understand why he was so reluctant to go after Elenia. I'd learned more about him from the severely broken English of the Count than I had spending time with Aaron himself.

"Shame."

I looked up. "What?"

Drakul made a face. "Shame."

"Shame," I repeated to myself. "What about shame? Are you talking about Alaine or me?"

"Shame. Alaine," Drakul grunted.

I ground my teeth together, wishing I could understand the ancient vampire better. Every other immortal creature seemed to speak multiple tongues with ease–it probably helped pass the time—so why couldn't he? It was arrogant of me to expect him to be fluent, of course.

"Why would Alaine feel shame?" I asked Drakul.

Drakul turned abruptly, heading down a side passage without warning. I hesitated. Was I supposed to follow him? Or was he done talking to me? This had to be the most contact he'd had with someone in a long time.

"Come."

"Yep, on my way!" I said, hurrying after him.

He took me past two corridors that had been blocked by cave-ins. We skirted around piles of debris from where the ceiling had fallen in. This section of the castle hadn't survived as well as the rest. Nor did it seem as occupied. Dust covered the floor, without any footsteps except those left by Drakul and me.

"What's down here?"

"Shame."

Drakul brought me to a door. It seemed no different than any other, but it was very obviously his destination. He gestured at me to go through. I approached the door, gently twisting on the handle and pushing it inward.

The room on the other side was dark. My wolf's sight lit the shadows in shades of gray. It was a bedroom. Or it *had* been. Someone had thoroughly trashed it. The bed was broken, the footboard half-ripped away, sheets shredded and cast everywhere. Paintings on the wall were covered in some dark, dried substance that my gut told me was blood. The table was in pieces, with high-backed wooden chairs cast to the four winds throughout the room. Tables were caved in as if a body had landed on them.

"What happened here?" I whispered, stunned at the ferocity of the attack. The sheer anger necessary to do something like this.

"Shame," Drakul repeated.

"Aaron, I mean, Alaine. He did this? Is that what you're trying to say."

"Alaine. Elenia. Shame." Drakul gestured as if expecting it all to make sense.

I shook my head. "I don't understand."

Drakul's eyes blazed with renewed intensity. "Shame," he repeated yet again.

"Yeah, I got that," I said, wandering into the room. Maybe there was something in here that would help unravel what the chatty vamp was trying to tell me. I doubted it. There was nothing left intact.

I walked to the middle of the room, turning back to Drakul as I took in the devastation, trying to figure out why someone would do this.

He said two names. Not one.

Spinning, I stared Drakul down. "Aaron and Elenia. They did this. This is because of a fight, isn't it?"

Drakul's eyes burned down to tiny spots. He moved his head up and down.

"How interesting," I said, considering the room and the location. "He brought Elenia here, to where he was born? They had a fight. In his room. Apparently, they have a bit more of a history than he's revealed."

Drakul turned and left the room without saying anything more. Perhaps it wasn't his place to.

My mouth flattened into a firm line. That was fine. Aaron would be here soon. Then he could explain this.

It's past time I got some answers.

CHAPTER FIFTEEN

I eventually found myself back in the great hall. Drakul didn't seem concerned about me exploring the rest of the castle ruins, but that didn't produce any of the revelations I hoped it might. Many of the passages were blocked from cave-ins, which drastically reduced the places I could go. I found a few rooms that looked more suitable for staying in, having been updated sometime in the past century, but that was the extent of it.

"Probably shouldn't be surprised," I muttered to myself as I sat on the throne, looking down at the table. "You can't even tell from aboveground that a castle was here once. It's all been overgrown. Of course, most of it would be gone by now."

Leaning back, staring up at the arched roof

overhead, I tried to picture what this place must have been like in its glory days. What had life been like for little human Alaine, long before he'd been turned into a vampire? What was his purpose? Was he a kitchen boy, destined to slave over ovens? Or maybe his lot was in one of the other trades. Blacksmith's apprentice perhaps, or maybe a hunter, stalking the surrounding lands to bring back meat for his lord.

Maybe he was the Lord's son himself. Being trained in the arts, how to fight, and act like a noble. Learning how to rule.

Running my fingers over the stone chair, I tried to imagine a young Aaron sitting in it, much like I was now, trying it on for size. How old had he been when he was taken? Vampires didn't age, which would put him probably somewhere in his twenties, maybe early thirties. Was he already sitting on the throne? Maybe he'd sacrificed himself in a noble gesture so that the rest of his people would live.

Questions burned in my mind.

Voices echoed through the chamber. I sat up straight, recognizing Fred. That was faster than I'd expected. Either he'd found Aaron without issue, or something had gone wrong.

If something was wrong, who would he be talking to, then?

I waited, trying to remain patient until Fred appeared, followed by Aaron and another.

"Fenrir," I said, standing. "Wasn't expecting to see you here."

The short, curly-haired man bowed his head respectfully. "I wasn't exactly welcome to stay in Seguin. So, when Aaron discovered you missing and set out to find you, I tagged along. We ran into Fred at the Broker's, and ..."

I nodded as Fenrir shrugged, the rest of the story obvious.

"It's good to see you," I said, meaning it.

Fenrir was the only other one like me in the world. A hybrid shifter-vamp cross. Only he was thousands of years old and had long ago mastered that dark, shadowy Hunger that lurked within us. It was something I would be working on for a long time to come if I survived the mission I'd set myself.

Even now, I could feel it, resting just out of reach in my mind. Never quite seen, but always felt. Ready to swarm forward and overwhelm me, turning me into a brutal killing machine at a moment's notice. Strong enough to attract the gods if I lost control.

A shiver struck me at the knowledge of what I could do. And the punishment. Fenrir had lost control once, many thousands of years ago. He'd killed hundreds, perhaps thousands. Each death enabling him to grow larger, stronger, than the one before it. To the point where he'd become a danger so substantial that Odin himself had ordered his capture, sending literal gods to take Fenrir down and imprison him for eternity in Mordathu.

I shuddered at the idea of being thrown in one of those green-walled cells. The prison for paranormal entities, Mordathu was located deep under Mount Olympus. Being sent there was a one-way ticket, though apparently, Fenrir had managed to find a way out. But I wasn't Fenrir. I was me. Joanna Alustria. I would be confined there for eternity if I lost control.

You're also avoiding something.

Sometimes, I really hated my inner voice.

"You went looking for me?" I asked, tearing my attention from Fenrir and letting it settle on the tall blond with bright blue eyes that pierced my hardened defenses with ease.

It was so good to see him again. Looking down at him, having his presence, made me keenly aware of how much I'd missed him.

Control yourself. You don't need him.

Maybe not. But I wanted him around. I liked having him close by. It was comforting and reassuring in ways that I didn't have the words for.

"Of course," Aaron said with his typical stoic bluntness, the words somehow conveying an attitude of "you should know better than to doubt that." "You left without telling me anything. For all I knew, someone had grabbed you."

"You don't have to worry about that," I said, getting up from the throne. I felt silly looking down at them. They were my friends. Well, Fred was. I didn't really know what to call Fenrir. And Aaron was more than a friend. How much more still remained to be seen, but I couldn't deny it.

There was a connection between us. Even as I descended the steps to stand in front of him, I could feel it, my heartbeat increasing with each step.

From another passageway, Drakul half-floated into the room, his giant sword strapped to his armored back. He and Aaron exchanged some words that sounded friendly, even with the harsh tones of their language.

To my surprise, Fenrir jumped in as the conversation died, speaking to Drakul. The ancient warrior focused his attention on Fenrir, speaking back with ... excitement? I watched the exchange, intrigued. I hadn't known Drakul was capable of emotion.

"Who would have thought it," Aaron said, clearly watching as well. "Two loners who have lived alone for ages, getting along."

"I mean, this is like the perfect place for them to hang out. Nobody's around or even knows it exists."

"I agree," Fenrir said before returning his attention to Drakul. The two of them wandered off down one of the passages, walking side by side, deep in animated conversation.

"Well, that's cute," I said, shifting awkwardly. "But what now?"

"Now?" Aaron asked, blinking at me.

"Yeah." I sighed. "Listen, I'm sorry for just upping and leaving, but I knew if I told you what I was doing, you'd just argue with me some more or try to stop me, and I didn't want to do that. I don't like arguing with you."

"Neither do I," he replied softly.

"I'll be over here," Fred said to nobody in particular, moving to the far side of the chamber to give us some space.

"I'm sorry as well," Aaron added stiffly. "For yelling at you. I'm just scared for you. I ... don't want to lose you, Jo."

"If you make me run and hide for the rest of my life, you *will* lose me," I countered gently. "I *have* to do this, Aaron. I have to. I need you to understand that."

"I do," he said gently, surprising me. He must have sensed just how stunned I was because he snorted gently and tossed his head over his shoulder. "Fred, um, talked some sense into me."

"It wasn't easy."

I grinned past Aaron to Fred. "I know."

Aaron harrumphed but refocused on me, his expression turning serious. "Fred says you found a way to revoke the Blood Letter?"

"Yeah," I said before telling him.

He went still, muscles in his jaw clenching as I laid out the requirements.

"I hate it," he said at long last.

There was probably a lot more he wanted to say. But it meant more to me than he might ever know that he didn't immediately jump to telling me *not* to do it. He was more than allowed to dislike it. Nor was he alone in that. I hated it, but I also didn't see another option.

"Yeah," I said, patting his chest. "I know. Me, too."

"Is there another way?"

Credit to Fred. Whatever sense he talked into Aaron in the short time he'd been gone had worked. Aaron wasn't telling me I couldn't do it. He wanted to know if there was anything else we could do instead. It wasn't a majorly different approach, but it was enough.

"I don't think so," I said heavily.

"Fine. Then, we do it here. Where I can protect you while you recover," he said, his eyes fiery with stubborn determination.

This time there would be no arguing with him. Which was okay. I wasn't feeling particularly argumentative on the subject either. Going to a hospital was certainly out of the question. I couldn't be around so much blood and vulnerable people. The darkness in me would only see them as prey.

"Okay," I said. "We'll do it here. In your home."

Aaron tilted his head at me. "There was a point behind those words, wasn't there?"

"I need you to tell me the truth," I said, matching his stare.

"Always," he promised.

"What happened here?" I whispered. "Who are you really? Tell me everything."

CHAPTER SIXTEEN

"Everything?"

I laid a hand on his chest without thinking, trying to push my way past his defenses. "Aaron, I know nothing about you. About your past. How can I be with you when I don't know you?"

"You know me," he said defensively. "You know who I am."

"I know who you are *now*. I don't know what made you what you are. I want to understand you. I want to know you. The *real* you."

"This is the real me. I am who I want to be. I'm not pretending to be someone else."

My eyes bore into his. "You know what I mean. I want to know your history. How you became the person you are today. It's obvious you weren't always like this."

"No," he said heavily. "You're right. I wasn't."

"I'll just see myself out," Fred called as he disappeared down a hallway.

I shook my head, smiling at his candor and terrible timing. Or was it perfect timing? Either way, it didn't matter. The two of us were alone now, and I'd broached the subject. It was time to see what came of it.

"Thanks, Fred," Aaron muttered as the silence lingered, shaking his head. "Okay. Um. Where to begin?"

"Here," I said, waving a hand at the castle around us. "Start here."

Nodding, Aaron motioned for me to take a seat. He pulled the high-backed wooden chair out from the side of the table and waited for me to position myself before gently sliding it in.

"Thank you," I said, falling silent as he took a seat beside me, his face blank as he ordered his thoughts.

"This is where it all began," he said. "Right here. Citadel Poenari, as it was called. Not much of a citadel anymore, I suppose."

"Time changes everything."

"That it does," he said with a heaviness I hadn't expected.

"Is that why Elenia would never expect you to come here?" I asked.

"What? Who told you that?"

"Fred. He suggested that this was a place he and I could lie low while I figured out how to deal with this whole Blood Letter thing. He said it was your home."

"It was," Aaron admitted. "A long, long time ago. But Fred was right. Elenia would likely consider this to be one of the last spots I'd ever return to."

"Why?"

"Because I haven't been here in over five and a half centuries," he whispered.

"What? Why?" Did it have something to do with the fight they'd had in that room?

"This place, this castle and the area around it," Aaron said, his eyes dimming, growing heavy with memory. "This is where I earned the title 'Prince of Darkness.' It's not something I'm proud of."

"Because you're Dracula?" I hedged, taking an educated guess.

"That is a name I was known by, yes. However, it came to mean more than just a name later on. There's another that I was better known as at the time. Perhaps you've heard of it. Vlad the Impaler."

I winced. I'd heard of it. "He ... you ... doesn't exactly have a good reputation."

"Nor should I," Aaron growled.

"Start from the beginning," I said.

Aaron sighed. "That would be somewhere around the eighth century. I'm not sure. Maybe the ninth. I was born right here, in this very castle. This section is much older than most suspect. The new castle was built later. When I returned."

I listened, enraptured. This was the most I'd ever learned about him. Seven sentences, and my knowledge of Aaron's past and who he was had probably tripled. I didn't dare speak for fear of stopping him.

"Although I didn't know it at the time, vampires were prominent in the area. They hid from plain sight, but local legends were full of stories of things in the night that would snatch unsuspecting victims. One day, they came for me when I was returning from a meeting of local lords. Our convoy was attacked. Many slain. I killed two of them. I guess that caught their attention because their leader appeared and bit me."

"I'm so sorry," I said, unsure of what else to say. It had happened so long ago that it felt silly even to say that much.

"They took me, and I stayed with them until I learned of the vampire city, Madrigal. I hated the idea of feeding, so going to a place where I didn't have to hurt humans appealed immensely to me. Once there, I made a bit of a name for myself. But eventually, even that came to an end."

"What happened?" I asked, practically on the edge of my seat.

"The queen and I became at odds," he said, anger tinting his words.

Still, you refuse to elaborate on her, I thought, making a note of it. *Why? What are you hiding?*

"And?" I pressed.

"Things didn't go well," he said. "I was forced back here. Drakul was living here, ruling as a vampire. He knew what I was and took me in. Claimed me as a son and protected me as best he could. Both from retaliation and also to try to cover up what I was doing, I suppose. I don't really know."

"So, you just appeared? Out of nowhere? And people believed you were his long-lost son they never knew about? They didn't question that?"

"Not quite," Aaron said, chuckling. "He claimed that I was his real son. Vlad the III, Vlad Dracula. Whatever you prefer. The real Vlad III died in an Ottoman prison, but it was easy to say that I had actually escaped and lived as best I could while slowly making my way home."

"I see. And the whole Vlad the Impaler business? What was *that* about?"

"I told you," he growled. "I'm not proud of what I did at the time. I wasn't in my right mind."

"So, you're really Dracula," I said, shivering unintentionally. "Out of legend."

Aaron looked at me strangely. "Yes, I am a vampire, Jo. But so are you. We're still just people."

"It's silly, I know," I said. "But Dracula evokes a lot of imagery for someone raised on human media. None of it favorable. Not to mention, there's a more real-life version still haunting this place. I mean, is he really on our side?"

"Drakul?" Aaron chuckled to himself. "He's an insufferable old bastard, but he won't kill you out of spite."

That didn't *quite* jive with the welcome Fred and I had received, but I let it slide. I didn't want to interrupt.

"That would be the third son," Aaron added quietly. "Radu 'The Handsome.' Though he's currently imprisoned in Mordathu. So, you're fine."

"If you say so," I said, still processing what I'd learned. It was a lot. Though, there was still lots missing. He might not be aware, but I knew he was glossing over his history with the queen. Something important had happened there. Not to mention, his return was still somewhat shrouded in mystery. How had he gone from hating feeding on humans to wanting to kill so many of them he became known as Vlad the Impaler?

"You can trust me, Jo. You're safe here. It might not be the citadel it once was, but it's still somewhere she'll never think to find us."

"For now," I said, deciding not to push for

more information on *why* she wouldn't come here. Not yet, at least. "It's still creepy."

"Maybe," he agreed. "But we'd still have come here anyway at some point."

"Why?"

"Because," he said with a grin, "if we're going up against that miserable bitch, then we're going to need all the help we can get."

"Help?" I asked nervously, stomach sinking.

Aaron grinned. "Drakul hates Elenia as much as I do."

"Great," I moaned. "So, he's going to be spending some time with us like an unwanted in-law?"

Cold filled his blue eyes. "You wanted to do this," he said grimly. "You said you wanted to take Elenia down and sit on her throne. If you want to do that, and *if* you expect to survive, you're going to need help, Jo. Are you prepared to take any help offered to you? Because I promise you that you won't like all of it. This is the way."

I swallowed, having trouble meeting his eyes, though I made myself do it.

"I know," I whispered.

Aaron's eyes searched mine. "Then, are you ready to do what it takes?"

CHAPTER SEVENTEEN

"I think so," I said nervously, wondering what else he had in mind. Just who was he thinking we'd have to turn to for help?

We were interrupted by Fenrir and Drakul, who returned to the main chamber via another hallway. Drakul carried a chest.

"Return," Drakul rumbled, speaking his broken English to Aaron instead of whatever language it was that Fred and Fenrir had used to converse with him. "Things?"

Aaron turned away from me to regard the old vampire as he set the chest down on the table.

"What's this?" I asked.

"He thinks I've come back for my ... stuff," Aaron said, staring at the chest.

"I told you that wasn't it," Fenrir said, shaking his head at Drakul. "He didn't come here for that."

Drakul said something in the other language. Fenrir fired back a reply.

"Enough bickering," Aaron said before they dissolved into a full-blown argument. "I will take it, thank you. It wasn't what I came for, you're right, but perhaps it will come in use."

Drakul turned his eyes to Fenrir, and I thought I saw a victorious glow twinkle through them.

"Yeah, yeah," Fenrir muttered, his lips twitching.

I looked back and forth between them, surprised at the ease with which they got along.

Turning back to us, Drakul focused first on Aaron, then on me. "Why you return?" he asked.

"For her," Aaron said, indicating me. "She plans to kill Elenia. You want to help?"

Drakul was still for a moment, the only movement his eyes as they darted back and forth between us. Then, quite possibly the creepiest thing happened. He smiled.

"Finally," he rumbled. "You go against her again."

Again? Had I heard that right?

"Yes," Aaron said.

"Good," Drakul ground out in his deep voice.

"Heart is healed. At last. This good."

I could no longer keep my mouth shut. "What's he talking about, Aaron? Going up against Elenia again? Your heart healed?"

Drakul's eyes darted to me. "You not tell? Bad."

Then, he began to chuckle.

"I really hate you sometimes," Aaron said as the old vampire crossed his arms, preparing to wait and hear what Aaron had to say to me.

"That's fine," I told him. "But he has a point."

Aaron looked troubled, avoiding my eyes as he stared across the room into nothingness. "I suppose he does. On many levels."

"What happened between you and Elenia?" I pressed. This was important. I knew it was. It had to be.

"We were in love," he said bluntly. "That's what happened. We fell in love, and I—I helped her."

Reaching out, I laid a hand on top of his, sensing his pain. "Whatever it is, it's clearly in the past. But you need to tell me. To talk about it."

"It's not easy," he said in a raspy voice. "It's all my fault, you see."

"What is?"

"Everything. All of it. Even your situation."

"But I thought Fenrir was the one who turned my mother?"

"I was," the old vampire-wolf said. "But I don't think that's what he's referring to."

"No," Aaron said, heaving a giant sigh and sitting back into his chair. "It all began about twelve years after I arrived in Madrigal. That's when Elenia and I met. We clicked instantly. Both of us young and power-hungry, eager to ascend the ranks in Madrigal. Out to prove ourselves to our elders."

I nodded. This was partly what I'd expected. That there was a deeper history between the two of them. The remnants of the room Drakul had shown me were not the result of a full-blown knock-down fight. It had the trappings of a lovers' quarrel.

"And so that's what we did," Aaron continued. "We plotted and schemed and ascended the very ranks of power together. Until about four hundred years later."

He paused, shaking his head, very obviously reliving the memories.

"What happened?" I pressed, sensing that now was the time to pry, to push for answers. I had to keep him talking now that he'd started. If I gave up, it would be impossible for him to start again.

"Then, we hatched the most ambitious plan yet, and I helped put her on the throne of Madrigal," he said hauntingly. "I made her queen."

"What?" I gasped. "But how could you? She's

insane."

Aaron looked at me, his normally bright eyes dulled with shame. "Love, mostly. I wanted the best for her. She also wasn't the woman she is now. Just like I'm not the man I am now. Power changed her. Warped her."

"You should have stopped her." The comment slid out before I'd had a chance to think about it. I tried to backpedal, but his response was practically instantaneous.

His eyes burned with blue fury. "Don't you think I *tried?*" he growled. "We ruled together for nearly two centuries. That's how long it took me to discover she'd gone insane with power. She'd begun working in the background, eliminating her rivals, making it look like accidents. Others were busy killing the low-level female vampires. Haunting the shadows and alleys. All to ensure that she would be able to rule forever, with no one to challenge her."

"He fight," Drakul rumbled, interrupting. "Lose."

"Thank you for the reminder," Aaron said with boundless dry sarcasm. "Yes. When I found out what she was doing, I confronted her. I tried to stop her. Even fight her. I failed."

"That's when you came back here?" I asked.

"You make it sound like it was my choice," he said. "I didn't 'come back.' I was unleashed on the people of this region. After Elenia spent months torturing me with a lack of blood, turning me feral until I was out of my mind, she let me go near one of the towns."

I stared in horror. "Oh, god. But how did nobody find out?"

"They covered it up," Aaron said heavily. "Drakul and a few others. They created the persona of Vlad the Impaler. All my victims were dead before they were impaled. Dead from my own hands as I fed on them."

"A cover-up," I whispered, stunned.

"It took me nearly thirty years to gather myself," Aaron said, leaning forward to rest his elbows on the table. "Three decades and countless innocent deaths. All because of her."

"Not Alaine fault," Drakul stated, eyes flaring bigger. "Not fault."

"I didn't want to do it. I didn't want to kill them."

He looked up at me, my heart breaking slightly at the haunted look on his face. I'd never seen him like that, so open and vulnerable, exposed. He was always the composed one, who had his head on straight. Never really letting emotions guide him. It was the opposite of the Aaron I had in front of me.

"I know you didn't," I said, sensing that he was looking for forgiveness from me. "Especially knowing what I know now about you."

"I don't want the title they bestowed on me. And I don't want the name originally given to me," he growled. "That person is dead. I stand apart from vampires. I might be one, but I am not one of hers. I've spent six centuries trying to create a name for myself to prove that."

"Yeah," I said. "I understand better now. I do."

"Can you forgive me?" he whispered.

"I'm not sure there's anything for me *to* forgive. This was all before my time. You were tortured, turned into a creature not of your own making, not by your own hand. You've dealt with centuries of guilt and done your best to make amends for it. I'm not sure anyone could ask more of you, Aaron."

"I can," he growled.

"Maybe. Maybe not." I smirked at a memory.

"What?"

"Oh, nothing. I was just remembering something. Now that I know she's the 'other woman' that people have mentioned when they see me with you."

"What is it you remember?" he asked.

I grinned. "Zeus likes me better than her."

Aaron stared at me. "*That's* what you took from all this? That he likes you better?"

"Of course, it's not *all* I took from it," I said,

laying my hand on top of his, letting him feel my presence. "But it's nice knowing that even some of the gods think I'm better than her."

"It's not hard," Fenrir muttered. "Have you met that bitch? Very unlikeable."

"Hey, let me have this little win, okay?" I said. "I just found out I'm going to kill his first girlfriend."

Fenrir shrugged, and I sobered, looking at Aaron, gathering his full attention.

"What is it?" he asked.

"You told me I would have to be ready to do whatever it takes to succeed. Now, I need to know the same from you, *Aaron*," I said, stressing his current name, the person he was. "If the opportunity presents itself, are you willing to take it?"

He flinched. "Take it?"

I nodded slowly, watching him closely for his reaction. "I have to know. Are you willing, and able, to kill your ex?"

CHAPTER EIGHTEEN

"**K**ill her?" he echoed solemnly.

I remained quiet, letting him process the question. Aaron wasn't an idiot; I knew he understood that there was only one way this ended. But had he truly contemplated that it might be *him* who had to kill her? If something happened to me, it was imperative that she still be removed from power.

"She has to go," Fred said, appearing nearby, silently admitting to having eavesdropped. "You have to know that."

"I do." Aaron sighed, looking down, but not before I got a glimpse of something I'd never seen in his eyes before. Not when we were staring down a hundred vampires eager to chop us up or the terrifying guardian spiders of Mordathu. He hadn't batted an eye when I'd summoned Zeus, having been more shocked than anything.

"What is it?" I asked, squeezing his hand, trying to reassure him it couldn't be that bad.

"I tried, once," he said, finally looking up.

I stiffened at the haunted gauntness that came over him, stealing the life from his features. Seeing this new side of Aaron was unnerving, but also, I thought, necessary.

"To kill her," he clarified. "When I first found out about the insanity she'd begun, culling us of all females, I stood up to her. Told her that what she was doing was utter madness and that she couldn't keep it up. But I failed. She was too strong."

"Aren't you older? I thought vampires grew stronger as you 'aged,'" I said, looking around to the others for confirmation.

Fred nodded at me.

"Technically, yes. But after twelve hundred years, the difference is minimal. Definitely not enough to make any difference in a fight."

"She's your equal, then," I said thoughtfully, reevaluating my perception of the queen.

"That's what she wants you to think," Aaron whispered. "That's why I went after her on my own. I thought I could handle her."

"So, what happened?" I asked, unable to hold back. Something must have gone horribly awry for him to be having this sort of reaction. Maybe it had something to do with why he'd vehemently tried to convince me not to go after her in the first place.

Maybe he was afraid that I would lose. That he would lose me. Because of whatever it is that he knows about her.

"She beat me to a pulp," Aaron stated bluntly, exhaling slowly. "I didn't see it coming. I landed the first blow due to sheer surprise, I'm sure."

"What?" I gasped. He'd said he lost. But I'd been picturing her getting a lucky blow in that stunned him. Imagining Aaron having his ass kicked was both tough and troubling.

"It's true," he admitted. "You can see the evidence yourself. The room's been left as-is since then. She handed my ass to me, then spent a few decades torturing me as punishment for breaking her heart."

"Bitch," Fenrir grunted under his breath, speaking for all of us with that one word.

"How was she able to do that?" I asked, glancing at the vampire-wolf shifter. "What gave her such a tremendous advantage? Is she like us?"

"No," Aaron and Fenrir answered at the same time.

"Then, what is she?"

"A vampire," Aaron said. "She's nothing more than a normal vampire. Ruthless and cunning, yes. Willing to do whatever it takes to survive.

Things I never thought possible of her when we first met."

He looked at me, his eyes haunted once more. Whatever it was that he was going to tell us, it wasn't good. I could see him searching for forgiveness already.

"What did she do, Aaron?" I said. "You need to tell us."

"She has blood slaves," he said heavily.

"*What?*" Fred hissed. "Those are outlawed!"

"I know," Aaron growled. "I helped her pass the law making them outlawed! All of this is my fault, you know. I helped put her ass on that throne, and then I helped her do everything necessary to secure her position. I was so naïve and blind."

"What are blood slaves?" I asked, looking back and forth between Aaron and Fred. "Why does that make her stronger?"

"You've experienced it," Fenrir said. "When you feed on fresh blood. The power that comes with it. The strength. It affects us all the same, though we get other 'benefits.' But take two vampires, everything else equal, and then let one feed on fresh blood. That one will have strength and superiority over the other."

"So, she fed before she fought you. Is that what you're saying?" I asked, disgusted. "On people she keeps around, against their will, draining them of blood to be stronger than everyone else?"

"Basically," Aaron said. "But it's worse than that. Human blood is the weakest of all. There's nothing extra in it. It's plentiful, however, and so it was the most commonly used among those in power in Madrigal before blood slaves were outlawed."

I felt a sinking sensation. "But humans aren't the only things that bleed," I said.

Aaron shook his head. "The stronger the being, the more their blood affects us. Most are too strong to keep chained. Not worth the risk of feeding on them. But some are superior to humans that are still available."

"Who?" I had to know.

Aaron bared his teeth unhappily, staring right at me. My stomach sank as I realized what he was about to tell me. The ugly truth that he'd been hiding all this time.

"Shifters," he said, his anger evident in the snarl. "She keeps a group of shifter blood slaves, whom she feeds from regularly so that she's always stronger than anyone else."

"And you didn't think to tell me this?" I asked coldly. "She keeps my people chained up, draining them, and you thought this wasn't worth me knowing?"

"I didn't know how to tell you," he ground out. "You had enough going on already, from the realization that you and your mother are vampire-shifters to going through your Soulshift to learning to control the darker side of our nature. Then, on top of that, that bitch put out a Blood Letter on you."

"You lied to me."

"I did *not* lie to you," Aaron growled dangerously, offended by my insinuation. "I would have told you if the issue came up directly. I simply did not bring it up to you because, at the time, it did not matter. You had other things requiring your attention."

"There are others," I said, not giving up. "Others who would love to know that she keeps our kind imprisoned."

"Is that what you want, Jo? A war between your people and hers? Are you going to send Johnathan and your already weakened pack up against her? Even if all your packs came together, Madrigal is far more heavily defended than you can imagine. It would be a slaughter on both sides, all over one woman. The population of Madrigal doesn't deserve your wrath. They don't know what their queen does behind closed doors. But they *would* fight for her if you tried to invade."

Grinding my teeth together in a fury, I searched for a hole in his logic but couldn't find one. He was right. If Johnathan and the other alphas found out what the queen was doing, they would march on Madrigal in force. It *would* be a slaughter. Thousands of shifters and vampires would die. All to get at one woman.

She's the one who needs to die. But maybe we can do this without the mass slaughter of innocents. I hope we can.

"And what if we can't do this any other way?" I asked. "What if invading Madrigal is how this has to end? I'm not saying it has to, but what if it *does*?"

Aaron looked down for a moment, thinking. When he lifted his chin to meet my gaze, his eyes were alight with renewed intensity, burning brighter than they had in a long time.

"Then I will lead the charge myself if that's how it must be," he snarled.

I chewed on my lip, considering his response.

"We'll see," was all I could bring myself to say before standing from the table, not meeting anyone else's gaze.

"Where are you going?" Aaron asked.

"To think," I said, trying to restrain the heat in my tone. "I'm still pretty angry that you took the decision away from my people. That you hid it for centuries from people who might want to know. How many hundreds, or thousands, has she stolen away to keep as her personal buffet? Or does she even steal them? People might notice that. Oh, god. Does she *breed* them?"

Aaron shrugged. "I don't know. I honestly don't know, Jo. You have to believe me on that."

"I want to," I said and turned away, leaving the hall behind.

It was true. I desperately wanted to believe that he was ignorant of how Elenia acquired her blood slaves.

But did I?

CHAPTER NINETEEN

Without realizing it, my feet carried me down the same hallway Drakul had shown me earlier. It was taking me toward the destroyed room. A room I knew now had been Aaron's. It was the room in which he'd tried to stop Elenia.

I followed the footsteps marking the dusty floor, letting them take me right to the room. Again, I stood in the doorway, surveying the damage. Now I could picture it. The way she'd thrown him through the table. And slammed him down into the bed, crushing the frame under the strength of her blow.

Aaron had tried. He'd tried to fight back. That had to count for something, didn't it? So why couldn't I look past that?

"Maybe I should have told you."

I stiffened as he spoke from behind me, but I didn't jump. Nor did I turn around.

Fingers gripped my arm, and Aaron turned me around. I started to protest until I saw the anger in his eyes.

"Maybe that was a mistake," he continued. "I don't see it that way, but you do, and perhaps we'll never see eye to eye on it. But that doesn't make me a terrible person, Jo. I didn't hold back information that could have changed your life or prevented everything that's happened to you from happening."

I didn't respond.

"*I'm* not the one keeping the blood slaves, Jo. I didn't help her get them or keep them. I fought against the ruling elite in Madrigal to have them outlawed. To stop everyone from drawing on them, human or not. I did that!"

His shout echoed down the hallway. I stared at him in silence, watching his face, seeing the emotions cross it as he relived his past. As he tried to get through to me.

"When I found out about her psychotic anti-female program? I fought against that, too. I tried to stop her. I nearly died, and she tortured me until I broke. Every day, she would tear me down a little further without building me back up. Then, she flung me out among humans when I was nothing more than a blood-starved beast. Leaving me to become a murderer of epic proportions."

What was I supposed to say to that?

"I have to live with that every day of my life, Jo," he whispered. "Every day. Tens of thousands of people dead by my hand alone."

"It must have been horrible."

"When I finally started to recover my mind, thanks to Drakul and some others, the true extent of what I'd done began to sink in. But did I give up and die? No, I didn't!"

"You didn't go after her again either," I pointed out, suddenly realizing that *that's* what bothered me so much. Aaron had tried once, and when he'd lost, he'd never tried again.

He jerked backward at my accusation, spine stiffening, while the sapphire orbs burned even hotter. "No, I didn't. I spent the next six *hundred* years helping people out," he snarled at me defensively. "Protecting people. Trying to do *good* by them and show them that my word was worth something."

"What do you mean?"

"My contracts," he said, some of his anger fading, deflating him slightly as he talked. "That's why they're so important to me, Jo. Why I value them so heavily, regardless of the pay. Those contracts are my word. They show that I am not like Elenia. That I am not like *them*. It is my proof that I am sane."

"What good is sane if she's still on the throne?"

"I did what I could," he protested. "I made friends and connections. I worked as actively against her as I could, without crossing the line into forcing her to come after me."

"And you never went after her either," I said. "You tried once, and when that failed, you said, 'nope, no good, I'm done, I tried.' You left them to suffer."

"You're right," he said. "I didn't go after them. Not because I didn't want to, Jo. Trust me, I did. I've thought about it for centuries, wishing I'd struck with a knife to her throat instead of a fist. How I could have ended this then. I've lived with the regret of knowing that I was the one who made it possible for her to do this. And do you know why I didn't go after her again, despite all that?"

"Why is that?"

"Because I'm not strong enough, Jo. With shifter blood in her, she will beat me. Every. Single. Time. There isn't anything *I* can do about that."

My eyes narrowed at the emphasis on that one word. "What are you trying to say?"

Aaron watched me in silence for a long time. "There isn't any way I can beat her," he said softly. "But *you* can."

"Me?" I said, confused. "What?"

"You can fight her. And win. You can be stronger than her, Jo. Than anyone."

I recoiled away from him as I understood what he meant. "You mean if I feed on live humans."

"Or shifters," he said. "Like her blood slaves."

"How can you suggest that?" I gasped, stunned.

"Think about it, Jo!" he said, punching a fist into his other palm to emphasize his point. "We *have* to find a way to beat her. Which means we're going to need someone as strong as her. Who can beat her in a fight. Think of all the *good* you could do."

"But you want me to feed on people!" I shouted, backing away from him, into the room itself. "On real people!"

The idea of feeding on someone had a dual effect on me. My mind and soul were thoroughly and utterly repulsed by the idea. My wolf agreed. She didn't mind the kill at the end of a hunt, but she didn't want to *feed* on them in that sense. Yet we were opposed by another presence, a dark, nonsentient *Hunger* that had me all but salivating at the idea, pushing the memories of the near-sexual ecstasy of feeding to the forefront of my mind.

I gasped and heaved, my chest rapidly rising and falling as I tried to calm myself. I couldn't let it get to my head. Feeding produced unparalleled pleasure in me, but I had to remind myself it wasn't real. It was fake.

"Feed, yes. *Not* kill. You'll have to pull away at the last moment. But then you go to another. And another. I'll be there with you, Jo. I will ensure you don't kill them."

I stared at him, horrified at how he kept pushing the plan and at the building arousal inside me. I wanted to hate it with my entire being, to deny it, but I couldn't. There would always be a part of me that was excited at the idea of feeding, and it shamed me.

"How can you endorse this plan?" I whispered.

"Because, Jo," he said solemnly, "if you make this sacrifice, think of how many people you will *save*. The blood slaves, present and future. Any newborn female vampires who will be hunted to the death, without ever realizing why, despite having done nothing wrong. If you take this burden onto yourself, all of that will go away."

I shuddered. "I can't do that," I protested. "You … you ask too much of me. I'm not that strong."

Aaron looked ready to push his argument, to try harder to convince me. He opened his mouth, eyes wide with fervent intensity. Yet, something stopped him dead in his tracks. He blinked twice and then abruptly calmed.

"Okay," he said quietly. "It was worth a try."

I sagged slightly at the change. "Does that

mean you're going to leave now? Because I won't do what you want?"

His face crinkled into a mighty frown. "What? Of course not, Jo. I wouldn't leave you."

That hadn't been *quite* what I'd asked, but I could see how he would think so.

"I was serious when I came to your door and told you that I wanted you," he continued. "I want you to be mine, Jo. That hasn't changed. Not one bit. I care about you a lot. I told you something drew me to you, and now I know what it was. You had vampire blood all this time. We just didn't know it. But whether you're willing to go that far to fight Elenia or not, it doesn't change how I feel about you."

"Okay," I said, not sure what else to say.

"I want you. I want to be *with* you, so I'll respect your decision on this. If we have to go up against her, just the two of us as we are, then so be it. I'll be at your side until the end, Jo."

I looked away, blinking back unbidden tears, not entirely sure where they'd come from. He was serious, I could tell that much, but why was I ready to cry over it?

"I'm sorry," I said, desperate to fill the silence with something, anything. "For getting so mad at you. I know you've tried hard to make up for it. I don't want to fight with you."

"Me neither," he said with a wry smile. "But I

respect your opinions and your decisions. I won't always agree, though, and I expect the same from you. It's not whether we fight or not that matters. We *will* fight and disagree. It's what happens *after* the fight that matters. That's what's important to me. Any couple will fight. That's normal and healthy, in my opinion, *when it's done right*."

I looked at him, taking something entirely different away from what he'd just said than what he'd intended.

"Are you saying we're a couple?" I whispered.

Aaron stared at me. "I'm saying I want to be. I've made no secret of that. The real question is, Jo, do *you* want to be one?"

CHAPTER TWENTY

"With me, of course," he added hastily a moment later, trying to break the tension.

I giggled. I couldn't help it. The sheer obviousness of his statement just struck my funny bone. As if I'd been considering being in a full-fledged relationship with anyone *but* him! There wasn't even another man in my life. Who would I even consider? Fenrir?

Was he actually concerned that I might be developing feelings for Fenrir? Just because he helped me learn about the darkness inside me, the Hunger, and how to fight it? Was he jealous of that?

For a moment, I thought about toying with him, of pretending, but I quickly chucked that idea out of my mind. Now wasn't the time for that, nor did Aaron deserve it. Not right now.

"You don't have to answer right now," he said. "Please, don't feel that pressure. I can wait."

He left off the implied, "I've waited long enough already, what's a bit more."

I turned away from him, stepping deeper into the room. "This is where it happened, isn't it?" I asked.

Aaron silently followed me in. "Yes," he whispered. "This is where I tried to stop her. And where she kicked my ass."

"I take it none of this damage was done by you throwing her around."

He snorted, a deep sarcastic noise. "I wish. I'd love to regain some of my pride and say we duked it out, and she happened to get lucky. Trust me, that would have saved me a lot of ridiculing once the truth made its way out. But no, none of this was done by me."

Sliding past me, he moved to stand next to the destroyed bed. "I was here," he said somewhat distantly. "She was across from me. We were arguing. I'd just told her that I had found out about the deaths of female vampires, how she'd gone insane with power."

"What happened next?"

Aaron closed his eyes. "I watched her heart break," he said softly. "She must have thought I would go along with her. I don't know if she was just insane or truly loved me that much to think

I would ignore it. I don't know, and I never asked. It doesn't matter. She stared at me as I told her that I couldn't support this, and she began to cry. Telling me that it was for the best. That she'd … that she'd done it for *us*, out of some sort of sick, twisted sense of devotion to me."

"What did you say back?"

"Uh, I told her she was insane if she thought I would go along with that." He winced.

"I take it that didn't go over so well?"

Aaron gestured around him. "Whatever gave you that impression?"

"Probably the one in the wall there," I said, pointing to a human-sized outline in the stone wall. "That impression. Made by you flying across the room into the wall?"

Aaron stared at me. "*Not* the type of impression I was talking about."

I laughed. "I'm sorry. I couldn't resist."

He nodded slowly. "She told me I had to do it if I loved her. So, I told her that I guess I didn't love her. Not the person she'd become."

I sobered quickly. "I'm sorry."

He waved it off. "I should have seen it sooner. The way the power had twisted her, warping her mind into something different. The woman I loved was long gone, had been gone for decades, if not more. I was too blinded by my love for her to see it."

"So, you hit her."

"Oh, yeah. I clocked her full in the face the instant I decided I had to stop her from going any further," he said. "I'll always remember the look on her face as she flew across the room. The shock and pain."

He wasn't talking about the pain from his blow. But rather the hurt of betrayal, I sensed, from the one she loved turning on her.

"Then, she came at me and flung me around, beating me until I was a hair from death," he muttered. "Not my most pleasant memory."

I moved to where he still stood at the foot of the bed. "You did the right thing," I whispered, wrapping him up in a hug. "And I respect you for that."

"Thank you," he said, slowly lifting his arms to return the squeeze.

For some time, neither of us spoke, simply swaying back and forth in time with one another. There was one question I had left, but it took me the better part of a few minutes to gather the courage to ask it. At some point, he must have felt it in my body.

"What is it?" he asked, moving me back a half step so he could look into my face, his eyes filled with worry and concern.

"Aaron," I said, halting and then starting again. "Aaron, I need to know something."

"Of course. Anything," he said, spreading his arms wide. "Whatever you want to know, just ask. I have not, and will not, lie to you."

I locked gazes with him, jade versus sapphire. I didn't want him looking away.

"Are you over her?"

Bracing myself for an immediate reply, a harsh denial of any current feelings, I once more found myself surprised by Aaron. He opened his mouth immediately, but perhaps upon seeing my face, he paused and truly considered the question the way I wanted him to. It wasn't *what* the answer was that mattered to me. It was the *truth* of it.

"There's a part of me, I think, that will always wonder about what could have been. If she hadn't become the person that she is now. I think I'll always love the person I fell in love with. But I love the memory of that person and the time we had together. I can't just forget it, but I can see it and see what I felt for her in the way I'm starting to feel about you. Much of you is similar to the person she used to be, but in you, there's so much more, Jo."

He smiled at me wryly, sensing my embarrassment, I'm sure. "I don't know how to describe it, but when I look at you, I'm overwhelmed by the goodness within and the strength of character, your willingness to do whatever you must, if you believe it to be the right thing."

"Thank you," I whispered as he trailed off and

looked at me almost eagerly, like a puppy hoping it had done the right thing. "For the kind words, but also for the honesty."

"I've had a long time to think about it," he said. "But the person Elenia is now? I can't love that. I don't love her. Killing her would, I think, bring some closure. I would no longer be reminded of what she's become or of the damage she's done. I could simply enjoy the memories of my past and move on with my future. A future that I very much hope includes you."

He stepped forward, wrapping his hands around my waist, making me feel tiny and safe. His fingers gripped my hips tight, and my bottom lip curled under my teeth instinctively.

"Pretty bold to be thinking about the future, given all we have to do to get there, don't you think?" I asked, my throat suddenly dry.

"Time waits for no man," Aaron said. "Or woman, in this case. I know what I want, Jo, and I'm not afraid to take it."

"Take it?" I half-teased. "Am I just a possession to you?"

"No, of course not," he rumbled, moving closer, blue eyes bright in the darkness, like their own tiny sources of light. "But that doesn't mean I don't want you to be *mine*."

Then, he lifted me by the waist so I could wrap my legs around his back as he kissed me. The scorching heat of his lips stole the breath from my lungs, making the world spin as I struggled to suck in more air. Heat rushed through me like a fire spiraling out of control.

A feral growl escaped Aaron as I clawed at the back of his neck, holding myself up, desperate to stay close to him even as he pressed against me, his own reaction building between us.

Cold stone pressed against my back as he slammed me into the wall with that calculated roughness that felt so good. I was tiny and small, and he simply moved me where he wanted me. I was his, and yet, despite the control over my body, I knew that he was mine.

We slipped into each other's embrace, a flurry of fingers removing clothing and undergarments, leaving us free as we sank to the floor, the thick carpet underneath one of the few things not shredded or destroyed.

This wasn't the way I'd envisioned things happening between us, but as our bodies merged and became one, my mind filling with *true* ecstasy, I knew that this was the way it was *meant* to be.

If I hoped to keep it, though, we were both going to have to survive what was to come.

CHAPTER
TWENTY-ONE

"This is quite the setup you have," I said as we walked across the parking lot toward the darkened office building. It was an hour after midnight, but nobody was home, it seemed.

Three stories high, with modern glass architecture from floor to ceiling, the building screamed *money*. The prime real estate overlooked a large grassy park next to the river, and the expensive glass building held clean but minimalist signs that indicated this was the home of Ironchill Holdings. It was the only building in the lot, with parking on one side, the park on the other, and thick strips of grass and trees separating it from other lots.

"Ironchill?" I asked, curious about the name as Aaron keyed in his code.

The security doors slid open with a soft hiss, and we went in.

"Blood has iron, and we keep it cold," he said with a shrug. "It's not very imaginative, I know, but I really don't care about that sort of thing."

"No, I like it," I said. "It's subtle and understated. Prevents you from standing out. Calling it 'Definitely Not Vampire Food Systems' or something would attract a little more attention."

Aaron barked out a laugh, shaking his head. "Yes, I can see how people might be a bit intrigued by that name. Good thing that was our second option."

I giggled, leaning my head against him as he guided us to the elevators at the back. The movement felt easy and natural. A barrier had come down between us after spending the night in his arms. It had been so casual and easy; I hadn't realized it was even there until it fell. But when I woke this morning, it was obvious that everything had changed.

For the better, it seems, though only time will tell.

We got into the elevators, and Aaron punched a code into another keypad. To my surprise, the elevator *descended*, taking us several floors down.

"Not going up?"

"Nothing there," he said with a shrug. "Decoy offices, nothing more. Unless you wanted to take a quick break ..."

I blushed at the suggestive tone. Part of me considered saying yes. After all, it *would* be both fun and pleasurable. I very much preferred *that* sort of endorphin rush to the one I was setting myself up for by coming to this building.

"Maybe later," I said, squeezing his arm, taking momentary joy in the way his bicep flexed under my fingers. "My mind is a bit distracted right now."

"Of course," he said, suddenly serious as the elevator came to a halt and the doors slid open. "My apologies."

"Don't feel bad," I said. "Normally, I would probably take you up on that. It's just, right now, with what's before me, I'm not really in the mood."

Aaron only nodded, gesturing for me to lead the way out of the elevator. "Don't worry," he murmured as he followed. "This is going to work."

"We hope," I said. "There's still a chance it won't."

"It's *going* to work," he growled.

I looked around the floor, shivering at the cold. Wisps of fog billowed down over giant storage cases that lined the walls. The cold air nipped at my skin, tightening it. Steel storage units perhaps twelve or fifteen feet high ran straight ahead of us, while in the ceilings above, generators provided the cold air necessary to keep the blood chilled.

Aaron started walking, ignoring the closest units. "We're going to want the freshest for this," he said, pointing at the end unit. "Last in, last out. This will be from this week. It's going to give you the biggest boost."

"Yay," I said, not excited for what was to come.

"You need to feed before this," Aaron growled.

We'd been over this topic many times, and I didn't feel like rehashing it. I hated it, but I was forced to agree with him. It was necessary. To survive the amount of blood that needed to be drawn from me to cancel out the Blood Letter, I would need to be as strong as possible first.

Which meant drinking a lot of blood.

I nearly retched at the idea but was stopped by the monster inside of me, its eagerness to taste blood overwhelming my disgust. That nearly set me off as well, but I held myself together, fighting the Hunger back.

I'm in charge. Behave, or you get none, I snarled at it within my mind, curious about whether it understood me or not.

Whether it knew what the words meant or it could feel my emotions, the Hunger subsided. It would get what it wanted regardless, so there was no need to fight me for control. That would only delay the feeding.

"I hate this," I muttered, slowly trailing after Aaron, unable to force myself to go faster.

He didn't say anything. Just reached for the first door and pulled it open.

"The sooner we're done," he said, turning to look inside, "the sooner—*get back*!"

I had a split second to pause when he flung a hand up to stop me from approaching. Then, the entire storage unit exploded, slamming Aaron back against the unit opposite. He reacted swiftly, bouncing off the door and flinging himself as close to me as he could.

He was halfway to his feet when the *second* storage unit exploded. The door blew off its hinges, spinning him around mid-flight.

"Back!" he coughed as smoke filled the room and alarms began to clang. "Get back!"

I started toward him, but the next blood storage unit blew up, the explosion knocking me on my ass. Aaron emerged from the smoke and grabbed me by the arm.

"Come on! We have to get some blood. They must all be rigged," he said, hauling me to my feet as we stumbled for the oldest blood at the front.

Behind us, the banks started exploding. Each one pummeled us with a new shockwave.

"Split up!" I shouted over the ringing in my ears. "Each of us goes for one!"

"Take as much as you can and get out!" he hollered, coughing again as he inhaled. "The code is 80014."

I braced myself against the wall while punching in the code, then flung the door open. In the middle of a room with bags of blood hanging from racks on a wall was a black box, which I assumed were the explosives. A big red clock counted down from four on the bomb. Moving as fast as I could, I swiped bags from the nearest rack and then dove for the door.

The bomb went off just as I cleared the door. I clutched the blood to my chest, trying to shield it with my body. I hit the floor hard as the door clipped me. A second later, warm heat ran down my side. It must have broken skin. There wasn't time for that, though. We had to get out of there.

Aaron emerged from his unit a second later, and then it went off. The shockwave hit me full-on, and I felt the blood bags I held explode. Immediately, the scent of iron filled my nostrils. My Hunger didn't care about the smoke in the air as it inhaled deeply. It had only one focus.

"No!" Aaron barked, slapping me across the face. "There isn't time for that. Come on. We have to get out of here."

I snarled, fangs sliding into place as I stared at him.

"I have fresh blood for you," he said, dangling one of the packs he'd managed to save in front of me. "Do you want that or the spoiled stuff in front of you?"

Lunging after him, I followed him into the elevator, eager for a taste. Once we were there, he dropped the blood and wrapped me up in a bear hug.

"Remember who you are," he said into my ear as we started upward. "Focus, Jo. Focus on my voice. On me. It's Aaron. You can do this. You can resist it. It doesn't own you. *You're* in charge."

I growled, feeling half-lost in myself, but something within his words lent fresh strength to my fight. While I battled for control, Aaron dragged me along, my body following his commands instinctively.

We tumbled out of the elevator and ran for the exit.

"Jo!" Aaron barked as we pounded through the parking lot. "Come on, Jo. Get yourself together. We're not out of this yet!"

We weren't? Slowly but surely I fought back the tidal wave of hunger and darkness, reasserting control of myself. I leaned heavily on memories of who I was, of what I was fighting for. My mother. My father. Aaron.

I know what real pleasure is, I snarled, calling up the experiences of the night before. Of my first time with Aaron and how wonderful it had been. *That* was true ecstasy, and I let the darkness in me know that anything it tried to summon would pale in comparison.

"Come on, Jo," Aaron urged. "Hurry up. I need you."

His words snapped me back to reality with an abrupt shock. He *needed* me. I was wanted by someone. I shook myself, looking up at him. "What is it?"

Aaron inclined his head in front of us. I turned and found myself standing face to face with a line of dark figures. The parking lot lights over them may have been shattered, but there was no denying the menacing figure standing at their head, sword sheathed over his shoulder.

"Corvis," I growled.

Also known as the Black Nacht, he was the head of the Nacht Bringers, Elenia's elite shock troops. We'd tangled several times before, most recently in Seguin, where I'd been forced to let him go, an unhappy truce that saved the lives of dozens of shifters. It had left a sick taste in my mouth.

Now, he was back for revenge.

"What unfortunate timing," Corvis called across the asphalt that separated his forces from our meager duo.

"I dunno, seemed pretty good to me," I called, my singed and torn clothing evidence of just how close it had been.

"Truthfully, we didn't expect to catch you," Corvis chuckled. "That was simply fortuitous timing. I was just here for the storage. But to have you caught in my web as well. Most exciting."

I gritted my teeth. This was supposed to have been a simple recovery mission. Grab some blood and get back to the castle as fast as possible. We'd traveled by portal, something I was getting used to, using the old hut in the woods. This time, there was thankfully no vampire bear to chase us. We'd then taken a taxi to the office. Fighting a bunch of elite vampire warriors was *not* something we'd planned for. Stealth had been our goal.

"We're so glad we could help," Aaron said, backpedaling and taking me with him.

"What are you doing?" I hissed under my breath.

"Buying time."

"But—"

"We got out early," he said, cutting me off. "Something about having to run from the bombs. Our exit time is still a few minutes away."

"It's also on the far side of them," I pointed out. "So going this way won't help."

"Sure, it will," he said. "It'll keep their attention on us."

"That might not be the attention we want."

"We don't have much choice."

He was right. Corvis had caught us completely flat-footed. The bombs were an unpleasant surprise, depriving us of the easy access to blood that I needed.

"Did we save any?" I asked.

Aaron patted his vest. "Only four," he said, dejected.

"Shit. Less than a quarter of what we'd wanted to take."

"It'll be enough," he growled. "It has to be."

"Concentrate on keeping them safe," I said as Corvis and the Nacht Bringers approached.

"And what? Let you get chopped to bits by the swords? No, I don't think so," he said, pulling the packs from his vest and handing them to me, not giving me a chance to say no. "They stay with you. *You* and them stay safe. This is about you. The plan requires you to succeed. Not me."

"And what are you going to do?" I asked.

"Plan B," Aaron said, pulling out a pistol from a shoulder holster I didn't know he had and firing three quick shots at Corvis.

The motion was so swift and unexpected that none of us reacted until the vampire hit the ground with a trio of slugs in his chest. The other vampires paused for a moment.

"He has limited capacity. Together!" another shouted.

The vampires came at us in a blob.

"C'mon, c'mon," Aaron growled as he backed up with me, holding on to his fire until the vampires were closer. "Hurry up."

A car came barreling up the road, tires screeching as it whipped around the corner and into the parking lot, scattering vampires as it came. The door opened before it had even come to a halt, letting out a woman, her long brown hair flowing behind her.

"Looks like you could use some help," Dani said as a sword appeared in her hands, runes glowing with purple energy down the blade.

The vampires came to a scrambling halt as my best friend in the whole world stepped up to meet them. She carved through the first one. The vampire didn't have time to scream before she took its head, whirling and taking the arm from another with smooth, even strokes.

Aaron and I reversed our course and charged, even as the vehicle's other occupant emerged, revealing a tall male with shoulder-length black hair. He whirled a hand in front of him, and a golden spear spun through the air before plunging deep into the chest of the nearest vampire.

The sight of the two newcomers was enough to drive the vampires back. They fled without much more of a fight. Not that I could blame them. They weren't equipped to fight a god. Let alone two.

"What the hell happened here?" Dani asked, coming up to embrace me. I hugged her back, wondering if it was my imagination or if I could feel her stomach protruding ever so slightly.

"Some really bad luck. I'm just glad we'd made arrangements to have you two pick us up after."

"I was surprised to get your call," Dani said, a bit of reprimand in her tone.

"You know why I don't come to you if I can help it," I said, looking at her.

Dani was tall and lean. She had gorgeous hair that hung halfway down her back and green eyes like mine, though hers were a darker, more olive color. If you asked her, she would say she was blocky and without curves, attributes of mine which she craved. But I looked at her and saw her lithe power—and wished I had her height.

The grass is always greener, I suppose.

"I am *not* made of glass," Dani growled.

"You're also carrying the first child of a shifter god to be born in millennia," I countered, crossing my arms.

If there was one person in the world who out-stubborned Dani, it was me, and I wasn't about to cave now.

"I'm also a god now," Dani ground out. "I can take care of myself."

"Gods can die," I whispered, reminding her of how she'd come into her power. "I won't be responsible for that. Not unless absolutely necessary."

"And this was necessary?"

"This?" I said, waving at the bodies. "This wasn't what I called you for, though your assistance in cleaning it up would be appreciated."

Dani tilted her head at me, eyes narrowing. "What *did* you call us for, then?"

I swallowed. "You're not going to like it."

CHAPTER TWENTY-TWO

"You're right," Dani said, scrutinizing my face. "I'm not going to like it. How bad is it?"

"Bad," I whispered, looking behind us as the building began to smoke, the fires from the underground storage area finally making their way to the surface.

"We need to clean up and get out of here," Aaron said, coming up to me and holding my hand.

Dani's eyes darted swiftly to our joined hands, though she didn't say anything. I knew I'd get the fifth degree about it later. When there weren't any boys around. Presumably, Aaron and Vir would exchange a few grunts about it, too, or whatever it was guys did to acknowledge changes like that.

"Give us a second," Dani said. "Just your friendly neighborhood cleanup crew, that's us."

"Next thing I know, you're going to start charging for this service," I said as purple magic began to glow from Dani's hands.

"Good idea," she muttered, focusing most of her attention on the magic. "But do we charge by the body or by the hour?"

"As long as there's a friends and family discount."

She glanced back at me. "You planning on racking up some more or something?"

"Not on this realm," I whispered as she cast her power over the nearest body, searing it cleanly into ash that swiftly blew away on the night breeze.

Nearby, Vir was doing the same.

"Where's this one?" Dani asked, pointing at a giant pool of blood lacking a body.

"Shit," I muttered, picking up a shell casing from nearby and pocketing it. A quick search nearby revealed two more.

"Shit, *what*?" Dani asked.

"They took him with them," Aaron said. "Which means he isn't dead. Tough bastard."

"Who?"

"Corvis," I spat. "Elenia's chief fixer."

"The Black Nacht," Aaron supplied when Vir

looked confused at the term. "Head of her personal guard."

"I'd really hoped we were rid of him," I said. "It was so satisfying watching you shoot him like that. Such a lame way for him to die. I found it fitting."

"I guess we'll have to do it the old-fashioned way," Aaron growled, looking down at the pool of blood before Dani scorched the pavement, removing the last signs of battle. There would be questions, but none that could be traced back to us.

Flames licked up from inside the building now.

"Sorry about this place," Dani said. "Your real estate investments have really taken a hit since you met Jo and me."

I snickered, briefly reminded of how demons had trashed his penthouse loft and mountainside chalet in their pursuit of Dani. To the best of my knowledge, repairs on both were still underway.

"I should bill you for it," he grumped as something else exploded inside the building, shattering glass.

"Probably," I agreed.

A moment later, sirens sounded in the distance.

"We should go," Dani suggested, motioning to

the car. "Get out of here."

"Yeah," I said, not looking forward to what would come next.

"Then you can tell me why you need my help."

I licked my lips, heading for the car's backseat. "Yeah. About that."

Vir got in and revved the engine while Dani sat next to him, and I climbed in behind her. I didn't want to have to face the glare I knew would be directed my way once I told her what was up.

"Can you move your seat up?" Aaron asked as he squished into his seat behind Vir.

"No," the shifter god said, putting the car in drive.

Dani cackled quietly to herself, something about revenge, but as we pulled out of the parking lot, her attention swiftly returned to me.

"Okay, spill," she said, turning her head as far as it could go. "What's so bad that you finally had to call me in?"

"Well, truthfully," I said, only wincing once, "we really only needed Vir."

Dani's face scrunched up. "What?"

"You told me already when you tried to cure my mother with your magic that he was the one who was good with the fine stuff. That you just didn't have the experience yet to really be great at it, right?"

"I suppose. But what do you need him for, then? What sort of fine magic are we talking about?"

I hesitated.

"Just tell her," Aaron said. "It's going to come out sooner or later. It's like a bandage. Ripping it off is always easier."

"Fine," I said, giving him a look, then glancing at Dani. "I need him to keep me alive while I get rid of this Blood Letter."

"How does fine magic work for that? If you wanted stuff blown up, sure. But this?"

"I found a way to get rid of the Blood Letter," I explained. "Which needs to go. If I'm going after Elenia, I can't constantly be dealing with others getting in my way at the worst time. It needs to go."

"A Blood Letter can only be revoked by the person who wrote it," Vir said, stating it like an absolute fact.

"True," I said. "But, then again, I'm not revoking it. I'm fulfilling it."

"You're going to kill yourself?" Dani asked dryly. "Doesn't seem very efficient."

"Just about," I said in a completely serious voice. "I found a loophole, one that will, if I survive it, allow me to *fulfill* the Blood Letter."

"*If* you survive?" Dani asked. "Warning bells are going off in my head at that."

"Yeah, they should," I said heavily, sighing.

"How do you do this?" she asked warily.

"It's called a *Blood* Letter," I said, emphasizing the important word. "Not a Death Warrant. The technical terms of the Bounty Hunter's Guild state that the letter can be fulfilled via proof of death *or* a certain amount of blood belonging to the letter's named person."

"You're right," Dani said coldly. "I don't like this. Absolutely not. How much blood do they want anyway? It's probably ridiculous. You're not doing it."

"Somewhere over two liters," I said quietly.

"That will be over half of her entire blood supply," Vir stated, surprising me with his knowledge of human anatomy.

"*What?!*" Dani shrieked, wide-eyed. "Fuck, no. No way. That will *kill* you, Jo."

"So will the Blood Letter if I don't do something about it," I growled. "I can't kill Elenia until it's gone, Dan. And the only *other* way to do something about it is if you drag my dead body into a Guild office. Given that I want to *live*, we'd better explore the alternative. Which is why I called you."

"You called Vir, you mean," she grumped.

"He doesn't have a cell phone."

"Now is *not* the time for jokes. You're asking us to help you commit suicide."

"I'm asking you to be my friend," I whispered. "I have to try. I called you because you'll give me the best chance of surviving. Between Vir's magic and my body's ability to regenerate as I drink blood, *hopefully,* I can make it through long enough to recover in time."

"In time?" Dani asked. "Are you in a rush to go after Elenia?"

"She has to be the one to bring the blood to the Guild," Aaron said, speaking up. "She must walk in, unassisted, and deliver it herself within one day of the first drop being taken. I assume it almost never happens, which is why nobody knows about it."

"That's impossible," Dani gasped. "You're going to be weak for ages."

"I *will* do this," I growled, looking defiantly at the car's occupants. "I *will* survive, thanks to all of your help, and then I *will* kill Elenia and put an end to her tyranny. Is that understood?"

"But, Jo," Dani whispered, pleading with me.

"Will you help me or not?"

"Of course," Vir said, glancing over at Dani.

My best friend, recognizing that she was outnumbered, slowly nodded. "If you don't need me for my magic, then what can I do?"

I bit my lip. This was going to be the delicate part, and she wouldn't respond well to it.

"Vir's going to use his magic. Aaron is going to,

well, hold me and feed me new blood to ensure I survive. And you ..."

"I'm *really* not going to like this," Dani groaned. "What is it, Jo?"

"Um. You see, I need somebody to actually *draw* the blood."

True to her word, Dani *didn't* like it. Which she made very, very clear to me. But in the end, she conceded.

Now all that was left was to actually do it and survive. No pressure.

CHAPTER TWENTY-THREE

"**W**hat do you plan to do with that?" Vir asked as I lay back on the couch, listening to the soft trickle of water as it flowed down a six-foot waterfall into the river that crossed through the middle of the room.

I looked up at the stone ceiling, feeling weird about being in Vir's private chambers, but he'd insisted that if we were going to do this, it would be in his sanctuary within the Direen. It was here, he'd said, at the heart of his powers in the realm of the shifter gods, that he would have the best chance of saving me.

There hadn't seemed any point in arguing. I just had to hope that Drakul and Fenrir wouldn't tear each other apart while we were gone. That hadn't seemed likely when we left, but throwing

Fred into the mix always made things murkier. Perhaps he'd be able to keep the peace.

Or perhaps they'll throw him out. Who knows. I have different things to worry about right now.

"Jo?"

"Huh?" I asked, glancing up. "Sorry, lost in thought."

"Understandable at a time like this," Vir said, offering me a gentle smile.

Dani and Aaron were nearby, doing the last bits of preparation for their ends of the task ahead of us. Meanwhile, Vir was preparing the magic he said he would use to try to keep me alive. The longer he had to study me, the better he could tailor his spell, apparently. Hence why we were preparing before the others were ready.

"Thanks. What was it you asked?"

"Those," he said, indicating the nearby blood packs, the full ones we'd gathered before the blood bank had gone up in flames. "What are they for?"

"To keep me alive," I said. "Aaron is going to feed them to me as we go, doing his best to keep me alive."

Vir shook his head. "That won't work."

"What do you mean?"

"You're a vampire," he said. "Your body absorbs blood. A human body digests it. Yours soaks it up. It enters your bloodstream due to the change in DNA from the vampire gene."

I stared at the full blood packs. "And if I start drinking someone else's blood ..."

"Then the blood we draw will not necessarily be yours," he said.

"And if the Guild finds out," I said, following his logic. "Fuck."

"Apt," Vir granted.

"What do we do? How do we handle this? How long does it take to enter my blood?" I asked. "Do we know? There must be *some* delay. Especially for it to get to the point where it would dilute my blood enough so it's not entirely my own."

"I don't know," Vir admitted. "But do you want to risk it?"

"We'll have to at some point," Aaron said, coming to crouch at my side. "If we do nothing, she *will* die."

I stared up at him, seeing the concern at the corners of his eyes. He was afraid for me. It was understandable. I was petrified. At first, it had been simply about dying. Lately, however, I was starting to become afraid of the things I wouldn't be around to see. Or experience.

Like a life with you, I thought, staring up at the vampire who had so recently become a big part of my world. That was what I didn't want to miss. Blinking back tears at the thought of not being able to experience many lifetimes with him, I tried to bring my focus back to the present.

This was the *only* way to explore what was developing between us. To chase the butterflies in my stomach that only he conjured. Not doing this would simply result in a life of misery, constantly running from one hideout to the next, hoping never to get caught. That was no life at all.

"You'll wait to the last second," I said firmly. "You must. My body will probably respond even if my mind is gone. But you can't give me any too soon. We must have *my* blood in there. Do you understand?"

"I'll wait," he agreed solemnly, voice steady and even. The only hint of his fear was deep in his eyes. In a place, I suspected, only I was allowed to see.

"Okay. Let's do this," I said.

Dani came over and crouched silently next to me, needle ready, the line hooked to a bag. She tied a strap around my arm, letting the veins grow more visible.

"Thank you," I said, catching her eye.

"Don't ever ask me to do this again," she said.

I swallowed. "I don't *have* anyone else to ask, Dan."

"Easy on the feels," she whispered huskily. "I need to keep my hands from shaking while I put this in."

"You'll be great," I said. "Just like you've always been to me."

The needle pricked my skin. I took a deep breath, exhaling slowly as the first bag began to fill. Part of me wanted to look down, to watch it, but I knew that would be a bad idea. I didn't need to see it happening. Soon enough, I would feel it.

In what felt like no time, Dani was already switching to the next bag. She carefully handed it over to Aaron, who packed it away into a cooler bag filled with icepacks. Nobody spoke, everyone concentrating on their own tasks.

"This is gonna work," I assured them all, starting to feel a little lightheaded as the third bag filled.

"I know," Aaron said, stroking my forehead. "We'll get through it."

As we moved to the fourth bag, my vision started to gray over. My limbs felt weak and heavy. I doubted I could get up from the couch at this point. Not that I intended to. We were going to keep this up.

"Now," Aaron said, his voice distant.

Purple light flared in the dim room, forcing my eyes closed.

"Jo?"

I stirred weakly, trying to confirm that I was still there, but my body wasn't responding. Even my thoughts felt sluggish. Detached. What had

I even been trying to say? The violet light grew brighter even behind my eyelids.

"She's fading," a female voice said. "We should stop."

"No!" a male voice barked. "She said to keep going. We keep going."

Where's Aaron going? What is he doing? I should probably ask him. He'll tell me. He'll tell me ...

"She's going to die if we keep this up. She can't take much more. Even with my magic."

"You don't stop. We see this through. It's what she would want," Aaron barked authoritatively.

"Six," a female voice said from somewhere far away.

The purple light was fading now. Growing darker. Whatever light was on, someone must have turned it off. That must be it. They wanted to go to sleep.

Sleep sounds nice. I could use some sleep now. Deep sleep. Restful. I'm so tired.

My head slumped.

"Jo!" someone shouted, but I shut it out. I was so tired. I just wanted to sleep.

"Jo? Jo? Can you hear me?" a male voice called. "Shit. She's not responding. What do we do?"

"Seven," a female voice said mechanically.

"Keep going. We're almost there."

"And she's almost gone."

"She'll make it," the strong male voice replied. "Keep using your magic."

"I am."

The voices continued to talk in my dreams as I faded away. Finally, I could rest.

"Jo? She's got no pulse."

"Give it to her."

Give what? I don't need anything. Just let me sleep.

I chased the darkness, letting it close over me, welcoming it with a warm smile. Just a short nap, that's all I needed.

Then, I knew nothing.

CHAPTER TWENTY-FOUR

Everything hurt.

What kind of dream is this? I thought, fighting through the mush to figure out what was going on. Where was I? What had happened?

I worked to take in a deep breath, but even the simple act of forcing my lungs to inflate was tiring beyond belief.

With agonizing slowness, I became aware that I wasn't dreaming. I was awake. My eyes were closed, and my body hated me.

"Jo?"

Aaron. I wanted to talk to him.

"She's coming around," he said.

"Good." That was a female voice. "Vir, you can let go now, dear. You can relax."

There was a groan and the sound of a body collapsing nearby. Almost immediately, everything went black. It was only then that I realized I'd been seeing everything with a purplish hue. What had happened?

"Come on, Jo," Aaron said, closer now. "You need to drink this."

The metallic tang of blood flooded my nostrils, provoking a hungry response, one that I couldn't fight. My mouth opened almost on its own, just a hair. I lay there, slack-jawed, until someone cupped my head and dribbled some liquid over my lips. Energy sparked and crackled through me.

I sucked in a huge, gasping breath and immediately collapsed again as the movements drained whatever new energy had been created.

"Here, take a bit more," Aaron said. "Try not to work so much. You're very weak right now."

More droplets spattered against my lips and teeth. Energy tingled for a moment before evaporating like dew under the rising sun. A faint ghost of life and zest, taken away from me as my body used it up. I needed more.

Someone else groaned.

"He'll be fine," said that same female voice. I knew her. I had to know her.

More blood was dribbled into my mouth, some of it making it onto my tongue this time. Sparks coalesced in my brain as neurons fired.

Dani! Her name was *Dani!* She was my best friend. I'd known her my entire life. We'd grown up together. She was here.

We continued the agonizing dribble of blood into my mouth for an eternity. Each time, Aaron paused, waiting for my body to absorb it. As the energy returned, however, so did something else. Something worse.

The Hunger. It gnawed away at my insides, demanding more. Blood was life. Life and pleasure.

Tingles shot along my spine as Aaron gave me the largest drips yet. Enough that I almost had to swallow before my mouth simply absorbed it. I shivered with sexual anticipation as my brain clicked enough to think ahead.

I was going to get to drink a lot of blood today. A *lot.* More than I had ever had in one sitting, except for when I'd fed on the bounty hunter Bianca. It was going to be *good*, the Hunger told me, its darkness insatiable. It wanted fresh, human blood, but anything was better than nothing.

Some other part of me, a weak, exhausted part, with no fight left in it, recoiled in disgust at the idea. I didn't like to feed. I didn't like blood. I hated what it did to me, what it turned me into.

"I think I've got it from here," Aaron rumbled as I took in another deep, throaty breath, my eyes slowly opening to reveal his gorgeous, chiseled face, a shock of blond hair hanging forward over his forehead.

"Yeah, I'm going to take Vir to get some food," Dani said, casting a worried glance at me. "You holler if you need something. Anything, okay? I don't have his skills, but I'm better than nothing."

"Of course," Aaron said. "I just think it best that this next part has some ... privacy."

Dani nodded. I saw it all happen, my eyes processing it and slowly feeding it back to me, but my mind was thick and sludgy, not moving. It wasn't until Dani was long gone, pulling a curtain across to give us privacy, that my brain finally registered that I should say something.

"Dani," I said hoarsely.

"*Hush*," Aaron said, stroking my forehead, his hand warm and clammy. "It's going to be okay, my dear. You're here now. We just need to bring you back slowly. To take our time, so you don't overdo it. You ..."

He shook his head, shutting his eyes, but not before I got a glimpse of some well-concealed emotions. My muzzy brain thought it might have been fear, but I knew that had to be wrong. This was Aaron, master vampire, Count Dracula himself! He wasn't afraid of anything. Was he?

Now that I felt slightly stronger, Aaron let more blood flow into my mouth. I gulped it down, my body reacting from the inside out. Heat swelled like a forge stoked to life, its fires slowly reigniting after having long been put out. My body did the same as fresh blood coursed through my veins, bringing forth my Hunger and its baser emotions. Its desires.

My breathing deepened, and pulses of ecstasy beat their drumbeat against my brain with each mouthful. It was inescapable.

"Here," Aaron said, giving me a straw.

I started sucking down more blood. Too much.

The sudden infusion of raw sexual energy pushed me to the edge. I trembled, gasping for air, my back practically arching as I shivered. I wanted more. I wanted it. Needed it. *Craved* it. My lips closed around the thin straw, and I sucked on it, pulling more of it into my mouth.

The blood smacked me back into the bed as I writhed, a tiny moan slipping out from around the straw. My tongue flicked against the top of it suggestively as I stared up at Aaron.

"Not happening," he growled. "You're far too weak. You just don't know it. You need to drink more."

I greedily sipped at the straw, the darkness overwhelming the part of me that was retching and practically throwing up at how badly I desired this. My fangs slid out, jutting over my lower lip as I regained the energy for them to come forth. Still, I drank more.

It filled me with a pounding need that only drinking could sate. I gulped down pack after pack, my body absorbing the blood before it made its way to my stomach. It leached into me, spreading from my brain to my toes, bringing me slowly back to life. An energy I couldn't ever recall feeling arose in me, urging me to get up, to move around.

"No," Aaron said as I tried to get out of bed. He placed a hand on my chest—just above where I *really* wanted him to touch, to grab, to *take*—and without any apparent effort, pushed me back down into the bed.

"I'm fine," I whispered, speaking my first words, my mouth finally working. "I'm just ..."

"Horny as fuck," he pointed out dryly. "And ready to hump anything that comes along. But your mind isn't working straight yet. I pushed you down, and that was with barely any *human* strength. You're not ready."

"Sit me up, then," I rasped. "So I can drink this faster."

Aaron looked unhappy, but when I started struggling to do it myself, he relented and propped me against a wall covered with cushions. No longer having to pause, I all but chugged the blood from the cup. He watched as my eyes rolled back into my head and my breath shortened.

I can't believe I'm doing this, a part of me thought as I all but had an orgasm in front of him. It should have been hot, in a way, but it wasn't. Not to me. I was drinking blood. So much of it, and I wasn't just liking it; I was *loving it.*

I knew Aaron would never let himself give in to the clear and obvious demands of my body. I might be fully clothed, but it was obvious that I was beyond aroused. He could have done anything he wanted to me right then. I *wanted* him to. Needed it. My body was ready for him in every way.

Yet, he refrained. I continued to drink and quiver with pleasure in front of him, in some sort of sick, disgusting mating ritual, but he never lost control. Even the scent of blood, and knowing how good it would feel for him to join me, drinking it and fucking, he never gave in. He sat still and calmly fed me blood pack after blood pack, taking the straw from one and putting it into the next.

Stop it, I tried to tell my body. *We don't need more. We're fine. Please.*

It didn't listen. It kept gulping it down. Taking more, even as it dribbled down my lips and neck, leaving my fangs a glistening, stained red. I fought with the darkness, with the Hunger, trying to overpower it, but it was in a feeding frenzy at this point, and I was too weak to fight it.

Tears streamed down my face, but I sucked it

back relentlessly, both knowing it was necessary and yet hating myself for it. This was what I was. Who I *would* be for all eternity. I would never be rid of it, always forced to deal with this darkness, this *evil*.

And then, just like that, there was no more. Aaron took the pack away and didn't replace it. I reached for it, for him, but he shook his head. "That's all we could get."

Part of me frowned, and as the haze surrounding my brain cleared, I was able to note a discrepancy between my memories and what just happened.

"How much?" I asked. "How did you get so much? We didn't save that much from your blood bank. I drank far more ..."

"Your clan," Aaron said calmly. "While you were out, and Vir was keeping you alive, Dani went to Seguin and took blood donations. She got as much as she could in a short time before coming back here."

I sagged back against the wall. My pack had given their blood. For me? I started to cry harder.

"Jo? Jo, what is it?" Aaron asked, suddenly concerned. "Are you okay?"

"Why does everyone support me?" I asked through the sobs. "They're donating blood to help make me better. I'm a monster. If they saw this, if they could see me now ... I don't deserve this."

"You're one of their pack," Aaron growled. "You're one of the good guys, regardless of what might be living inside you, and they know it."

I shook my head. I didn't want to hear it.

"You need to rest now," Aaron said, stroking my head, leaning in to kiss it. "You must regain enough strength to finish this."

"We got it, then?" I was referring to the necessary amount of blood.

"We got it," he confirmed. "And you still have eight hours to recover and take it to Mr. Orrin. But you have to do it. Unassisted. So that means getting stronger. You might feel strong now, but you're still too weak to walk."

"Eight?" I whispered. "That's it?"

Aaron's jaw tightened, and he looked away momentarily. "You were out for a long time, Jo," he said, clearing his throat softly. "I, uh, we almost lost you."

"I'm back now," I said, touched by his caring and his fear for me. He was in the same position he'd been in when I'd started it all. Had he even moved? Sixteen hours he'd been by my side. Never leaving. "And, uh, thank you."

He smiled. "Anything for you, Jo."

I couldn't match his smile. Not with blood crusting my mouth and the taste of it still so strong on my tongue. But I could pat his hand.

Reassure him.

"You have a few more hours' rest," he said. "We're going to try to get some more blood."

"No," I whispered, shoving aside the vampire part of me and its desire for more. "No more. Please."

"You have to do it," Aaron growled at me. "You've come this far, Joanna Alustria. Are you going to give up now, just because you have to drink some more blood and feel good? Or are you going to do what's necessary and walk into that office and deliver this damn blood yourself?"

I glared at him. We both knew the answer to that.

CHAPTER TWENTY-FIVE

I tottered into the reception area, the cooler clutched to my chest with all my strength. Aaron had been right; I was far weaker than I felt. Despite drinking down more blood than I'd had taken out, my body was far from recovered. Clearly, it wasn't a one-to-one ratio. I took another step forward, wishing Aaron could have accompanied me inside.

He was standing right outside the door, having carried me into the building and up the elevator. I would have fallen well before if he hadn't. But that wasn't part of the rules. I simply had to walk into the office and deliver the blood, *my* blood, to Mr. Orrin without assistance.

I'd thought I could do it. Right now, however, the rectangular waiting room seemed like it stretched on for eternity. The secretary's desk was against the wall on the far side of the room from me. Behind her was the long solo hallway that led to Mr. Orrin's office. *That* was where I had to go.

Staggering forward, I approached the desk, even as the room spun and started to elongate itself before my eyes. The secretary looked up at me, her face blank, though her brown eyes screamed disdain. She didn't want to deal with me and whatever my business was.

Weren't her eyes green last time? I wondered, my brain going off track as I stared at her. It didn't matter. I had a mission to accomplish.

I took another step, my legs screaming with the effort; the muscles in no way recovered enough to walk. Yet, walk I did. My arms were looped through the cooler's handles, and I kept it close to me. It was also strapped around my middle and over my shoulders, but if I dropped it, or if any of the blood packs fell out, there was no way I could pick it up and then stand again.

Come on, you bitch. Ask me why I'm here, I thought, glaring at the secretary. I was the only person in the room, and she wasn't on the phone. Yet, she made no effort to start the conversation. Instead, she *waited* for me to cross the room. Making me go to her before acknowledging my presence.

Setting my teeth, I vowed that I wasn't going to give her the satisfaction of seeing me crumple over. I would walk up to her desk and make the bitch do her damn job. She was going to get up off her perfect little ass and walk her unnaturally perfect legs down that hallway to tell Mr. Orrin that I was here. I didn't care.

A tiny sigh escaped the woman's lips as I took another two steps. I was somewhere between halfway there and seven miles distant, judging by how hard it was to take each step. My energy was fading. I had to get there.

So, I took a step. And then another.

"Can I help you?" the woman asked once I was finally standing right in front of her desk.

I looked longingly at the flat surface of the desk, wanting nothing more than to lean on it and rest my weary body.

Do that, and you won't get back up. And that might count against you in some way.

Even as the idea came to me, I recognized the trap. The Guild wasn't going to make this easy on me. If they accepted my blood, they would make Elenia very unhappy. It might be done by the book, but I doubted they wanted to deal with unhappy customers. So, it would be in their best interests to make every little thing a failure point.

"I'm here to see Mr. Orrin," I rasped. "About the fulfillment of a Blood Letter."

The secretary looked me up and down and

sighed. "Very well."

She lifted the phone from the desk and pressed a button on it. I was surprised she didn't get up and talk to him in person, making me wait even longer.

Perhaps me saying that I was here about the Blood Letter means she can't wait? I don't know.

Neither did I care. All that mattered was that after a few words to Mr. Orrin, the secretary got up from her desk.

"Follow me," she snapped. "Don't take too long. Mr. Orrin is very busy."

I knew what that meant. *Take too long, and he won't be available to see you. So you had better walk faster.*

Which would tire me out more. And leave my legs more likely to give out, causing me to fall to the floor. And thus failing.

Bitch.

I stared right at her, wishing I had laser beams for eyes as I forced myself down the hallway, one step after another.

Left. Right. Left. Right. Right. Right. Left.

Sometimes I didn't even step. I simply dragged my foot up. Having my hands tucked against my chest worsened my balance, but it didn't matter. The cooler was the important part. That was what mattered. I had to keep it safe. I had less than an hour to go until the first blood would no longer pass whatever test the Guild put it to.

Amazingly, I made it to the door. The world was spinning, I was sweating profusely, and my legs were shaking like we were in the middle of an earthquake. But I *made* it. The secretary, looking even more frustrated, opened the door, admitting me into the darkened room.

I wobbled my way through the door, only narrowly missing being caught by the secretary as she pulled it shut. I gave her a brilliant smile and stuck my tongue out at her before making my way toward the desk, where Mr. Orrin sat cloaked in shadow.

"Miss Alustria," he said in his gender-neutral voice.

Although he was called "Mr. Orrin," I had to wonder if that was perhaps part of the disguise. A way to confuse people about "his" true identity. Either way, that was how I went along with it.

"Mr. Orrin," I said, my voice weak and soft. "I've come to fulfill the terms of a Blood Letter."

"Indeed?" the shadowy form mused. "Whose?"

"Mine," I stated, looking at the cooler. "This is my blood. Over two liters of it, as per specifications. Enough to claim the letter and have it revoked."

There was silence. "How did you learn of this?"

I grinned. "I read the fine print."

Orrin sighed in frustration when I refused to elaborate. "Place the blood on the table," he commanded.

With my fingers shaking, I slowly undid the straps of the cooler, making sure to keep one arm linked through the handle as I did. The weight grew heavier as the straps came free, and I grimaced, struggling to hold it up.

"Don't drop it, Miss Alustria," the voice admonished. "I won't be picking it up."

Glaring at him, I fumbled with the last strap. It came free, and my arms sagged. I cried out, hauling back. Muscles in my back screamed in protest, too weak to support this extra weight now that it was free. I tilted forward, my arms slowly lowering against my will, even as I tried to command them to raise.

No! I was going to lose it. I was going to fail, right here, now, when I was so close. This wasn't possible!

I leaned forward, dragging a foot closer to the desk. This wouldn't happen. I wouldn't *let* it happen. Now not. Not when I was on the edge of succeeding.

Bending at the waist, I flung the cooler with all my might toward the desk. It clipped the edge, spun, and landed on its side, pushing papers and other items out of its path as it came to a halt in front of Mr. Orrin.

"There," I gasped, forcing myself to stand upright without touching anything. "All yours. Now revoke this letter."

Mr. Orrin was silent for a moment. He had to be evaluating my delivery method, deciding whether it would be acceptable. I bit my lip so hard it bled as I waited for him to do something, *anything*.

"Analyze it," he said at last, grabbing it and passing it off to someone else, someone I hadn't realized was there until their footsteps sounded in the room.

The cooler disappeared into the hands of whoever it was while I struggled to penetrate the intense darkness around Mr. Orrin. Just how many other people were in the room? I had thought we were alone, but that was obviously not the case.

Time seemed to stretch on. Mr. Orrin said nothing. We waited, and my legs began to tremble even worse. My strength was fading. I didn't know if I could sit down at this point or not. The Blood Letter hadn't officially been revoked. If I fell, I might still fail.

All my attention boiled down to staying upright. To not falling over, to not slumping against the desk. Stand up, and wait for word. There could only be thirty minutes left at this point.

Not that I could stand for that long anyway. But I have to try.

An eternity passed before there was movement. I heard a muffled voice, and then, once again, there was silence.

"Well?" I challenged sharply. "Did they tell you that it's good? That it's all there?"

Mr. Orrin clasped his hands in front of him. Something about the way he did it told me he wasn't happy.

"Good," I growled, swaying heavily, though there wasn't a breeze in the room.

I was just that weak.

"It appears that you have, somehow, succeeded, Miss Alustria," he said reluctantly. "The terms of your Blood Letter have been filled. It has been revoked."

"Thank you," I said, meaning it.

"You must remember that this doesn't mean another cannot be placed on you," he added.

"I know," I said. *But I'm not going to give her the chance.*

"So, what will you do now that it's lifted?" he asked.

I glared into the darkness. "Probably something even stupider than this."

CHAPTER TWENTY-SIX

"Jo."

I looked up to see Vir approaching. He walked up to the bed—his bed, technically, though I had commandeered it during my convalescence. Not by choice. I'd stumbled out of the Bounty Hunter Guild's offices and woken up in it. Since then, I'd tried to take the couch, but two gods and a twelve-hundred-year-old vampire were hard to resist when they told you to shut up and stay in bed.

So, I did as commanded, and I stayed in bed. Truthfully, I was too weak to resist, even mentally. Today was the first day I was feeling up to moving around. Although I was drinking blood regularly, it was a slow process not only to recharge my body but also to heal it from all the damage I'd done by draining it nearly to death.

"Hi," I said as Vir took a seat nearby. "I've been meaning to thank you, by the way. For holding on as long as you did while I was out."

"You are most welcome."

Vir bowed his head, acknowledging that for nearly sixteen *hours*, he'd maintained a healing trance around me until I finally woke on my own and could feed on blood. His was the groan that I'd heard upon waking. Apparently, he'd passed out, but I didn't recall that much, to his dignity's thanks, I'm sure.

"Hopefully, by tomorrow, I'll be ready to go," I said. "At least I can give you and Dani the bed back. I feel like such an intruder."

"You aren't," Vir said, raising a hand, stopping my protests. "And that is not why I came to see you either."

I noted the lack of humor in his voice, the solemnness in his eyes.

Ah, shit. Here it comes.

"You want to know about the rings," I said with a sigh.

Vir nodded.

There was no avoiding it. I was surprised that Aaron hadn't informed him about it. Then again, maybe Vir hadn't asked, deciding to wait until I was alive enough to ask me. That was more his style.

"I needed information on how to beat the

Blood Letter," I said. "I got it."

"And the rings?"

"My payment," I said softly, having a hard time meeting his eyes.

"You did not lose them?"

"What?" I said, pushing myself up into a seated position. "No, of course not. I gave them to the Broker in exchange for the information I needed. The bastard must have known what they were, or at least some of what they could do, so he robbed me of their powers, powers which would have helped me get through this much easier."

"Ah," Vir said. "The Broker. I suppose I shall have to pay a visit to him."

"Did you ever meet him?"

Vir shook his head. "No. I was trapped in the Direen long before he rose to his current station. Still, I have heard of him. It is past time we met."

"Yeah. Sorry about the rings," I said. "I didn't really see any other choice."

"You did what I would have urged you to do," Vir said. "I gave them to you with the knowledge you would do best by them. I have no regrets."

"Thank you," I said, relief lifting my spirits.

Vir nodded, patting my leg before rising and departing. In the background, I heard the crackle of the fireplace. I couldn't see it from where I lay. The bed was blocked from the rest of his home by an L-shaped wall. But I could still hear it. It sounded lovely. And warm.

Slowly, I swung my feet out from under the covers and onto the floor. My arms trembled as I pushed myself to a sitting position, but they didn't threaten to fail. I was getting stronger.

If I could make it into Orrin's office and out again, I can make it over to the fire, I told myself sternly before taking two breaths in preparation for the next step.

"And *up*," I urged, pushing up and standing in one motion. It wasn't smooth, and I nearly went down in a flail of limbs, but I made it. Now it was a simple case of walking a few dozen steps. I could do that.

I'd gotten about halfway before Aaron caught sight of me and realized I wasn't Dani. He surged to his feet in a blur and was at my side in less time than it took me to take half a step.

"No," I said, snatching my arm back. "I'm going to do this myself."

Aaron started to protest.

"You can walk at my side and catch me before I fall. But I'm doing this *alone*."

"But you're not alone," Aaron whispered.

"I know," I said, smiling at him as I took another step. "I have you. And two awesome friends. I have you to catch me if I fail. I'll take that. But I also need your support in my decisions."

Aaron looked at me with exasperation, and he hovered over me the entire way to the couch, but he didn't try to hold me up again.

"Thank you," I said, half falling and half sitting back into the couch, basking in the warmth of the fireplace. "For a lot of things."

"You're welcome. You deserve it."

I shot him a surprised look.

"You do," he said insistently, taking a seat next to me. "You're the strongest woman I know who's still essentially human."

Dani snorted from where she sat in a loveseat with her nose buried in a book. "Rude."

Aaron mock-glared then looked back to me. "I'm serious. What you just did? Nearly killing yourself, just so that you can have a chance at taking out Elenia so that *other* vampires can live a better life?"

"That's not quite why I did it," I whispered. "It was *my* Blood Letter, after all."

"That was part of it, though," he countered. "Whether you want to admit it or not. It was the most selfless thing I've ever seen a vampire do, I think. Elenia would never in a thousand years contemplate putting herself in harm's way to help others. She would sooner sacrifice a thousand of our kind than risk even a hair on her head."

I looked away, embarrassed at what he was saying.

"That is what separates you from the likes of her, Jo," he said, uttering words that he knew would get through to me. "Her caring for herself is what makes her a monster and why she's unfit to rule."

"I know."

"It's also what shows that you *aren't* a monster," he said forcefully. "That you *aren't* like her, in any way. You are her better, and we would be better off as a race with you on the throne. I can see that. So can these two. The rest of my team knows it. They would follow you anywhere they would follow me. Probably even further. You're a hero to them, Jo."

Now, I blushed. "Stop, please. I'm just me. I'm not a hero. I just want to *exist*. I want my mother to exist without needing those damn drugs. Your team, they all deserve to find mates. To have someone they can love, who won't be executed on sight. That's what I'm fighting for."

"I know," Aaron said, smiling broadly. "But they know it, too, and that's how they see you. You're a beacon for change to them."

I sagged even deeper into the couch. "Oh, god. That's not good."

"What? Why not?"

"Because, Aaron. What if I fail? Yes, I got rid

of the Blood Letter, but the odds of me failing to kill Elenia are still astronomically high. She's got a thousand years and more experience on me."

"And you've got your shifter heritage."

"Which will drive me insane if I tap into both at once."

"Fenrir is still here," he pointed out. "And besides, you won't be alone."

I looked at him.

"I'm going with you," he said quietly. "And if the opportunity presents itself, I'll plunge the blade into her chest myself. She *needs* to be stopped. By any means necessary."

"I agree," I said. "And it's about time we started working on that. Don't you?"

Aaron's eyes glittered with fervent intensity.

I matched his look with a feral, wicked smile. "Assemble the team."

CHAPTER
TWENTY-SEVEN

Fenrir and Drakul were the first to show up, to my surprise. I'd expected the team members in Seguin to arrive first, but when Vir blinked into being in the center of his sanctuary with those two in tow, I had to wonder if that was any sort of indicator of their willingness to join our hunt.

They kept to themselves, however, sitting by the fire and talking somewhat animatedly—for two vampires at least—in whatever language Drakul spoke. I eyed them, wondering what was going on there. I hadn't expected them to have much, if anything, in common.

"The others will be here soon," Vir said, coming up beside me. "Dani won't have taken much longer to get to Seguin and back."

We'd sent Dani to get the other members of

Aaron's team since they all knew each other, but they were taking longer than expected.

"They should have been back ages ago," I said. "Here to Seguin is a short hop. I don't understand."

"Maybe they were in the midst of something?" Vir suggested. "I don't know."

"Me neither," I muttered. "And that's what's got me worried."

Vir patted me on the shoulder. "It will be fine. They—" He paused abruptly, looking up. Then, he smiled at me. "They're here. See, as I said, everything is okay."

But as Dani and the five other members of Aaron's team blinked into being, dropping their connected hands, I knew that Vir was wrong. Very wrong.

"What is it?" I asked as Dani approached, face somber. "What happened?"

A glance told me everyone was there. Nobody was limping or otherwise visibly hurt. So it wasn't about the team, then. Something else had gone on in Seguin.

"Your dad found me," Dani said, rushing on at my moan of dismay. "Everyone's still alive!"

I sagged, and Aaron was abruptly by my side, his arm around my waist. I leaned into him, basking in his support.

"But ..." Aaron rumbled. "What happened?"

"He gave me this." She fished a letter out from her leather outfit, handing it to me.

I reached up to take it, my arm stiff, robot-like in its movement as dread overtook me. What was so bad that he'd had to write me? Johnathan said he'd protect my parents, and we hadn't heard of a fight. Dani would have told me that right away. Which meant something *else* was going on.

Focusing on keeping the trembling down, I unfolded the letter. To my surprise, it wasn't in my father's handwriting at all. It was cursive and flowy. A female hand had written it.

No more. Wishing you all the best on the upcoming Wild Moon.

Much Love, Elenia.

I frowned, looking up at Dani. "No more what? I don't get it."

"Your dad said he got that in the mail. When he should have been getting more of your mom's pills."

My blood turned to ice.

She knew. She *knew*.

"Sonofa*bitch!*" I swore, turning away. "She's going after everything. Trying to destroy me and my life."

"What happened?" Aaron asked.

"I never knew who sent my mom her pills," I said. "But whoever it was, Elenia got to them. She won't get any more."

Aaron hissed. "When the next Wild Moon comes ..."

I nodded. "She'll be unable to resist. She'll shift. Become like me. And Elenia will order her death."

"Shit."

I wasn't sure who uttered the oath, but it about summed everything up. The next Wild Moon was only six days away. I would need at least one more day to finish recovering and get the entire team ready to go. So we had five days to pull this off. To overthrow a ruler who had to know we were coming for her.

Needing a moment to think, I walked over to the fireplace. Everyone else followed me, taking seats.

"So, what are you going to do?" Fenrir asked, surprising me by speaking up.

Still, he'd given me the opening I needed to state my mission to everyone.

CHAPTER TWENTY-EIGHT

"**I**'m going after her."

I swept my gaze over our team. It had taken most of the day for Dani and Aaron to gather everyone, and I was feeling much better. My strength was returning swiftly, although I was ready to vomit at the idea of drinking any more blood.

What I wouldn't give for it to taste like a good red wine. That would at least make it a bit more passable.

Instead, my lips and teeth were stained crimson from the metallic liquid, and my nose was likely to give me hints of the iron-like tang for weeks. The darkness in me, that shadowy *thing* that longed to feed, should have been overjoyed at the literal buffet I'd been feeding it, but no, I couldn't even get that lucky.

Not only was it insatiable, always craving more no matter how much I gave it, but now it was clamoring for the real thing. It wanted to *feed*. Thankfully, I was in charge, and without a Wild Moon to give it that terrifying level of power, where it and my wolf merged, *I* would stay the boss.

"If you're going after her, why are we here?" Fenrir asked.

Beside him, Drakul muttered something I didn't understand.

"He wants to know why he left his castle to hear something he already knows," Fenrir supplied.

"Because," I said, meeting everyone's eyes one by one, "I can't do it alone. I need your help."

There was silence. Drakul and Fenrir exchanged glances. The two of them were sitting on the smaller couch while members of Aaron's team hung around and sat on the back of the bigger one, and Vir lounged in the single recliner with Dani perched on his lap.

Aaron stood next to me for moral support. I knew he was in. He'd already said so. It was the others who I hoped to recruit. I wasn't going to assume anything of anyone for this venture. It was too likely to be a suicide mission for that.

Stop thinking like that. There's a chance. There's always a chance.

Hope for the best. Plan for the worst.

"You know I'm in," Fred drawled, finally breaking the silence. "Never could stand that bitch. If this is my chance to help take her down, then I'm *so* in."

"Well, shit," Jaxton said with a fake sigh, glaring at Fred. "Now I have to go. Someone has to make sure you don't screw it all up."

"So, does that mean I'm going to do the same for you?" Dave said.

Jaxton, Aaron's second-in-command, rolled his eyes skyward, then scanned over the rest of the team, receiving whatever passed for affirmatives from them.

"We're all in," he said after a moment. "The more, the merrier, right?"

"And the better chance of getting yourselves all killed," Fenrir pointed out.

"So, you aren't coming?"

Fenrir exchanged looks with Drakul. The silver-haired warrior grunted something that I didn't understand, but the head shaking was clear enough.

"This is foolish," Fenrir said, nodding at his newfound companion. "This group is not enough to get to Elenia. Not now. You will fail. We hope that you don't die, but more than this group is needed."

"We could go," Dani said from nearby.

"No," I said, shaking my head.

"I am *not* made of glass, damn you," Dani snarled, rehashing an argument we'd already had.

"But the child inside you is, my love," Vir said. "Which is why I should go."

"I will *not* deprive your child of a parent," I growled at him. "So sit your ass down. I grew up with the closest thing to no mother. It might have been easier not to have had one at all. I don't know. But what I *do* know is that I won't be a party to doing that to anyone else. Hate me if you want, but I would rather die and have your child grow up with both of you than me live and one of you have to sacrifice yourself so that I make it out."

"That's not fair," Dani whispered. "We could help. A lot."

"Of course you could. And if we get trapped and she's holding us prisoner, guess who gets to play the negotiator for our freedom. If we fail and she does anything but kill us outright, I expect you to come to free us *without* trying to blow everything up."

"No promises," Vir muttered. "If you're not here to say no ..."

"Beggars can't be choosers, I guess," I said, shifting my weight around unhappily. I still didn't like the idea, but it was the best I would get. "Besides, we're going for stealth. We're not trying to blow the door inward. If stealth fails, then maybe you two can come along. Fair?"

"No," Dani said.

"Too bad," I growled. I knew it was a bit foolish to leave them behind. Vir and Dani were literal gods. Their strength could make a huge difference.

It would also put a massive target on their backs. Everyone would know they had gone to war with another realm. It would open them up to blowback and retaliatory strikes. If they or, God forbid, their *baby* should suffer because of that, I would never be able to live with the guilt of it. I could deal with Dani being upset with me. She'd get over that. That's what best friends were for.

"We could really use your help," I said, turning to Fenrir. "Are you sure you won't come?"

Drakul spoke up again.

"What are they saying?" I whispered to Aaron.

"Uh, nothing nice," he said, cringing slightly at a particular word from Drakul. "He thinks your plan is foolish and wants no part of it."

"Oh," I said, feeling dejected.

Aaron's hand found mine, squeezing it. "It'll be okay. They'll come around, I think."

"Maybe." I watched the pair go back and forth. "They seem … different since we left them."

"They do," Aaron said. "Don't they?"

"Fast friends," I said, testing the waters for his reaction.

Aaron offered a noncommittal grunt, which confirmed that his thoughts were likely paralleling mine regarding the pair. Something had changed with them after meeting each other.

"We have reconsidered it," Fenrir said at last. "And the answer is no. Not unless you come up with a better plan."

I didn't *have* a better plan. If I did, that's what I would have put forward to them. There weren't a lot of options or choices open to us, and I had to take what I was given.

"Okay," I said, trying to shrug off their refusal to come along. It was surprising, at least in regards to Fenrir. I'd thought he was on board with getting rid of Elenia. It would certainly make his life easier if nothing else.

Nothing you can do about it. Those two are old and probably beyond your way of understanding.

"When do we leave?" Jaxton asked, pulling the conversation back on track.

Casting him a grateful glance, I forced my mind to the task at hand. If those two weren't going to come, they weren't going to come. End of story.

"Soon. We'll sneak in via one of the entrances Aaron says should be lightly guarded. We'll have to get in with minimal noise, so make sure you equip yourself for stealth. From there, we make our way to Madrigal as fast as possible without leaving a trail. Get into the palace. Kill Elenia. Get out. It's simple, which should help us stay effective. She'll be expecting some sort of wild, complicated plan."

"You should go simpler," Fenrir said. "Just storm the city and kill anyone who tries to stop you."

Aaron bared his teeth in anger at the useless suggestion.

"And just *what* army do you suggest we use for that?" I asked, irritated by the lack of faith and his behavior change.

"I'm just saying you'll have the same shot at success. This plan is suicide," Fenrir growled. "She'll be ready for this. Waiting for it. Take some time and come up with something better."

"We don't *have* time," I snapped. "In case you missed the part where my mother is going to join us in this life as a hybrid monster with the next full moon, which arrives in a few days. I will not let her go through that alone, having to fear for her life and becoming a danger to everyone around her. Am I understood?"

"Dani and I will help with that," Vir said softly.

I looked at him.

"We'll bring her here. She won't be affected

by the Wild Moon." Vir's eyes hardened. "And I mean *we* will bring her here," he growled. "I won't risk anyone else. Not after the last time that we tried to move her. Dani and I will do it. We can also keep your father safe from her. That will be our contribution. If all goes well, you come back, and we will take you to Shuldar to help your mom and you through the change. Together."

Vir's tone brooked no argument, so I didn't bother.

"Thank you," I whispered. "I appreciate that."

Drakul said something to Fenrir, who looked irritated and replied. Drakul shifted, his armor making an intimidating noise as he stared at Fenrir long and hard.

"Fine," Fenrir said, throwing up his hands. He looked over at me. "We'll go with them for the Wild Moon. I will help your mother as best I can."

"Thank you," I said softly. "I appreciate that."

Fenrir shrugged. "Helping her is a good plan. This is not."

"*Enough*," Aaron barked, losing his patience with the vampire-wolf. "We know how you feel about it. You've said it enough. You don't need to say any more. Got it?"

Fenrir shrugged.

"We'll need to go back to Seguin," Jaxton said. "Get a proper load of gear from Johnathan's vaults. If we're going in just us, we'll need to go heavy. More than we brought with us, that's for sure."

"That's easy enough," I said. "We'll leave from there once your team is set. Will that work, or do we need to do something else to use the entrance you have in mind?"

"That'll be just fine," Aaron said.

"Then, let's move," I growled. "Time is ticking."

CHAPTER TWENTY-NINE

"**H**old up."

Aaron's barely audible command brought our entire column to a halt. We automatically crouched while Jaxton deployed the team around us so that we had various angles covered by their guns.

"What do you see?" I murmured, keeping my voice low, without any harsh whispers that could be carried on the soft breeze.

"Guards," he said, frustration evident in his voice.

I knew he'd hoped to get closer without being spotted, but the odds of that were against us at this point. Elenia was on high alert. She'd taken out a Blood Letter on me, and now, she'd threatened my mother. She *had* to know we would come after her.

The hope was that she wouldn't be prepared for the seven of us to come together, loaded with enough weaponry for an infantry battalion. Modern weaponry at that, something generally eschewed by the paranormal community, as I was finding out. They had old-fashioned notions of honor and the like.

Guns were not their favorite.

Too bad for you, I snarled mentally at Elenia, beyond eager to exploit that shortcoming.

"How many?" I asked, not wanting to peek around the corner. I wasn't used to this sort of stealth movement, and I didn't want to give us away by moving too quickly or doing anything else that might alert the guards ahead.

We approached the Realm of the Undead's entrance by climbing a chain-link fence and coming through the rear of an old water park on the outskirts of Kellar. It was still in use, and even now, the dull thrum of pumps and machinery could be heard as the water cycled through, keeping things clean for the morning when guests would come again.

Everything had been going swimmingly— *hah!*— until we'd reached the dirt road behind the slides and wave pool. That was when we'd nearly been spotted. An employee of the park, or maybe a security guard, had nearly pinned us in his headlights as he fired up a truck and came around a bend ahead unexpectedly.

We'd managed to duck into the tall grasses on either side of the road, but it had been close. Now, we had to contend with more guards.

"Three," he said.

"Vampires or human park security?"

"Vamps," Aaron replied immediately, confident in his assessment.

"How can you tell?"

He looked back at me, not impressed at having his judgment questioned. I shrugged. Too late now, I'd already asked.

"The giant swords strapped to their backs and the fact they're hanging around an old dumpster might have something to do with," he said dryly, still keeping his voice low. "Instead of near the offices and within the park itself, where security guards might actually be somewhat useful."

I nodded an apology.

"No time to waste," I said. "Do it however you want, but take them out. We can't get stuck on this side of the gate. We have to get through it and start making our way to Madrigal."

Aaron nodded. He made a flurry of hand gestures to Jaxton, who then pointed at Alexi and Fred, motioning for them to accompany him. They crept farther along the wall of the building we were using for cover. Fred joined them, and one by one, he boosted them up onto the roof. The trio disappeared, with Fred rejoining us.

I didn't hear a sound as the vampires got into position. I waited with my shoulder against the wall as Aaron carefully watched the guards.

My ears twitched with a trio of loud coughs, all sounding almost simultaneously.

"Go," Aaron whispered, and he rushed to his feet. I followed. We raced across the ground while Jaxton and the others dropped from the roof to join us, weapons held across their torsos as we ran.

The suppressors on their assault rifles had kept the noise to a minimum. There were no shouts from anyone, and nobody seemed to hear the guards crumpling to the ground. All three were down and out, lying limply in various positions.

"Alexi," Aaron said. "Deal with them."

Alexi and Pieter started hauling the bodies into the overgrown bushes behind the shed. We couldn't leave any sign of our passage. Nothing that would raise the alarm or give away our presence. To vampires *or* humans.

Half a dozen people running around with rifles in the dark would surely provoke alarm if anyone employed by the water park saw us, that was for sure. We didn't want that. The goal was to ensure we had an open way back as well.

Once the bodies were gone and the piles of blood were covered by kicked-over dirt, Aaron turned our attention to the dumpster itself. It was one of those open-topped ones, where the thin side could also be opened, like a storage container. It was rusted to hell, the ochre flaking metal a darker orange than the bin itself, and based on the weeds and even a tree growing up around it, it hadn't been moved in a long time.

The lock on the door, however, was shiny and new-looking. Aaron grabbed it, and with a flex of his arm, he tore the lock from the rusted dumpster. I saw that the lock hadn't even been warped. He'd simply ripped hard enough that the anchors of the dumpster had come free.

Must have been to keep curious humans out.

"Everyone ready?" Aaron asked. "This is going to take us to the outskirts of Madrigal itself. We'll come out behind a building. Alexi and Pieter will scale the building and secure guidelines for the rest of us to follow. Once there, we should have a decent enough view to see what our path forward will be. Got it?"

There were no questions. We'd already gone over this. Aaron was just rehashing it to be certain.

As was his way, Aaron took the lead. Fred came up behind him, and the others fell in line, sandwiching me halfway through to keep me sheltered. I wasn't carrying a gun. Not because I didn't want to, but because I had no experience with one, and as Aaron had vehemently told me when I'd asked for one once, now was *not* the time to learn.

He had promised to teach me. If we survived.

We will survive, I told myself, banishing the offending thought to oblivion.

"All right, let's do this," Aaron said, lifting the securing arm that kept the doors closed and hauling it open.

Then, he raced through the opening and disappeared into thin air. The bin's interior was full of junk, but as we followed Aaron through, we never made it. As we crossed the perimeter of the bin, we abruptly crossed over and emerged into the vampire's realm, just as planned.

The bright bone-white light that infused every aspect of the realm tore at my eyes. I hissed, blinking furiously. I needed my eyesight back, fast. There was no time to waste. We were in the belly of the beast, and one wrong move could set us back, or worse, doom us all to a horrible death.

The last thing I needed was to be blinded by sunlight.

Nearby, Aaron and Fred were wrestling guards to the ground. I started as a loud *crack* heralded the death of one of the guards, his spine severed thanks to Fred wrenching his head around. Aaron took longer, but he made less noise as his arm squeezed like a vise around the guard's throat, blocking oxygen and blood supply, before finally crushing his trachea.

The body flopped for a few seconds longer, then was still. Aaron let it go, getting to his feet, his distaste for the death clear for all to see. I knew he hated killing his own kind when they were just following orders, but we had no choice.

That's why we have to do this. So that such orders stop being issued.

Alexi and Pieter had already ascended the side of the building, and moments later, a pair of ropes dropped down.

"Up you go," Aaron said, motioning for me to take one of them.

"Don't be long," I said and grabbed the thick rope, hauling myself up.

I walked up the side of the building, the motion only possible thanks to the extra strength from being both a shifter and a vampire. I could never have managed such a climb otherwise. Even then, I was nearing my limits by the time I reached the top. I made a mental note to work on that some more. The other vamps were barely breathing hard.

We crouched low, letting the lip of the flat roof obscure us as best we could. Half the team moved to the very edge and lay down, staying entirely out of sight while Aaron and I surveyed our path through the city.

To the palace itself. Where *she* would be.

"Uh, are you seeing this?" I asked, staring at the sight before me in dismay.

Our plan wasn't going to work. It couldn't.

The boulevards were choked with vampires. I'd never *seen* such a teeming mass of them before. Huge columns of them marched along the wider streets, while patrols walked or jogged through smaller passages. Elsewhere, civilian vampires were organizing themselves into groups.

"She's mobilizing the entire damn city," Aaron breathed. "Just to stop us."

"Are we sure it's that? Could she be going after Hades in strength?"

"It's possible," Aaron said. "But what would she do if she beat him? The demons will come back eventually as more people from our walk of life die. Hades can't be killed while he's in his own realm, at least not by her. So, what would it accomplish?"

"I'm not sure," I confessed. "I was really hoping there was another reason to it, that's all. If this is all for us ..."

"Then, we're screwed. There's no way we're getting through all this."

Even many of the rooftops had groups of vampires on them. None had spotted us yet, concealed as we were by the lip that ran around the edge. But finding a way to the palace wasn't going to be possible. Not through all *that*.

I lay down on the roof, removing myself from sight.

"Well, *fuck*," I said.

What the hell did we do now?

CHAPTER
THIRTY

"We need to head back," Aaron said, his dejection mirroring my own.

He looked frustrated, and who could blame him? We'd come so far, right to the edge of Madrigal, our target all but in sight, and now we were stymied. Unable to proceed, thanks to the extreme paranoia of the queen. It sucked.

"Is there no other way? No secret passage we can take?" I asked.

"No."

I looked up at the curt reply. "Hey, this isn't my fault. I'm trying to explore our options here, okay?"

Aaron hissed, but not at me. "I know. I'm sorry, Jo. I just thought ... I thought things were finally going to change, that's all. That we could make a difference that I've longed to make for centuries. To see it so bluntly denied is *frustrating.* Still, I should not have taken it out on you."

His hand reached out to squeeze mine. I squeezed it back. There was no need to hold grudges simply because he was upset. I was, too.

"Anyone else have any good ideas?" I asked the rest of the team as they lay on their backs, rifles held across their body, at the ready, just in case.

"We could cause a distraction," Fred said. "Try to draw attention to another part of the city. Create a path for you two to get to the palace."

"That would be suicide," Aaron said, gently refusing the offer.

"He's right. We're not letting you get killed just so we *might* succeed. Thanks for the offer."

"Don't mention it," Fred said, relieved. "I didn't much want to do it anyway. It was just an idea. Really the only idea."

"Yeah," I said grumpily, staring across the roof at the ropes we'd used to climb up. The exhilaration of being strong enough to pull myself up the two stories was long gone by now. Crushed by the overwhelming sense of failure. "We'd need a bigger diversion anyway. A much bigger one to get through all that."

"Too bad we can't use Fred's ego," Dave said, injecting some levity into the moment as we all chuckled.

I continued to stare at the ropes, my eyes unfocusing as I furiously tried to come up with something, *anything*, that would let us continue.

"Shit," I mumbled to nobody in particular. I didn't have any good suggestions either. It was like Aaron had said. We had to turn back.

"Let's get out of here, rethink our strategy," Aaron said, pointing at the ropes.

"Yeah, I think you're right," I said, just as the rope on the right twitched. "Did you see that?"

"I did," Aaron hissed, snapping his fingers.

The team rolled to their knees in a heartbeat, weapons up and aimed at the ropes.

A face appeared over the edge of the roof. The vampire's eyes went wide, just as four of the six rifles fired. There was an explosion of blood, and they dropped out of view.

Shouts went up from below.

"He wasn't alone," I cursed. "Damn. We've been found. Aaron, we need another exit, now."

"We've been spotted," Alexi said. "Six buildings over. Five-man team. They heard the gunfire."

I looked over my shoulder in the direction Alexi indicated and cursed like a sailor. I could practically *see* the shockwave as knowledge of us spread through the city.

"We're going to be in a *lot* of trouble in a few minutes if we don't get a move on right away," I said. "Can we just take out the vamps below the ropes and go back the way we came?"

Pieter rushed to the corner of the roof, stuck his head out over the edge, then yanked it back real quick as a flurry of what appeared to be crossbow bolts shot through the air.

"Would not recommend," he said gruffly, unfazed by the close brush with face impalement.

"Aaron?" I said. "You know Madrigal the best. Get us out of here."

"We don't have a choice," he growled. "We have to go through them. Nothing else is close."

"Weapons free?" Jaxton asked.

I frowned, looking at him. There was something in the way he asked the question.

"Yes," Aaron said.

Jaxton said something in a language I didn't know, but a curse is a curse in any language. He nodded at the others. They rushed to the edge, and a moment later, a flurry of flat discs went over the edge, pulled from their equipment harnesses.

"Plug your ears and open your mouth," Aaron warned, crouching down.

I hurriedly did the same, just as the alley below us blew up. Fire and flame rushed skyward, an expanding ball of heat washing over me, forcing my head to turn around.

"Well," I shouted over the ringing in my ears.

"If they didn't know we were here before, they do now."

"Go!" Aaron shouted, pointing at the edge of the roof.

I swallowed. I didn't want to go down there. I didn't want to see the carnage the modern weapons had wreaked on an unsuspecting populace.

Most of whom were probably innocent, only following their queen because they didn't know any better. Now, they're dead. We killed them.

"Their blood is on *her* hands," Aaron snarled as we headed for the lip, where the burnt remains of the ropes smoldered on the roof. "She forced our hand. Remember that."

"Maybe," I said, unconvinced.

There was a very loud *crack*, and the building shivered.

"Uh," Jaxton said, from where he stood on the lip itself, ready to go over the edge.

Then, he was gone as the building crumbled out from below him. It spread out. We turned to run, but the building collapsed faster than we could react, tossing us to the ground as it tumbled into ruin.

Mortar dust filled the air as we landed amid the debris. I cried out as something slammed onto my leg, slicing it open. More debris washed over my head, and something decently sized clunked me in the temple, leaving me dizzy. That was the worst of it, though.

Coughing violently on the dust that I'd inhaled, I pulled my shirt up over my mouth, trying to filter the debris as best I could.

"Get up!" I shouted. "Come on. We don't have time! Let's go!"

The sound of coughing reached my ears. At least someone else was alive. I stumbled forward through the dust, trying to find them. The footing was uneven, and I had to keep one hand to my face to hold my shirt over my mouth, which made climbing through the rubble difficult. I finally saw a shadow and reached for them, hoping it was Aaron.

I lunged closer and came up short as I saw a face I didn't recognize staring back at me. Brown eyes, long brown hair, and, worst of all, a wicked sword in his right hand.

It was one of the Nacht Bringers. And he wasn't surprised to see me. The sword came up and around.

Shrieking, I fell backward, narrowly avoiding the razor-sharp blade as it went for my throat. Falling to the ground, I closed my hands around the first thing I could find. A chunk of steel. Growling in anger, I wrenched at it, yanking it free from the rubble. I was no swordsman, but the simple strike the Nacht Bringer came at me with was easy enough to parry.

I hadn't processed what to do next as the two pieces of metal *clanged* against one another mightily, but as it turned out, I didn't have to. Two holes suddenly appeared in the vampire's head, and he crumpled backward.

"Come on," Alexi said, emerging from the rubble. "We must go."

"Yeah, tell me about it," I said. "Thanks for the assist."

"Don't mention it."

We stumbled through the debris until we reached a strangely empty area. The building had fallen around the doorway back to Earth, but on the one side, it had gone *through* the opening. The rest of the team was assembled there. Dave held Pieter, who'd clearly broken a leg. The vampire's face was white, and he had a fixed grimace, but he didn't say anything.

"Got her," Alexi said as Aaron sagged with relief at the sight of me.

"Thank you. Okay, through you go. Let's get out of here, fast."

Alexi led the way, followed by Fred, then me, Dave and Pieter, then Jaxton.

The cool air was a marked contrast to the dusty confines we'd left behind. There was a layer of dust surrounding the container and piles of debris. We all pitched in to quickly toss it back through before Dave closed the door.

"It's the best we can do," Aaron said. "Elenia will have it cleaned up and fixed once she sees what happened. But we can't let them catch us."

Keeping the existence of the passageways between Earth and other realms secret was paramount and something that all creatures worked together for, as I understood it, even during hostilities.

We headed back the way we came, Pieter gasping in pain as Dave swept him up into his arms and carried him. I tried not to imagine how excruciating the pain must be with every bounce. I doubted I could hold up under it.

On we ran, with our tails tucked between our legs. We had failed. Badly. Despair loomed large, threatening to swallow me whole, and for a good reason.

This was all my fault.

CHAPTER THIRTY-ONE

We were all in a black mood by the time we exited the portal. I blinked, expecting the brightness of the white gates of the Direen. Instead, I was greeted by the inside of a dilapidated hut.

"Why did you bring us here?" I asked, forcing myself to hold back my anger as I pushed the rickety door open. I didn't want to destroy it just because I was mad.

The sun was out, but the canopy overhead was so thick that minimal light filtered through. Shadows whirled like crazy as the branches creaked and groaned overhead. Dead tree branches snapped and fell to the ground, disappearing into the carpet of desiccated tree debris. I shivered, wondering if the vampire bear was out there.

"Do you really want to go back to Dani and Vir and tell them what happened?" Aaron said as he started away from the hut, the others following.

I didn't have much to say to that. Confronting them with the failure of our mission, *my* failure to find us a better plan, was not something I was eager to do. We would have to notify them eventually, but for now, Aaron seemed as content to sulk in the mood as the rest of us.

Nothing bothered us as we trekked through the woods. Even vampire bears must be smart enough not to deal with seven really angry and heavily armed interlopers. We descended down the ridge, past the castle's ruins, and then crossed the river. I paused to scoop up some of the frigid water and wash my face down, cleaning off the dust.

The others followed my lead. It seemed to calm some of the impotent frustration and rage that filled us. I sighed heavily, scanning the group.

"There's no way we can go back in like that now," I said, gesturing with one hand for us to continue.

Fred nodded in agreement.

"She'll be expecting us to pop out of any old secret hole," Dave said. "Sneaking in just isn't going to happen. Not unless anyone knows a passage she doesn't."

"I don't," Aaron grunted. "We discovered them all together. So every secret one that might not be known to others will be known to her."

"It's not your fault," I said, rubbing his back as we entered the cave, Fred and Dave pushing the barrier closed while Jaxton held Pieter. "There was no way you could have known that we would need it so many years later."

"Maybe if I wasn't so naïve," he said crossly.

"You were in love," I said. "That's no reason to hate yourself. You couldn't have foreseen the need to betray her a thousand years later."

"Should have been more cautious," he grumped, but his heart wasn't in it.

Not having a better plan was my fault. I was the one who had gathered everyone together to go after her. It was my responsibility to do better, and I was determined that I would, going forward. I just didn't know how.

We made our way to the great hall, where Pieter was laid out on one of the long tables. I turned away as Fred and Jaxton set his leg. Then, they pulled out a plastic vial of blood from Pieter's reserves and upended it into his mouth, giving him some energy to heal. Once that was done, we all sat down.

I stared at the ancient grains of the wooden table, tracing them gently with a finger. Malaise was setting in, dragging us all down as the silence thickened. Everyone felt like they'd failed. I thought about telling them not to be so sad, that this was my responsibility, but I couldn't even bring myself to do that.

"Oh, *great*, they came back here, too," I moaned as metal scraping against the wall announced Drakul's presence as he half-floated into the hall from one of the passages, his sword scraping against the wall.

Fenrir followed and surveyed us swiftly, shaking his head.

"So, how did that go?" he asked.

With a snarl, I launched myself at him, going up and over one of the tables and taking him to the ground. He saw me coming from a mile away, and with a slight turn as we went down, he tossed me across the room. I caught a glimpse of him rolling to his feet before I hit the wall and slid down.

The sound of half a dozen safeties snapping off filled my ears.

"Do that again," Aaron hissed, "and it will be the last thing you do. Am I clear?"

"I'm fine," I said, waving to get their attention from the upside-down crumple I'd formed in the corner. "Totally fine, see. He didn't hurt me. Just defended himself. No need to start a firefight."

Aaron stared at Fenrir for a few moments longer. "We could have used you," he said accusingly.

"For what?" Fenrir said as Drakul moved to his side, the two of them staring at the weapons still pointed in their direction. Though Aaron had backed off, the rest of his team were still ready for a fight.

"Your knowledge," Aaron said, waving at them to lower the muzzles as he came over to help me up.

"Thanks," I mumbled.

"What knowledge?" Fenrir asked as I patted myself down, shaking my clothes back into place and generally trying to act like nothing out of the ordinary had happened.

"Of the palace, for starters," Aaron growled. "Maybe you could have helped us find a way in that we didn't know about. Then, we might still have succeeded."

"I don't know that place," Fenrir growled. "I never spent time there. I lived among an enclave of vampires here on Earth. I lost myself for a time, and then Odin sent his thugs Thor and Loki after me to imprison me for eternity. Or are you not familiar with your lore?"

"And some 'eternity' it was that you were imprisoned for," I said. "Lots about you doesn't seem to be true."

"Well, I don't know the palace," Fenrir said. "And like I told you, this was a dumb plan that you shouldn't have gone forward with."

I snarled again, but Aaron restrained me from lashing out.

"He's not worth it."

Glaring at Fenrir, I shook my head. "What happened to you? I thought you were on our side."

"Whatever gave you that idea?" he snapped. "Because I helped you not go crazy? Look at how that turned out for me. Got attacked by a damn mage and nearly sent back to Mordathu! Yeah, that's enough for me, thank you. I should have stuck with laying low, staying out of sight of everyone. Which is what I intend to do now."

He glanced at Drakul, who nodded.

"I'll be staying here. If you come up with a better idea, let me know. Maybe I'll tag along," he said, the two of them heading off down the hall.

"Better idea," Jaxton scoffed. "What sort of better idea?"

"Probably the one he suggested the first time around," Dave said wryly. "Storm it with an army."

"We'd never get an army of shifters to do that," Fred said. "And there aren't enough like us of our own kind to do it, that's for sure. Maybe we could start an advertising campaign, recruit enough over time, but I doubt it. Elenia would try to shut that down immediately. We'd just be making ourselves a target."

"What about Dani and Vir?" Jaxton suggested softly. "We could use their help."

"If we do that," I said, "she'll go after the shifters. I bet she has teams poised to attack Shuldar and Seguin the second those two get involved. Which means they'll be stuck defending and unable to help us attack. It's easier not to get them directly involved."

And it's better for Dani that way, too.

"Well, who then?" Dave asked. "Where else are we going to get an army? Just go up to the nearest military base and ask the humans to help?"

"You're right," I said, looking at all of them. "*We* could never assemble an army ourselves."

Aaron's eyebrows came together swiftly. "Why do I get the feeling I'm not going to like what you have to say."

"Because you aren't," I said quietly. "I have an idea."

"But …" Aaron prompted.

"But it's a bad one. A *really* bad one," I said. "But it just might work."

"What is it?" Aaron asked softly.

I sighed. "I know where we can get the army we'd need."

CHAPTER THIRTY-TWO

"Well?" Dave said, spreading his arms wide. "Don't keep us on the edge of suspense here! Tell us, where do we get this army? We'll round them up and storm the palace and finally be rid of that bitch."

"It's not going to be quite that easy," I said, cringing away from Aaron's imploring look.

"Where are we getting the army from, Jo?" he asked.

"Um," I said, hesitating. This was stupid. Beyond stupid, really, it was insane. Only an insane person would think to do this.

"Jo …?" Aaron prompted again.

I sighed, shaking my head. I'd opened my mouth. There was no going back now. "Screw it. Fine. We need an army? We go to the one person who has an army and who also hates Elenia."

Recognition dawned a moment before I said the name.

"Hades."

Aaron's face exploded in a mixture of shock and anger. "Absolutely *not!*" he bellowed.

"Do you have a better idea?" I countered, raising my voice. "Or are you just dismissing it out of hand without truly thinking it through? Because it might be a bad idea, but you know it could work."

"If Hades doesn't kill you first!" he protested. "You told me that the last time you were there, he said not to come back because you won't get a warm welcome."

"That's why we go together," I said. "I'm not stupid. I won't wander in there alone. We go together and say we've come to bargain. Maybe we take something along to appease him."

Aaron looked ready to erupt into another angry outburst. I reached up and pressed a finger to his lips.

"*Think* about this before you start going on. Take my safety out of the equation, you adorable, protective idiot," I said softly, lessening the impact of my words. "Think about the *idea* and not me."

He pursed his lips together, compressing them into a flat line.

"She's right, you know," Fred said, leaning forward onto the table. "Nobody else has an army. Plus, Hades already has motive to want her dead. It's a good bargaining chip. We tell him he helps get us in, then we kill the queen, and the war between realms stops."

Aaron glared at his subordinate, but Fred just laughed it off.

"Don't look at me like that. I might work for you, but you know damn well I'm not your inferior to be silenced. She's got a good idea, and you're letting your feelings for her color your response. Take your emotions out of it and *think*, fearless leader."

"You know," I said, leaning around Aaron to address Fred a little more directly, "I *think* I was already calming him down. You don't need to rile him up."

"Sure, I do," Fred chuckled. "He deserves it for dismissing you like that."

"He's just scared for her," Dave said. "Can't blame a guy, can you? He cares for her. A lot. Wants to keep her safe."

"More like he probably fears that if we succeed, she'll end up on the throne, and he worries that he'll lose her again," Jaxton said softly.

Aaron looked around at everyone, but he didn't speak.

"You all agree with her?" he asked, nostrils

flaring with anger.

"We don't have to *like* something to realize it's our best shot at success," Jaxton said after taking a quick visual survey of the other members.

"She's right."

All eyes turned to Fenrir.

"There's your better idea," he said when I lifted my eyebrows in silent question. "And it's actually a pretty good one."

"Absolutely not," Aaron snarled, storming out of the room.

"Aaron!" I called, too shocked by his behavior to do much more, but he ignored me, tromping down one of the hallways, making nearly as much noise as Drakul.

I stared after him until he was gone around a corner.

"Well, go on," Fenrir said, breaking the silence.

"What?" I looked around the room at the prompt, noting that all eyes were focused on me and me alone. "What am I missing? Why am I going after him? He's in a mood for no reason. I don't want to deal with that."

"Because," Jaxton said softly, "he's in a mood 'cause of you."

"Me? What the heck did I do? Is it because I brought the idea up?"

"Of course not," Jaxton said, shaking his head.

"He's worried about you. Just won't admit it. Not here, around us at least. Has to be all macho. You know how it is."

"You're saying he's mad because he's scared? But he can't admit to being scared because ..."

"Because he's a man who grew up twelve centuries ago and has certain ingrained notions of women and 'how to be a man' that you're going to spend decades undoing if he doesn't get any therapy? Yes, pretty much," Dave said dryly.

I shook my head at him. "Where did he *find* you people?"

That brought a round of laughter from the group, but still, none of them went after him. Which meant I would have to do it. There was no way I was walking into the Underworld without him, that was for sure.

"Okay, here I go," I said.

"Have fun," Dave said with faux innocence.

I stuck my tongue out at him and then followed Aaron down the hallway. I had an inkling of where I might find him based on the exit he'd chosen. Coming to a halt, I knocked on the door to his old room.

There was no response, but my wolf's hearing picked up the sounds of someone breathing inside.

"Aaron," I said, resting my palm on the door. "Aaron, it's me."

When he still didn't say anything, I took a breath and opened the door.

I'd been prepared to be lambasted and put on the receiving end of a verbal tirade of epic proportions, but it wasn't anything like that at all. Aaron was sitting on the floor at the foot of the bed, knees drawn to his chest. His head was resting on his arms, which were crossed over his knees.

"Hey," I said, closing the door behind me and moving to him, taking a seat next to him. "What's wrong?"

This was so uncharacteristically unlike him that I approached the situation with hesitation, moving slow, thinking slow. What was making him like this?

He lifted his head slightly to look at me with those bright blue eyes that had snagged me so thoroughly once I'd let him in. They were troubled and full of what I thought was anger. But why was he so angry?

"Talk to me," I said, getting in close to him.

"About what?" he said gruffly. "We're going to do it anyway."

"I have to," I said. "But why is that so upsetting to you?"

Aaron sighed. "It's … not easy to admit to."

"What isn't?"

"Down there," he said slowly, looking straight

ahead. "The Underworld. Hades. I … I can't."

"You can't go?"

Aaron scoffed, then looked at me sharply, perhaps because he realized I was serious. "No, no, it has nothing to do with that. I'd go anywhere for you, Joanna."

My stomach leaped into my chest at his simple proclamation.

"No, it's not that. It's taking you there. He's a god. Abaddon is one of the demon kings. And he's going to be *pissed* if you go back."

"I know that," I said, stroking his hair, which was now nearly finger length. I liked it longer like that. "We'll just have to make him see reason."

"Don't you get it?" he insisted. "If … if he *doesn't*, if he refuses to listen to us, I can't protect you from him, Jo. I can't stop him from killing you. Or worse, throwing you into the pits … alive. I'm not strong enough."

I practically wilted, somehow sad and irritated with him all at once, but also swooning. It was a confusing series of emotions. "*This* is what that outburst was about? Because you can't kill Hades if he tries to hurt me?"

"Yes." He stiffened a little, sounding stronger. "I *just* found you, Jo. I'm still learning how to trust again, to let myself be open with you. If that's taken from me now, I don't know what I'd do."

Wordlessly, I snuggled into him. I almost wrapped him up in my arms, but given how he was currently feeling about his masculinity, I let him hold me instead. Make him feel big and strong. It wasn't his fault that he couldn't defeat a literal god. That wasn't what I wanted from him anyway.

"I don't need you always to be my protector," I said, listening to his heartbeat and enjoying the gentle weight of his head on top of mine as his strong arms kept me close. "I need you to *support* me."

"And I will," he said fiercely. "I will follow you into the flames of the Underworld itself, Joanna. I just feel impotent that I might not be able to get you out if things go to, well, hell."

I couldn't begin to imagine what that must have cost to him admit.

"I think it's a good sign," I told him, laying a hand on his, letting our fingers intertwine.

"What? That I'm not strong enough?"

"Not that," I said. "Stop it with that. I don't want your protection. I want your support. Get that through your skull. But no, I was talking about your ability, your willingness, even to admit this. You're opening up to me. Baring your soul. To me. Thank you for that."

Aaron was silent. "He told you never to come

back."

"I know," I said, sensing that this was his way of moving on, of accepting what was going to happen and changing the subject. "But I don't have a choice. He'll either see reason. Or we'll make him. Somehow."

CHAPTER THIRTY-THREE

"**A**re you sure you're ready for this?"

I glared at Fenrir. "Really? *Now* is when you're going to ask that?" I gestured at the misty gray portal that would take us from Earth to our first step into the Underworld.

"Last chance to back out," he said with a shrug, brushing aside a stray curl that had fallen onto his forehead.

Fenrir stood at the front, with the rest of the team strung out around us. I hadn't realized it at the time, but having him along would make life much easier. He was the only one of us who could take a portal directly into the Underworld. Otherwise, we would have had to journey to another realm first. In the past, we'd gone through the vampire's realm.

I didn't much like that option now. A direct flight was far more appealing, especially since we were running out of time. My mother had been safely transported into Vir's stronghold in the Direen, much to my relief, but she was swiftly running out of pills.

Can't let Elenia put a Blood Letter on Mom before I kill that Queen Bitch. That would just be the definition of bad luck.

Only four days remained until the Wild Moon. While it seemed we would get lucky and my mother wouldn't go through what I did, thanks to being off Earth, she would still return to normal without the drugs. And I wanted to be there for it. I wanted to meet her for the first time.

I shunted that thought aside. I'd spent too long thinking about what I'd say to her already, but that distraction could prove fatal. I had to focus on the task at hand. We were entering a hostile environment. Once Hades realized I was there, he would come for us. And we had to be ready.

"She's ready," Aaron said defensively when I didn't immediately respond.

"I'm not backing down," I confirmed as Fenrir glanced in my direction. "Whatever it takes to get to Elenia, I'll do it."

"Everyone double-checked?" Aaron asked, reaching out to squeeze my hand as the team sounded off.

I squeezed back, showing my appreciation for him sticking up for me. It was a relief to know that he had my back and was driving us forward as much as I was. We were in this together. Both had our reasons for seeking Elenia's demise, which also strengthened our dedication to one another.

Once she was gone, we could truly begin to explore these feelings and what they entailed for the future. We just had to survive plunging into the Underworld first.

Drakul just grunted, adjusting his sword in its sheath.

"Whatever," Aaron muttered dismissively at the crusty old vampire. "Let's move out."

As a group, we approached the portal. Hands were linked to shoulders, ensuring we stayed connected and all ended up at the same place.

Heat washed over me like a wet cloth, the first confirmation I had that we'd succeeded in reaching the realm. Bright red-orange light was the next, the sky the same color as the land around us.

We emerged onto a flat, blasted hellscape that stretched for miles in every direction. The ground was dried to the point of cracking, a maze of spiderweb-like fractures spreading out endlessly around us. There wasn't a tree, shrub, or bush to be seen. Ahead of us rose mountains. Behind …

I shuddered at the inky gray-black that marked the edge of Hades' realm. What happened if someone stepped out there, I didn't know. Nor did I have any interest in finding out.

"Long way from where we need to be," Jaxton said gruffly, glaring at Fenrir.

"Did you want me to bring us out in the middle of some of his troops? Near a well-used entrance, perhaps? I'm sure that would have gone over well."

"Might have saved us time," I said, starting forward. "It won't be long before he realizes I'm here anyway. That way would have simply meant we had an answer sooner. We don't have time to waste trekking across this."

Yet, we advanced into the wasteland anyway.

"Out here, the lord of this realm will have to send someone to intercept us," Fenrir explained, carefully not using Hades' name to avoid drawing his immediate attention to us. It wasn't wise to use any god's name within their realm unless you were on good terms with them. "They'll likely not want to fight all of us, being more willing to carry a message back to him."

"He might have a point," Fred said. "Out here in the badlands, nothing ever happens. If his highness isn't paying attention, he'll send a minor demon to investigate. That might actually work in our favor."

"Still should have told us," Aaron said.

"Nobody asked," Fenrir retorted with a shrug.

It bothered me how distant Fenrir had grown. What was going on with him? Maybe we hadn't been best friends, but he was withdrawing from everything around him recently.

Ever since he met Drakul ...

I mused that over for a bit, wondering if the answer could be as simple as I thought it might be. If it was, perhaps I should go easier on him. After all, there were others who had acted like this. Were they for similar reasons?

My eyes shifted back to Aaron.

Fred grunted. "We have a problem."

Instantly, all attention was on the vampire who always seemed to know a bit more than he let on. I didn't have time to worry about that now because my gaze was fixed on the tip of his out-stretched finger. On the "problem" he'd pointed out.

A problem soaring through the sky toward us, on wings blacker than night.

"Either he's really far away ..."

"Or he's *really* big," Aaron finished as the figure in the sky grew larger.

And larger.

"Yep, we definitely have a problem," Fenrir said, shuffling sideways.

Away from me.

"So much for sending a minor demon," I said, watching what could very well be my doom approaching us, knowing there was very little I could do about it.

Just standing there and taking it would be hard enough. As the giant approached, he brought with him a dark and oppressive energy. Its presence slammed down through the stifling heat, slapping me and the others to the ground. Not even Fenrir could resist the might of such a being.

My wolf was going crazy, trapped inside my mind, howling at me, begging to be let out. She was faster; she could run away from this. Take us to freedom, anything that would stop the fear from his presence spreading through us.

Together, we fought back, though I didn't grant her the freedom she longed for so badly. Now was not the time to unleash the beast within me. Not yet.

A miniature wave of dirt and debris was kicked up from his mighty wings as Abaddon, one of the Underworld's Demon Kings, landed half a football field away with as much grace as a delicate bird. The shockwave of his landing would have spilled us from our feet if we weren't already on all fours, desperately trying to stay upright.

He towered above us, nearly sixty feet tall,

excluding the trio of horns sprouting from his forehead, reaching toward the hellish sky. Twin eyes the same color as his wings looked down at us, evaluating the group before him. They had no pupils, which only added to his imposing look.

Not that he needed to look any more imposing, given the giant double-bladed ax he gripped casually in one clawed hand, its shaft as wide as I was tall. The gray metal of the blades was alight with carved reddish symbols, the runes glowing with evil intent.

"My master warned you not to return."

When Abaddon wanted to make an impression, he certainly could. The force of his voice tore at my eardrums. I clapped my hands over my ears, but it was far too late by then. I fought a whimper from the pain. Showing weakness in front of a being like him didn't seem like a smart idea.

Against the fear wreaking havoc on my body, I forced my head to turn so I could stare up at the beast.

"I know," I shouted back. "But I wasn't exactly graced with a plethora of options. This was the best of the bunch, which should tell you everything you need to know."

The demon king studied me ominously as I spoke and for several long heartbeats after. "Why have you returned?" he asked at long last.

"You can tell your master that I've returned because I'm here to bargain."

"You are bargaining," Abaddon rumbled. "With your life."

"Tell me something I don't know," I muttered as the mental pressure lifted at last.

Abaddon must have heard me because he smiled wide, revealing two rows of razor-sharp glossy black teeth. "Very well. I tell you this. If your bargain is not interesting, my master will permit me to toss you into the Pits of Tartarus."

"Well, shit," I cursed.

His grin grew wider. "Alive."

CHAPTER THIRTY-FOUR

"I told you he wouldn't want to see you," Fenrir said as we all stood up, brushing ourselves off while Abaddon waited in the distance.

"And I told you that I wasn't backing down," I growled, brushing past him and walking toward the demon.

Fenrir snorted, but he followed, as did the others.

"Are we walking back?" I asked.

"No. Come," Abaddon said, crouching down, extending both his hands toward us. "I will carry you."

I swallowed against the sudden dryness in my throat. By doing this, I would be stepping straight into the belly of the beast. A quick squeeze of his hand and we would be nothing but paste to be washed off.

Though, that would be preferable to letting him cast us into the pits while alive. At least we would be dead first.

"Anyone see a better choice?" I asked as the team approached with extreme hesitation.

My wolf was all but clawing at my mind, trying to get out. She did not want to submit to anyone, and the dangerous spot I was about to put us in did nothing to calm her. I hoped she would tire herself out soon because I would need all my mental focus to deal with Hades.

Loaded up in both his hands, Abaddon closed his fingers around us and then reached for the sky, jumping high into the air as his wings swept downward, the mighty *whoosh* of air a reminder of just how big he was.

As if I need a reminder. Not with these tree trunk-like fingers closed around us, ready to turn us into pancakes if Hades flicks a finger.

"Let's just hope he goes for it," Aaron said from at my side. "I really would hate to fly all that way to be rejected."

I closed my eyes, blowing air out from my nose at his attempt at humor. It worked for a moment, but the bleak oppressiveness of our situation quickly flooded back in. The odds were so against us. Even if we survived our meeting with Hades *and* he agreed to furnish us with an army, there was still one monumental task for us to complete.

Killing Elenia.

If the Vampire Queen was as strong as Aaron said, our job would be near impossible. I did my best to radiate calm and control, but internally, I was slowly concluding that we were going to die. I'd known from the outset that we *could*, but more and more, I felt like that was my destiny.

The wind rushed over us as we descended swiftly. Leaning forward, peering through the cracks, I spied the walls of Hades' stronghold approaching. We were there already. A major commotion drew my attention next.

"Something's going on," I said as figures streamed from the castle, pouring out through the main gates.

The others rose, eagerly peering around. I followed the column of demons—what else could they be—but I lost them somewhere in the hills on the far side of the citadel. Abaddon's thick finger blocked my view.

"A battle," Fred observed. "I can see fighting."

"Vampires?" I asked.

"That would be my assumption, but too far away for me to tell. All I can see are two lines marching toward one another. Too hard to know for sure, but I can't imagine anyone else would be so bold. Whoever it is, it's a major strike. Probably a thousand or more, at least."

I grinned, hope sparking in my stomach.

"Why are you so happy about that?" Aaron asked.

"Don't you see?" I said, looking at him and the others with me. "She's attacking. We got here at the perfect time. He's going to be extra pissed at her and hopefully more willing to go with our plan."

The shock of Abaddon's landing dropped us to his palm. Moments later, we were spilled to the stone ground as rank upon rank of demons marched past, covered in an assortment of arms and armor.

On the wall over the gate, a lone figure stood, observing the activity. He wore nothing but black pants and a matching black vest pulled tight across his powerful frame. His hair was black and curled, clinging to his skull. I couldn't see his eyes from here, but I remembered them from when I met him in his spire. They would be dark brown, capable of piercing you to the soul in a heartbeat.

"My lord," Abaddon rumbled. "I have returned with the interlopers."

"You should have killed them," Hades snapped, his voice easily carrying down to us. He did not turn away from the battle.

"They say they come to bargain," Abaddon replied, unfazed by his master's tone. "I thought it wise to hear what they had to say. They were aware that returning was unwise, so there must be a reason."

"Oh, there's a reason," Hades said, turning at last, his eyes miniature blazing suns, visible even from this distance.

Casually leaping from the wall, he landed in front of us, the fires even more intense this close up.

"Look," he snapped, glaring up at Abaddon. His hand stretched out and waved in a circle. A sphere in the sky turned opaque, revealing a party of demons carrying a limp figure away from the fighting.

"Azazel," I whispered, recognizing the teleporting demon from my last trip.

"Yes, Azazel," Hades raged. "Look closer."

The image zoomed in, and I gasped. Azazel was covered in cuts. From head to toe, the wounds were open, black blood trailing behind the group of demons that rushed him away.

"Corvis' work," Aaron growled. "They must have gone toe to toe. I guess we didn't kill that bastard after all."

"Indeed," Hades snapped. "How convenient for Corvis that *you* happened to arrive at just the right time to siphon my best warrior away. Now Azazel will be weeks in recovery, if not months.

Do you have any idea how much work he does? This is all your fault."

My jaw dropped open. "*My* fault? We had nothing to do with this. Nothing at all. Bad timing, that's all, nothing more. We're here to *help* you with this."

Hades snarled, leaning in close to me. I scurried backward as the heat of his eyes singed my skin.

"You could help me by having never come back as you were told. I warned you that there might be a hot reception. Now you will reap the consequences of your actions."

He clapped his hands, and four demons that I'd never seen before simply *appeared* around him. No blinking, no poof of smoke. One moment they weren't there, and the next, they were.

Each one was seven or eight feet tall. They walked on reverse canted legs and had four arms, each one ending in fingers that looked like they could curl in either direction. One hand per side held a traditional sword blade, while the other held shorter, thicker blades. I didn't know their name, but they were perhaps eight inches long and six inches wide, with a zig-zag along the blade side.

Two black eyes watched us while they waited for their master's command.

"Take them to the dungeons," Hades ordered.

"Let them sweat out the truth. Eventually, they will admit that they are secretly helping. At least one of them. Probably *him*."

Hades' finger pointed at Fenrir. "And I gave you shelter for so long."

Fenrir barked laughter. "You're crazy, Hades. You know damn well that we had nothing to do with this. You're just pissed off that you're going to have to do all the work Azazel does while he recovers. And we're your convenient scapegoat. Trust me, though, you want to hear what the girl has to say."

"No, I don't," Hades said calmly, gesturing at the demons. "My Enkk will gladly kill you if you try to run or fight."

I glared at him as the demons marched us away. The last thing I heard was Hades barking at Abaddon, telling the demon king to get out to the fighting and stop it already.

Then, we were swept into the bowels of the castle. There, the Enkk held us at swordpoint, while other demons, the hoofed and horned Axotl and the monkey-frog Djinn, removed all our weapons and gear, leaving us with nothing but our clothes. After that, one of them patted us down roughly to ensure nothing was hidden or had been missed.

Convinced that we had nothing left on us that could be of use, the Enkk herded us into darkened cells. The door clanged shut behind them as they retreated, leaving us in near pitch black. There was just enough light to make out the shapes of the others in the cell around me.

"This isn't the way I thought I'd go out," Dave muttered once we were alone.

"Yeah," I said, slumping down against the stone wall, feeling the heat of it warm my back already. "Me neither."

CHAPTER
THIRTY-FIVE

We'd all been pitched into the same cell, which didn't leave much in the way of personal space for any of us. We spread out as best we could, most of us using the wall to sit or stand against.

Fred was one of the few who hadn't done that. He was leaning on the bars, tapping against them, one by one.

"What are you doing?" I asked, watching him curiously. Was he just bored? It seemed more like he was searching for something.

"Looking for the false bar," he said.

"The what?"

"Each of these cells was built with a way out. Just in case. One of the bars in them is fake and will give way if pressure is properly applied to it."

"You certainly know a lot about this place," I said. "Been here before?"

"Something like that," Fred said, refusing to elaborate.

I cast a glance at Aaron, but he shook his head. Whatever it was, neither of them was telling. By now, everyone was watching Fred with interest as he made his way across the front of the cell, block by block, testing each piece, including the cross-welds.

"You don't seem to be finding much," Fenrir pointed out as the vampire neared the far edge of the cell.

"So I've noticed. I think they must have removed them, though they don't look like they've had any work done. I—" He cut himself off as his fingers rapped against one cross-weld.

To my ears, it rang the exact same, but he'd heard something different. He grabbed the bar and wrenched it. The metal protested, and Fred grunted this time, putting lots of muscle into it. The metal began to turn with a shrieking sound.

Abruptly, an Enkk was there, its sword moving between bars until the point of it pricked under Fred's chin. Fred froze, rising onto his tiptoes as the Enkk made its threat clear without saying a word.

"Okay, so we won't be doing that," Fred said as the sword lowered, and he backed away from the edge of the cage. "Not while those things are still watching us."

He made his way to the back of the cell, keeping a wary eye on the Enkk until it simply wasn't there anymore.

"Damn things give me the creeps," he said, glaring at the emptiness beyond the bars. "Hate them."

I laid my head back against the wall, letting it rest against the stone, feeling the slow pulsing warmth reaching out to tingle my skin. I was out of ideas at this point and needed time to come up with something. Perhaps after the battle was over, Hades would come to talk and listen to our offer.

That was about all that I had, which felt an awful lot like giving up, but what more could I do? The Enkk were outside our cell, waiting to pop into existence to skewer us if we so much as tried to escape. Even if we somehow got past them, there was Abaddon and Hades to deal with.

Things were bleak.

"Anyone else feel like this is getting hotter?" Dave asked, lifting a hand from the ground. "It didn't feel that bad to my hand when I first sat down."

I put a hand down on the ground. "Feels about the same to me," I said.

Alexi, who was seated on Dave's other side, lifted his hand that rested between them. "Ow," he said in his harsh accent. "It is definitely hotter."

"It's fine over here," I repeated, touching the floor.

"Not here," Dave said, moving away. "And I think it's spreading."

It didn't take long to confirm his theory. Within minutes, I could feel the floor warming around me. Once it was too hot to stand, we scooted across the cell to the front, pressing our backs to the cool metal of the bars, eager for any bit of relief. The Enkk appeared outside the cell, but they only watched.

"This isn't good," Aaron said, breathing slightly faster now as the temperature in the cell continued to rise. The stones were heating the very air now, making it more difficult to breathe.

"Why not just kill us?" I asked, confused. "Seems less resource-intensive."

"No idea. Maybe this is his idea of fun, torturing us by slowly cooking us alive?"

"Well, it's working," I said, sweat beading on my forehead and temples, soaking the back of my head as it dripped through my hair.

It wasn't long before my clothes were soaked as well, with my body trying to regulate its temperature. The men all doffed their shirts. I waited as long as I could before doing the same, standing against the front of the cell in just a sports bra. Not that it made much of a difference by that point. We were getting close to overheating, and it had been maybe half an hour at this point.

"We're going to die if we don't cool this place down," I said.

"How do you suggest we do that?" Fenrir said, miming looking around. "I don't see a giant bucket of cold water or snow around here, do you?"

I stiffened in shock. "Not snow, no," I said, grabbing Aaron by the shoulders. "Frost. You need to make frost. Try to cool the stones down!"

He looked at me, unsure of it. "That's a lot of frost," he said. "I've never done that much."

"All of you, at once," I snapped, pointing at his entire team. "Stand in a circle, try to do it together."

With no better ideas, Aaron gathered the men around him in the middle of the room.

"Together," he ordered. "One. Two. *Three*."

A blissfully refreshing wave of cold rippled through the room. The stones hissed as a cold front formed around their feet, instantly blanketing the room in fog as the cool moisture met the heated air.

I gulped down huge lungs of the air, my body shaking as goosebumps popped up under the layer of sweat. It was the most wonderful thing I'd ever experienced, and I basked in it, as did the others.

Then, it was gone. The stones melted the frost, and heat eventually cleared the air. Leaving us right back where we'd been.

"Again," I ordered.

The vampires worked in concert. This time they hit the room with their waves of cold three times in succession, leaving them gasping from the effort. The stone floor had cooled significantly, and we all managed to recover slightly.

Nearly five minutes passed this time before it wore away. I could see heat shimmering from the stones in the corner now, where it had first grown warm. They were once again turning the heat up in here, baking us in our own sweat, like turkeys basting.

"You have to do it again," I said to Aaron. "It's our only hope."

Nodding, his face drooping with exhaustion, the six vampires once more tried to spread the cold. Alexi stumbled. Pieter, still weakened from the energy his broken leg had required to heal, dropped to one knee, shaking. Fred stood around stoically, putting on an indifferent front.

"It's no use," Aaron said as the cold front quickly disappeared, once more dropping us into a bath of heat. "We can't create enough cold to make a difference."

"Fuck."

The single word cut through everything but the stifling heat.

"But you could," Aaron added. "You're stronger, Jo."

"I've never done it before," I pointed out. "You said yourself it takes practice to 'vamp out.' Now doesn't seem like a time … But then again, what other options do we have?"

"Precisely."

"Okay," I whispered to myself, moving to where the team was, trying to focus. "Let your vampireness go. Call it up, and then let it spread."

Fear. Hunger. Rage. Those were the three keys of the vampire that lived inside me, the *thing* that longed for blood above all else.

I'd always avoided it, trying to keep it in the shadows, pretending like it wasn't there. I couldn't do that, not now. Not if we wanted to live. So, I reached out to it, feeling its presence.

Come forth, I commanded. The darkness came into me, flowing swiftly. More and more. I clenched my jaw against the fury that was swept along with it, the rage pushing blood into my muscles while my stomach gurgled with hunger. My mouth started salivating, and then my fangs popped free with a hiss.

"Here."

I popped my eyes open to see Aaron with a vial of blood.

"Where did you get that?" I said around my fangs, holding the caged vampire hunger within me at bay by focusing on his face, reminding myself that I was in love with him. I used other positive emotions to stay in charge. Love. Caring. Friendship.

"We always carry spares," he said with a cringe as his team also retrieved their vials.

From between their legs.

"Was this—"

"Taped to the inside of our legs? Yes, yes, it was," he said hurriedly. "But we don't have time. Doesn't matter where they were. You need to drink."

"You should have used this," I said. "You can already make frost."

"Not frost," he said ruefully, pulling the cap. My nostrils flared as the scent quickly reached me. "Only cold. *You* could make frost, though."

I suddenly no longer cared why that was different, why it mattered. Somehow I knew it should, but between the heat, and the taste of the warm blood as it caressed my tongue, I just did not give a shit. Not anymore.

There was one thing, and one thing only, that mattered. *Feeding.* Hands batted away my fingers as they clawed for the vial, and one by one, the other members upended their backups into my mouth in an orgy of wonderful sensations.

"Now harness it," Aaron whispered in my ear, his tone almost seductive, given the sensations running through my body. "Hold it tight, compress it down into a tiny ball as hard as you can, until you can shrink it no more. Then let it *go*."

I focused, trying to do as he said. Nearby, Alexi fell to the ground as his eyes rolled up into his head. Instantly, his skin blistered as it touched the heated rock. Fred and Dave pulled him up as fast as they could get to him, but his face, arm, and chest were already a wreck.

They were counting on me. If I failed, we all died.

I found the vampire in me and compressed it down. I pressed it from the outsides of my mind, clamping down with an imaginary vise, spinning it tighter and tighter. My limbs began to tremble from the effort. Aaron grabbed me by the ribs and held me upright, stopping me from pitching face-first to the floor.

Finally, I reached a point where the energy of the Hunger, so bottled up, was as strong as my mind. An equilibrium.

"*Release it*," Aaron whispered.

I stopped squeezing.

A globular cold front raced out from me. It froze sweat and shattered the stone prison, sending sharp shards everywhere, slicing us all open. It turned the heat in the air to fog and then ice, which dropped to the floor in a tinkling wave that spread away from me. The ground turned white for nearly ten feet in every direction as I froze it *solid.*

"I *did* it!" I gasped, staggering for breath in the super-chilled air, while my body slumped from the effort, weakened from the energy that had taken.

"Yes," Aaron said calmly. "You did. That ought to get his attention."

From somewhere outside of the cell, a terrible roar could be heard, echoing down every corridor and passageway, seemingly coming from the very bowels of the Underworld itself.

And all at once, I knew why it was a mixture of pain and anger.

I had just released frost. In the heart of the Underworld.

"He's definitely going to kill us now," Dave drawled into the silence that followed.

CHAPTER THIRTY-SIX

"If we're going to die, then I'd rather get him all riled up, so he just offs us swiftly out of spite instead of cooking us to a nice internal temperature of charbroiled," I said. "But you do whatever you want."

Dave looked at me, a little hurt. "I never said I disagreed with you."

I closed my eyes and sighed. "Sorry, Dave. That wasn't called for."

Before he could reply, a warm front gusted through the hall outside our cell. The temperature quickly rose to an uncomfortable level. Nervously, I backed away as the frost inside the cell showed signs of melting.

"Who *dares* show such disrespect?" Hades howled, arriving behind a wave of billowing fire, the flames flickering out and dying swiftly.

His black vest stretched to bursting over his chest as he breathed heavily, his rage at my actions tearing away his self-control.

"You," I growled, surprising myself with how much backbone I displayed even in the face of fury from a god known to be spiteful and quick to anger.

Hades focused on me, his normally dark brown eyes filled with a white-hot flame. Literally, there were flames burning where his pupils should be.

"What did you say?" he hissed, the sound like hot metal being shoved into cold water.

"I said that *you* were the one who has been disrespectful," I said, standing my ground. If he were going to kill me, it wouldn't be with me cowering in the corner.

Although the others didn't speak up, I felt their presence nearby. They, too, were going to meet their deaths with some courage.

"Me? Disrespectful? I was not the one who unleashed the cold on my home."

"No, but you treated us like nothing when we came in good faith to bargain. To *help* you. Instead, you decided you would cook us alive and serve us up for dinner. If that's not being rude, then I don't know what is. You forced me to do that to save myself. Either way you look at it, this is *your* fault, Hades. Not ours."

I braced myself for the inevitable wave of fire that would flay skin from bone and reduce me to little more than charred ash that the Enkk would sweep from the cell.

The God of the Underworld trembled with rage as he stared at me, struggling to come up with a response.

"Ask Abaddon if you think I'm wrong," I said, shrugging.

Hades lifted a hand, a ball of fire so bright it hurt my eyes to look at it. "I could kill you without breaking a sweat."

"Of course you could," I said, staring at the ground, shielding my eyes with one hand against the light. "Finally, something we agree on. You're the god, and we're in your realm. But think about that for a second, Hades. We, I, *willingly* came here, to your realm, to bargain with you, knowing that you didn't want me to come back. Don't you think that maybe, just maybe, there was a good reason behind it?"

The ball of pure sunlight faded until I could look at Hades once more.

"I should just kill you and be done with it," he muttered. "Such insolence from a nobody."

"Yeah, but you're curious now," I said, smiling in victory.

I had him, and we both knew it. He wasn't happy about it, but what did I care? As long as I could live through it, I didn't care much about his feelings.

"Perhaps," he admitted. "But if I don't like your plan, I will still kill you."

"Do you ever get tired of threatening people with that?" Fred called. "You need to come up with something more original."

Hades turned his attention to the big, gruff vampire. His eyes focused on him, looking beyond the surface in a way I couldn't. Fred didn't even flinch.

"*You*," Hades rumbled. "So you escaped my hounds."

"Like always," Fred said dryly. "But that's not the point. You should listen to her."

Hades' hands clenched into fists. "You do not tell me what to do. You are not welcome here, ever again, understand me? Or I will speak truths you do not wish others to hear."

Fred snorted. "Two can play that game," he retorted but declined to say anything more.

I looked back and forth between them. Who *was* Fred?

Hades growled in irritation, then snapped his fingers at me. "Fine. Speak. Tell me why you returned."

I grinned at him. "I want to kill Elenia for you."

Leaving a god speechless was a damn good feeling. I bathed in it, luxuriated in the moment, splashing it all over myself and not caring who knew about it. If I had his mild curiosity before, now I had his attention.

"Quite the proposal," Hades said, looking at me with a bit more interest.

I didn't like that part. Being the focus of a god when he wasn't dismissing you was a tad unnerving.

"I told you I would have a good reason for coming back."

"But there is more," Hades said. "You did not need to come here to kill her. She resides in her own realm."

"Actually, I did need to come see you first," I said.

Hades' face split open into a grin. "Oh. That is rich. You need my help, don't you?"

I bowed my head in his direction. "Winner, winner."

"I am listening," he rumbled. "Make your case. It had best be good."

"First, I want to know if me killing her will sate your need for revenge and end the war between realms."

Hades stroked his chin.

"She was the one who helped steal all those souls from you and funnel them into the Direen," I pointed out. "Nobody else could have orchestrated that. Your fight isn't with the regular vampires. It's with her. So, if I kill her, we have peace between realms."

"If I help you kill her," Hades said, "then the throne will be empty. And only a female vampire can sit on it. I would be assisting you in becoming the new Vampire Queen."

"You would," I said, fighting back a shiver as I verbally accepted the idea.

"Most interesting," he said, lips curling upward. "Most interesting indeed."

"So, will you help us?" I pressed, eager to get out of the cell and back to work.

Time was ticking, and the longer I spent locked up, the worse it would get. I didn't know how quickly Hades could assemble the army we needed, nor could I be assured that our journey to the queen would meet with immediate success either. My mom could survive in the Direen for some time, but I would *not* let her live her life there.

Nor would I be somewhere else when the last of her meds fully wore off and she returned to normal. Whatever her normal might be after taking the pills for so long.

If I'm nervous, I can only imagine how Dad feels. He's missed his mate for over two decades now. He remembers her how she was and is likely terrified to find out who she is now.

"What help of mine do you need?" Hades

asked. "You have yet to specify. I will not blanket agree to help without knowing what it is you require first."

Smart.

"The queen has mobilized Madrigal," I said bluntly, seeing no use in dancing around the issue. Either Hades would help, or he wouldn't. "We can't get in on our own. Teams of vampires watch the entrances while more fill the streets. There's no way for us to get to her like that. She's too well protected."

"What do you expect me to do? Kill her for you?" Hades growled.

"No," I countered. "I want you to provide us the distraction to draw away most of her guards."

"What sort of distraction? If she has the entire city up in arms, that would require quite the contribution on my part." Hades sounded skeptical.

I hesitated, feeling like I was losing his interest. My mind raced, trying to come up with an alternative. Was there another way Hades could help us succeed? A way that required less effort from him, making him more willing to cooperate?

I didn't see one.

So, I went for broke. What was the worst that could happen? "I need an army," I said bluntly.

Hades goggled at me. "You never cease to amaze me with your demands, mortal," he said, shaking his head. "An army? You intend to invade?"

"Yes," I said bluntly. "The army will draw her forces away from Madrigal. It has to. Otherwise, you'll slaughter her troops if she attacks piecemeal. When the bulk of them come to fight, my team and I will slip away, enter the palace, and put an end to her once and for all."

"Ambitious," Hades said. "And if you fail?"

"Then she's going to be really angry with you," I said. "But what else is she going to do? She doesn't have the strength to invade the Underworld. It would ruin her to do so."

"And you would be dead," Hades said grimly. "Therefore, I would get my revenge on you."

My chest tightened. I hadn't thought about *that* particular angle yet. Torture in the afterlife did not sound particularly enjoyable.

"Having Elenia off the throne *would* be good, yes," Hades mumbled half to himself. His eyes traveled from me to Aaron and then back. "Though, I wonder if you're ready for all that would come with it."

"I am," I said as strongly as I could muster.

Hades chuckled. "We shall see. If I am to give you command of my army, then I will require ... *assurances* of your sincerity."

I licked my lips. "Such as?"

CHAPTER
THIRTY-SEVEN

"If this goes badly, it will leave me wide open for attack," Hades stated. "Elenia may not be able to kill me or conquer the Underworld, but there are many other things she can do to severely hurt or hamper me while the heart of my realm is undefended."

"How would she do that?" I asked. "Wouldn't she be too busy defending her own?"

Hades snorted. "Not if she sees the attack coming and plans for it."

"How could she possibly do that? The only people who know the plan are right here." I neglected to add Dani and Vir to that list because I knew they would never go to Elenia and tell. I trusted them with my life.

"It's the people here that I don't trust," Hades growled. "Not for this task, at least."

I turned to look at the team. Who could he mean? "Fred ...?" I had no real idea.

"Is that what you're calling yourself?" Hades chuckled. "No, I dislike him, but I trust him."

"He means me," Aaron said, stepping forward. "He doesn't trust me."

"Your arrival here is still suspicious," Hades said. "It was almost too perfect. If I am to give you command of my army and lend you the strength you need, I must know that he isn't a double agent."

"He's not," I said, rolling my eyes. This was ridiculous. Aaron was *not* a double agent!

"Do you know that he's the one who got Elenia to where she is now? That he put her on the throne?"

"Yes, yes," I said. "They were in love, and together, they ascended the ranks until she was on the throne."

"No," Hades said. "I mean it literally. *He* is the reason she is on the throne. The previous queen died by his hand. Not hers."

I looked at Aaron. He nodded slowly, confirming the story.

"Okay, so?"

"You said it yourself. They were in love."

"Right, and?"

"And people do things for love," Hades said

pointedly. "Like betray those they pretend to care about."

I stared at the god. "They haven't been together for *centuries.* Are you telling me you truly think he's been apart from her for this long, all because the two of them somehow knew this moment would come to be?"

"Stranger things have happened," Hades said. "Trust me. I was there for some of them. Long-term planning is not unheard of in immortal beings."

"I don't believe it."

"When Elenia was elevated to the throne, she continued funneling souls from my realm into the Direen for Irr to use kill his fellow gods," Hades said, naming Vir's insane brother, who was now thankfully dead. Dani had seen to that.

"I know the history," I said. "What I don't understand is how you think it's related."

"Elenia would have known that at some point I would find out. That I would discover she had assisted Irr. That I would be furious and want revenge. She would want a plant, someone who could pretend to be against her while feeding her information so that she could succeed."

"That *does* sound like her," I said, forced to admit it. "But it's not Aaron. It can't be."

Hades' lip twitched. Had he been waiting for me to say something like that? Did he know about Aaron and me? He couldn't.

"Perhaps you are right," Hades granted. "But I am not willing to trade on 'maybes' and 'possiblys.' I require hard *proof*."

"Okay, I can't argue that. But how do you want him to prove that he's not a double agent?" I asked, looking around at the others to see if they had any suggestions. "Obviously, asking her is out of the question."

"Indeed. I think the best way would be for him to demonstrate his loyalty to someone else."

"He'll never pledge his allegiance to you," I said, trying to refrain from breaking out into laughter. "Come on, Hades."

"She's right," Aaron said firmly.

"I wasn't talking about myself," Hades said, grinning. "I meant *you*."

My laughter stopped abruptly. He wanted Aaron to show his loyalty to me?

"Absolutely *not*," Aaron said emphatically. "She's not ready for that."

I whipped my head back and forth between them. "Ready for what? What are you two talking about?"

"He wants Aaron to claim you," Fred explained.

That put to bed any rest that Hades knew something was going on between Aaron and me. How he knew, I wasn't sure, but he did.

"He already has," I said. "If it means what I think it does."

How lovely *this* was. Having my sexual laundry aired out in front of a god and the rest of Aaron's team. I'm sure the jokes would be endless.

"In the ancient way," Hades said. "I want to see him formally relinquish his claim on Elenia so that he may take you."

"Ew," I said, cringing. "You're not going to watch, thank you very much. That is private time."

"He wants me to bite you," Aaron said in a hard tone. "To quite literally *claim* you as my own. Not sex."

"Oh." I frowned. "But I'm already a vampire. I thought I had to be human for that? To turn me."

"Turning someone is different than feeding on them," Aaron said, staring past me at Hades, anger plain to see on his features. "Just more of the same. *Claiming* a vampire is ..."

"Permanent," Hades said. "Until the claim is relinquished for another. Which is why I require this test of loyalty."

"I never claimed Elenia," he countered.

Hades scoffed, disbelieving. "You two were thick as thieves for centuries. Everyone could see you were in love."

"She wouldn't let me," Aaron said heavily.

"From the start, she said it was because she wanted to change the way things were done. That women shouldn't be the property of men and that since they could not claim anyone, the practice was unfair."

"And you did not see through this?" Hades asked.

Aaron's lungs rose and fell with a slow breath. "Like with many things, I later found out she'd lied to me. It was all part of her plan. I assume that she didn't want me connected to her. So that I didn't know about her plans. In hindsight, it was naïve of me, but as everyone knows, I loved her."

"Be that as it may," Hades said, "I still require my proof. This is my offer to you. An army to help you put her on the throne if you do this."

Aaron laughed sharply. "I'm not helping put her on the throne. She is damn well capable of doing that herself. I'm going along to undo the mistake I made in putting the *last* one on the throne. Nor will I claim her, not for you. That is not your right to ask or demand."

"What about if I ask you to?" I said, breaking in before he could go on. "Would you do it then?"

He frowned at me while Hades waited impatiently. "You would be giving yourself to me, Jo."

I'd already done that.

"Forever," he added.

I hadn't done that.

"You don't seem fazed by this," I said, staring up into his eyes, the azure rings of his irises inviting me in with their calm, measured gaze.

"I'm not."

"Why?" I asked, losing myself in him, forgetting about everyone else at that moment. Just then, none of them mattered, only this one, this man.

Aaron's mouth curved upward into a faint smile. "This isn't the path I saw us getting to it," he admitted. "But I held hope that we might find ourselves here at some point. I would never have forced it on you, but that's not the same as saying I did not *want* it. Like I want you."

My heart skipped a beat at his words. It wasn't the first time Aaron said he wanted me. In fact, our entire adventure began with those words when he'd shown up at my parents' door. He'd said the same three words then, like now.

Only this time, it was *my* reaction that was different. Back then, I'd dismissed him, told him he was crazy, and it would never happen. And now ... now I wanted him back.

"Okay," I said, throwing caution to the wind. "Do it."

Aaron frowned at me, his body language suddenly changing dramatically. "No."

CHAPTER THIRTY-EIGHT

No? Had he just said no? I shook my head, thinking my ears and brain must be playing tricks on me. After all the kind things he said to me, all the words about wanting me, about wanting to claim me. Had they just been lies? What purpose had they served him?

"I *knew* it!" Hades hissed, and heat blossomed from him. "Traitor."

Aaron lifted an arm to Hades, still staring at me. "I am not a traitor."

"You said no. You can't do it, can you?" Hades growled. "Because you are bound to *her*."

"I *won't* do it because you've got us crammed together in a cell like dogs," Aaron shot back. "You will free us and give us a room so that we may be together. I will not share this moment with anyone else but Joanna."

Oh. That was not what I'd been expecting, but it suddenly made sense. From the way Aaron talked about it, claiming was an intimacy on the level of sex. Of course, he would want privacy.

"So, you still want to—to claim me?" I asked, stammering ever so slightly over the word, still getting used to the terminology.

"With all my heart and body," he said. "But not in front of these idiots or Hades."

"Hey!" Dave barked. "I resemble that remark."

The entire team chuckled at the comment, though none of them objected.

"Consider this *your* good faith gesture," Aaron said to Hades.

"I do believe giving you a demon *army* is a pretty good faith gesture," the god said.

"This is a gesture to indicate you will follow through with *that* gesture," I said.

Hades shook his head. "Whatever. I suppose it makes no difference. You can't escape." He snapped his fingers at two of the Enkk. "Take them to guest quarters and ensure they aren't disturbed. When they are done, summon me."

Wordlessly, the four-armed demons moved to carry out his orders, one of them opening the door so we could leave. While they didn't communicate with each other, they seamlessly positioned themselves with one to guide and one to follow us, ensuring we did not sneak away.

"And feed them," Aaron said as he passed Hades, pointing at his team. "We're all on the same side here."

"For now," Hades agreed, motioning to the remaining Enkk to carry out the command and provide food.

I hoped he would provide the *proper* food. If we were going to storm Elenia's palace, I needed the entire team to be in peak form. That meant they needed blood.

"We could use some, too," I commented.

"Any *other* requests?" Hades said dryly, not denying the request.

"Not yet."

The god grimaced, then flickered out of existence without another word, off to tend to his realm. Hopefully, that would involve sending out the word to raise an army like the one we'd seen marching out of his stronghold upon our arrival.

As we climbed the steps out of the dungeons into another part of the vast subterranean complex at the heart of Hades' realm, my heartbeat sped up. Just what was I committing myself to? Vampires didn't deal in human lifetimes. Aaron was already twelve centuries old. He could live twice that again if nothing killed him. And now I would bind myself to him for as long as we both lived.

Which could be a very, very long time indeed.

Was I ready for this?

Sensing my hesitation, Aaron took my hand and squeezed it before locking his fingers through mine.

"You can say no."

"It's not that I *want* to say no," I said, not pulling my hand away. "But I don't *really* know what I'm getting myself into by saying yes. This is all so new to me, Aaron. I don't know things. Am I making the right choice? Do I even *have* a choice?"

"Of course you have a choice," Aaron said instantly. "I will not force you into this."

I tightened my hand on his. "I'm not talking about *you*, Aaron. If I don't do this, Hades doesn't give us his army. People will suffer and die because of it. People who don't deserve to."

"Like your mother," he said softly.

"Yes."

"Whatever you choose, I will support you," he said. "I will fight to the end if need be. If we have to try to storm the palace, the two of us, then I will fight by your side. I am yours, Joanna Alustria, and no one else's."

The Enkk led us from the staircase into a hallway. We followed behind in silence, Aaron letting me muse about the decision ahead. There was no need for him to say more. I knew how he felt. The rest was up to me.

"What happens to me if you claim me?" I asked.

"We would be bound. Our minds joined."

"So, we would know what the other is thinking?"

"Feeling," he said. "To an extent. It deepens the connection already there."

"Oh."

"It would also mark you as mine to any other male vampires. If they bit you, for any reason, it would burn them," he added, as we came to a halt in front of a door.

How the Enkk knew where to stop was beyond me, but it was evident that this was the guest quarters we were assigned. They waited for us to open the door and then moved to stand on either side of it.

We were still prisoners, it seemed.

"Would you have any control over me?" I asked, surveying the room.

"No," Aaron said, doing the same.

It didn't take us long.

The large space was sparsely but expensively furnished. Thick carpet covered the floor while a large four-poster bed sat against the wall to the right. Directly adjacent to the door were his and hers desks, floor-length mirrors, and wardrobes. Everything was carved from rich brown wood, stained to bring out the grain to perfection.

All the finishes were done in gold. Handles, knobs, trim. All of it.

Other than those furnishings, however, the room was empty, the walls bare. I spotted a door that must have led to the bathroom, and that was it.

"He really loves to entertain, doesn't he?" Aaron murmured humorously as the door closed behind us, courtesy of the Enkk.

"Absolutely. I can just imagine Hades at a dinner party in the Underworld right now. Can't you?"

Aaron cackled with laughter.

I, meanwhile, sat on the edge of the bed, surprised by how comfortable it was. Aaron continued to pace back and forth in front of me slowly.

"So, how do we do this?" I asked, trying to diffuse the tension. "Is there a ritual or something?"

"No. Nothing like that. You just … let me take control, and I'll do the rest. *If* you're ready for it."

I reached out and grabbed his wrist, stopping him so that he faced me.

"I don't think I'll ever be *ready* for it," I told him, standing and moving into his personal space. "But it's what I *want.*"

"Are you sure? It will hurt."

"No, it won't," I said, pressing a hand to his

chest as his fangs slid out. "All I'll feel is you."

CHAPTER THIRTY-NINE

I looked up at him, past the fangs, losing myself in his eyes. There was something different about them. Darker, more mysterious. Like shadows at the edges, swirling in circles, pulling me into their deep depths. I inhaled sharply, stunned by the intensity of the pull, the desire I felt to leap at him.

It was a mix of sexual and sensual, emotional and physical, but I held absolutely no doubts that it was *real*. Something pulled me into him, and after a brief moment of confusion, I stopped fighting it, succumbing to it. I gave myself over to him, releasing control.

Aaron took over from there. Fingers gentler than the caress of a summer's breeze pulled my hair back and to one side, exposing the pristine skin of my neck. I trembled each time his fingers grazed my flesh, my chest rising and falling as my breaths became shorter. Faster. My pulse quickened, thundering in my ear as he bent to kiss me.

The searing heat of his mouth stole the air from my lungs, the tease of his not *quite* forceful touch bringing me up onto my tiptoes. I wanted more, and I went for it, leaning into him. His hand snaked around my back, gripping my hip and squeezing. Without any effort, he lifted me high into the air until I was above him, looking down.

At some point, my leg must have kicked up because, when he set me down, only one foot made contact with the floor. It didn't matter. Aaron held me steady, our lips pressed together, opening as our tongues flirted playfully for the barest, briefest of moments.

The outside world faded to gray as we became fully wrapped up in one another. I couldn't recall feeling this way when we had sex, but then again, he'd never quite looked at me like *this* before. His hunger was plain to see now, but it wasn't violent. It was seductive and promising. It called to me, and I ran to answer.

Fingers caressed my jaw, and I shivered, letting him turn my head to the side. This was it, then. This was how it would happen. I was going to be *his*.

And that will mean he's mine, I thought with a

wickedly sensual smile. Whether he knew it or not, I would get something out of this as well.

Him.

For all time, for all eternity. We would be bound together.

"Are you ready?" he asked, his voice fluttering as he kissed his way along my jaw and down my neck.

Licking my lips, buying myself a moment to steady my nerves, I nodded. "Yes. I am ... Are you?"

A deep chuckle shook him from the belly outward. "You caught that, did you?"

"Maybe," I said, squeezing him tight. "But it doesn't matter, not really. You can be like that around me, you know. I like to see that side of you. The human side. Strong and powerful is good most of the time, but sometimes I like to know that you have emotions. And being the only one you share them with, well, that makes me feel even more special."

"You *are* special," Aaron said, kissing my neck, his lips easily finding the vein. "Especially to me."

Goosebumps flowed down my spine and across my chest at the promise of what would come next.

"I know," I said, stroking the back of his neck. "You've shown me that."

"I promise to keep showing you, for all time,"

he whispered into my ear, his hot breath causing me to gasp. I'd never been this on edge before, antsy and nervous about what was to come. Not the first time with him, not my first time ever. This was something new, something different.

And I couldn't imagine sharing it with anyone else.

A giggle slipped through my lips at that thought.

Aaron pulled back, frowning slightly. "What's so funny? What did I miss?"

"I was just thinking," I said, still smiling. "All this time, you've been the experienced vampire who knows everything, helping me find my way in this new world. We've gone from partners to friends to lovers, and now, something more. But you've always known what was going in the world around us."

"And that's funny?" he asked, looking at me like I might have lost a marble or two.

"No, what's funny is that, for once, this is a first for you as well as me. *Neither* of us has done this before. I like that."

Aaron considered my words for a moment, then nodded in agreement. "I do, too, Jo. I'm glad that I never claimed Elenia. That my first time is with you."

"Thank you," I whispered, stroking his cheek.

"For what?"

"For trusting me," I said. "For trusting, in general. After the way she hurt you, betrayed you. To open yourself up to me, it's very flattering."

"Of course, I trust you. I love you, Jo," he stated as if that answered everything.

"What did you say?" I gasped, stunned.

Aaron suddenly looked away. "Um, I mean, if you don't, that's fine. I just, I didn't mean to make things weird. I—"

"I love you, too," I said, grabbing his chin, forcing him to look at me.

The words felt *right* coming off my tongue. Not only that, but they felt appropriate, given what we were about to do. This wasn't the sort of thing we'd do if we didn't care that strongly about one another. All of a sudden, I was glad he'd said it. That we'd brought it out into the open.

"You do?"

"Yes," I said. "I love you, Aaron."

"I love you, Jo."

He swept me up in a giant, crushing hug. I returned it with force until he grunted and set me down, both of us chuckling at the reminder that I was just as strong as he was and could give a mean bearhug myself.

Not that I'm going to let that stop him from doing things like picking me up ... or other things.

We settled on our feet, laughter slowly fading,

though the smiles stretched to our ears.

"I'm ready," I whispered as the moment lingered. I turned my head to the side. "I'm ready to be yours."

Aaron stroked the side of my head, kissing my lips tenderly, the edges of his fangs brushing against them and my face as he kissed lower and lower. I trembled, nerves abruptly getting the better of me until he held me tight in his arms.

This was it. I closed my eyes as his fangs pierced my neck. There was a momentary burst of pain, but then I only felt warmth.

The shadowy Hunger inside me swept forward toward the site of the attack, a rush that left me heady and weak-kneed. Aaron didn't let go, continuing to feed on me.

To *claim* me.

My Hunger found something in my neck and rushed forward. I *felt* it happen, like the click of plugging something into an outlet. My body lit up like a Christmas tree, and I moaned loudly as my pleasure centers were instantly overloaded. There was only one outlet, and I shook and gasped for air as I climaxed in his arms.

It was the most intense thing I'd ever gone through. I struggled to maintain focus. I wanted to *remember* this moment, this event. This was the beginning of the rest of my life—whether it was long or short remained to be seen—and I was going to cherish it for as much time as I had remaining.

Blood trickled down my neck as Aaron withdrew.

Even though his teeth were gone, a part of him was still there. Still inside me.

Just not the part I was used to. Though, judging by how his pants had tightened, I wasn't going to be missing out on that either.

"I can feel you," I gasped, touching the rapidly healing wound on my neck while staring at him.

And I could. A flicker of emotion and surprise at the very edge of my awareness that was absolutely *not* from me. It was someone else, and I felt the surprise that appeared on his face come through that link.

"I can *feel* you," I repeated in a tiny voice.

"Can you feel this?" he asked, and a second later, love and unconditional caring came flooding through the link.

"*Yes!*" I hissed, trying to send the same back.

Aaron's face lit up, and pleasant surprise and joy came back to me.

"Now come here," I growled, running a hand down his front and past his belt. "I want to see what else we can feel."

When my fingers dropped past his buckle, I got the answer, and both our eyes widened.

"Oh, my," he growled excitedly as clothing flew everywhere. "This is going to be fun."

"Just don't take too long," I admonished, biting a lip in anticipation. "We still have a war to fight."

"I know. And once we've won, I'm going to take a long, *long* time to do this properly."

"That had better be a promise," I said, lying back onto the bed, enjoying the feel of arousal that came through our link as his eyes feasted on my body.

Yes, this would be fun indeed.

What comes next, not so much.

CHAPTER FORTY

I thought we'd need to demonstrate our new bond to Hades somehow, give him proof that Aaron had actually claimed me. But it never happened. We eventually emerged from the guest quarters and let the Enkk escort us to Hades. He'd taken one look, and that was all he needed. Whether it was just that obvious or being a god gave him the power to see things we couldn't, he was convinced without us having to lift a finger.

Yet, as much as he'd been convinced, I hadn't missed the surprise on his face when he realized it. He hadn't expected Aaron to go through with it.

I always knew he was a better man than you expected, I smirked.

Now, as the rest of the team and we climbed the wall surrounding Hades' stronghold, I leaned into Aaron. "Why didn't Hades think we would go through with it?"

"You noticed that, too, did you?" he replied.

"It wasn't hard to miss," I said dryly.

"He's been excessively paranoid this whole time," Aaron said. "So maybe this was just part of it? Perhaps he never truly believed that I hadn't claimed Elenia."

"Even if you had, though, that wouldn't stop you from being able to give up your claim on her and take me."

"No," Aaron admitted. "But I guess he thought I wouldn't."

"Or couldn't," I said. "If he thought you were a double agent this whole time, he would think you'd refuse at the last moment. Or maybe you'd do something and tell me that was claiming me since I wouldn't know any better."

Wry humor filtered through our link. I could tell what Aaron thought of that.

"You're far too smart to let me hoodwink you like that," he said.

"Flatterer."

There was no verbal response, but I could feel him laughing again, and I sent my own back to him.

"Are you two done talking about me?" Hades called down from the wall, where he waited for us to arrive. While we had to climb the stairs, he could teleport himself.

I knew from experience that he could have taken us with him. Vir and Dani blinked around the Direen all the time and had taken others along. Making us climb the stairs was just Hades being spiteful.

I sent more amusement to Aaron but didn't reply to the god lording over us. I got Aaron's agreement in return.

When we finally crested the top stair, Hades gestured to the exterior of his stronghold. Glancing at him, we walked to the edge.

"Damn," I whispered, taking in the view before me.

"I agreed to provide an army," Hades growled. "I keep my promises."

"Nobody accused you of not," I said.

The army stretched out and away from the walls, thick ranks of demons standing in formation. At the head of it, wearing nothing but a black loincloth the size of a small house, Abaddon waited patiently, holding the shaft of his ax while its head rested on the ground.

"I think this will work," Aaron agreed as we looked at the vast number of demons called to assist us.

"It had better," Hades growled. "This is most of my forces, minus a few units to guard various entrances, and of course, those necessary to guide new souls across the river."

"It'll do," I said. "All we need is to create a big enough diversion to have Elenia move the bulk of her forces out of Madrigal so that we can get to her."

Hades growled at the vampire queen's name. "What I wouldn't give to be there when you kill her."

I thought about teasing him, telling him he was more than welcome to come along, but thought better of it. In his realm, Hades was effectively invincible. However, if he left the Underworld, he would, in a way, become mortal. Still immensely powerful, but he *could* be killed. It wasn't worth the risk.

Not when he had us to do the fighting for him.

"Abaddon will command the troops," Hades added. "I am not prepared to relinquish actual command to you. You will tell him what you need, and he will see that my army does it in the best way possible. Is that understood?"

"Yes, that's fine. I don't want command anyway."

"In addition, to help you get into her palace ..." Hades snapped his finger and pointed behind us.

I turned to see a group of Enkk, outfitted for combat, holding the gear they had confiscated from Aaron and his team earlier. Eight of them in two ranks four deep stood still.

"They will go with you. Use them as you need."

Hades' eyes burned brightly. "But do not fail. Either kill her or find another place to flee. I will not tolerate failure."

"Yes, boss." I surveyed the army again, awed by the sheer number of demons. Details were hard to make out this high up, but it was an impressive display of force.

"I have a question," Dave said, raising a hand.

"It's not a classroom, Dave," I said, shaking my head.

"Uh, right," he said sheepishly. "Anyway. Um. How are you going to get all these troops into her realm? She's not just going to wait around peacefully."

Hades grinned. "You'll see."

I waited for more explanation, but Hades didn't offer any. Just a cryptic smile. It didn't really matter how, as long as he could, so I let it slide.

"Are they ready to go?" I asked.

Hades grunted an affirmative, staring proudly out over his army. I had to wonder if he'd ever had cause to assemble his might like this. It was almost cute. He looked like a proud papa watching his baby do something for the first time.

"All right," I said to Aaron, breaking the spell of the moment.

He waved at his team to grab their gear, and we filed out, heading down the stairs and then out onto the battlefield toward the giant demon king, who stood ready and waiting for the command.

The Enkk traveled behind us. I had no idea how we'd command them. Hopefully, they would just do as Aaron told them. Although I'd been the one to ask Hades for an army, I had no doubts about who was in command of this part of our mission. I had little combat experience. Aaron would lead us.

"A lot of vampires are going to die today," Jaxton observed as we walked past rank after rank of restless, shifting demons. "Many of whom have no idea what they're fighting for."

"I know," I said heavily. "And that's something I aim to change. When I'm on the throne, things will be different. There will be changes."

"Good," Aaron said. "I support that wholeheartedly."

"I will not be a tyrant," I said. "And I expect the six of you to tell me if I start to become one."

The others nodded.

"Damn," I said, shaking my head. "I don't even *want* to be queen. Far too much temptation. I can already taste it now, and it terrifies me. All those people, willing to do as I say? Without even knowing me? No, we can't have that. They need to know what and why they're fighting if it ever comes to that again."

"It won't," Aaron said. "Because you won't be like her. You'll be *better*."

"I'll try," I whispered, suddenly overwhelmed by the looming responsibility if our mission succeeded.

"You'll succeed," he stated, and I couldn't detect any doubt. Not in his words or the support that came through our link. "I believe in you."

I took a quick breath. "Let's just think about surviving what's about to come, shall we? Then, we can move on to fixing what's broken."

"Agreed," Aaron said.

"They'll be waiting for us," Fred pointed out. "Elenia. Corvis. The Nacht Bringers. All of them."

I growled. "Good. It's about time we ended this." Looking up, I caught Abaddon's eye and nodded. "Let's do this."

The demon army stirred to life.

CHAPTER FORTY-ONE

Abaddon turned and walked across the blasted hellscape of the Underworld, crushing reddish rock under each of his gigantic three-clawed feet. Clutching his ax in hand, he approached a tiny rip in reality, where a few dozen demons stood guard.

The others and I flinched when he barked a command. The words, though I couldn't understand them, hurt to hear.

"If we try to funnel this army through that door, we'll be slaughtered," I said. "It can fit two abreast and none of the heavies."

"Just watch," Fred suggested.

I eyed him sideways, then shrugged, my attention returning to the demon king as he reached down to the doorway.

"Holy fucking shit," I gasped, not minding my

language as I watched Abaddon.

Giant blackened fingers pushed through the tiny opening. The demon king braced his feet, and with a guttural roar, he started to stand up. Looking on in disbelief, Abaddon stretched the doorway open. He lifted and lifted, pulling it up ten, twenty, *thirty* feet, and more.

Then, he held it with one hand, bending down to grasp his ax, and used the damn thing to wedge the doorway open. The mighty weapon trembled for a moment but held. Lowering his shoulder, Abaddon started pushing the split in reality, sliding it open like it was a barn door, so easily did it move under his tremendous strength.

"That'll do," I whispered, awed as the opening stretched over a hundred feet wide. "Remind me never to tangle with Abaddon, okay?"

"If all goes well, we'll never come back here," Aaron pointed out. "So you'll never have to worry about that even being a possibility."

"And if it goes badly, I'll come back as a powerless soul, so again, nothing to worry about. Perfect. I'll be quite happy never to have him be on the other side."

The demon army seemed to agree. Their roars and growls grew in volume as Abaddon gave them a passage into the Realm of the Undead that would fit enough of their army to make a difference.

Heads turned to me as the demon king slowed to a stop, muscles straining now.

"They are ready," Fred whispered.

"So, what are we waiting for?" I said.

"They await your orders, I think," Aaron said from the corner of his mouth.

"Oh. Um. Move out!" I called nervously, hoping that was the right order.

It was.

Horns brayed up and down the lines as the demon army dressed its ranks and headed toward the silvery-gray portal.

The foot soldiers advanced first. Most of these were the rather human-like Axotl, with their reverse-canted knees, hoofed feet, and spiked tails. Their faces were vaguely humanoid, minus the fur, flat noses, and, of course, the two upthrust fangs jutting out from their jaws. The front ranks carried shields, while those behind held long spears. Others had swords strapped to their backs.

Banners waved and fluttered in a breeze that I couldn't feel as the army moved toward the split between realms. Orders were barked, grunted, growled, and chittered in a dozen different species equivalent of "stay together, don't mess it up!"

Eventually, our turn came, and we started forward, tightly ensconced in the middle of the army. Our purpose was not to lend a hand in the fight but to sneak away once the battle was in action.

"Okay, everyone ready?" I asked as the first ranks neared the portal.

Weapons slid from safe to semi-automatic, while Fenrir and Drakul simply shook themselves loose, each ready to do battle in their own particular way. It was unlikely we would face resistance until we reached the palace, but we had no idea what was on the other side of the silver-gray wall.

As we got closer, formations of Djinn lifted from the ground on their tiny wings. The monkey-frogs hovered close overhead, moving with the rest of the army as it was swallowed up by the portal.

My heartbeat increased with each step as our turn approached. Soon, we were marching straight into the other realm without slowing down or taking time to see what we were getting into.

After all, ranks of demons were coming behind us. If we tried to stop, we'd be smashed flat.

"Oh, shit!" someone yelped as the noise of battle assaulted us as we crossed over.

The vampires weren't just expecting us; they were *ready*. Massive formations of warriors were already slicing at the head of the emerging army of demons, swords cutting them down as more demons plowed onward, running over the attacking vampires.

Above, Djinn streaked downward with ferocious primate roars, targeting their ground-bound prey, ready to wreak havoc. However, as they got close, the vampires crouched, lifted their wrists, and let loose a hail of bolts from contraptions mounted to their forearms.

Djinn fell, screeching before being quickly silenced by the deadly bolts. Other demons were taken down by vampires carrying razor-sharp swords. However, as more demons poured through the portal by the second, the front was not only stabilizing but widening.

I watched as an array of giant catapults groaned and shook as vampires fired silver-white balls toward us. I watched as they hit the ground and cracked apart with a blistering hiss, the cold air sucking all heat from the surroundings—including the demons themselves. Whole ranks were frozen solid, only to be smashed to pieces as vampires road through them on horses, using clubs to break apart the ice statues.

A repeated croaking sound went up, and the ground trembled. I whipped my head around just in time to see a thick arrowhead formation of alligator-horses trot by. The long-snouted mouths were the sole weapons the demons possessed as the four stallion legs churned along effortlessly.

The two cavalry groups clashed, and the vampires swiftly found themselves retreating as powerful jaws tore them from the saddles and flung them to the ground, where they were quickly crushed.

"This is madness," I whispered, overwhelmed by it all.

"This is war," Aaron said darkly, grabbing my elbow and moving me forward, so we didn't get in the way of "our" army.

Beyond our advancing army stood what had to be the entire assembled might of Madrigal. Vast formations of vampires stood ready and waiting to charge into the slaughterhouse. Clad all in black, they stood motionless, still, waiting to enter the violent chaos of the vortex between the groups.

More attacks from catapults and other, heavier siege equipment were set loose upon the demon lines. Chittering svipul, eel-like dogs, darted to the sides in thick lines, worrying at the flanks of the vampires and driving them back, forcing them to split their attention.

The ground trembled, and a monstrous form appeared through the portal. Walking on four legs, each the size of a school bus, the massive beetle stormed forward, its black chitinous shell glittering in the off-white light of the vampire realm.

It leaned in low over the vampires, and with a

gush of air, flame spewed forward, incinerating an entire block of the bloodsuckers. I gasped as the heat bloom washed over us, even from this distance. I couldn't imagine what it would have been like to be closer.

In response, half a dozen vampire formations split apart, revealing wooden contraptions topped with a wicked-looking metal point. Giant crossbows *twanged,* and the six-foot-long bolts flew through the air, impaling the beetle-thing. It reared up high on its two legs, screeching in pain, just as another bolt took it in the stomach.

The entire carapace split apart as fire spilled from the mortally wounded demon, washing over the demons closest. The creature galloped through the formation in its dying throes, trying to rid itself of the bolt embedded.

"Run for it!" Aaron shouted as it headed our way.

We raced to the side, ducking around and between marching formations of more demons than I'd ever seen before. We ignored their growls and shouts of anger as they were jostled and lost their step.

Moments later, the beetle's continued spew of fire wiped them from the battle.

Eventually, the giant beetle crashed down, death finally overcoming it. The oncoming demons marched around it. The battlefront grew wider, and we watched from our vantage point as both sides poured reinforcements into the fray.

"Are we close?" I asked as the Enkk shadowed us.

"Just about," Aaron said. "But I'd hoped that we'd get closer to Madrigal before the armies met. Having them right here is about the worst that could happen. We'll easily be spotted leaving this formation. There's nothing around us."

He was right.

"We need transportation," I said.

As if anticipating this, a dozen of the croco-dile-horses swerved out of the mass and came toward us in a trot. Their broad backs looked exactly like any horse I'd ever seen. But their necks were scaled, and their heads were most certainly *not* horse-like. It was much larger, about three feet long, lined with razor-sharp teeth.

"I take it this is our ride?" Aaron said.

The lead creature tossed its head in a remark-able recreation of an impatient stallion.

"I guess we have our answer," I said, stepping up to the closest of the beasts.

A thundering crash sounded as two new for-mations crashed together, drawing my attention back to the battle at hand.

A battle *I* was responsible for. I had wrought all of this death and destruction. My actions.

"All of this to kill one person," I whispered, shaking my head.

"All of this to put a stop to *more* of it," Aaron said. "We are only doing what we must, to stop her. She is doing this because she *wants* to."

"Perhaps," I said. "But I can't help but feel a bit responsible."

"Then take your responsibility," he growled. "And shove it and a sword straight down her throat. Make sure that this isn't done in vain."

I bared my teeth. He made a very good point.

"Come on," I said, hopping astride the beastie as best I could. "Let's go kill the queen."

CHAPTER
FORTY-TWO

With the others clinging to the scaly necks of our mounts, the beasts took off, heading for the right side of the demon formation. As we did, the rest of the demon cavalry joined us, picking up other groups as we went, until nearly two hundred of them galloped around us.

"I thought we wanted to be stealthy?" I shouted at Aaron, desperately clinging to my mount as my hair whipped out behind me.

"No chance this far out," he called back. "They're going to punch a hole for us. Then, we ride as fast and as hard as we can."

"They'll see us," I growled, jealous at the easy way he rode the beast, making it look effortless.

"So, we had better not take too long, then, shouldn't we? Get in quick, don't stop for anyone, and get the job done. Once Elenia is dead and you're on the throne, they'll obey you. You can end this."

"I guess."

I fell silent as we rounded the edge of a formation of Axotl and plunged through a gap and then another. The croc-allions, as I named them, pivoted sharply, and their *croak-croak-croak* battle cry sounded.

"Oh, *shit!*" I howled as we charged the vampires, our little group safely ensconced in the middle, while the Enkk casually ran alongside us, easily keeping pace.

The thick legs of the croc-allions—*horsi-gators?*—churned easily through the flimsy vampires, crushing them underfoot or simply darting their heads down and crushing them between their powerful jaws.

It was over in seconds, and we emerged out the far side, the bulk of our escort peeling off and slamming into the side of the vampire army, killing as they went. They drew the vampires' attention, allowing us precious moments to accelerate and pull away *behind* them.

I had to hold on for dear life. The ground flashed past underneath as we got up to full speed and cruised, swiftly distancing ourselves from the vampires behind us. I groaned and clung tighter to the neck of my mount. My thighs would be bruised for a week from trying to squeeze tight and stay on.

"Guys, we might have a problem," Jaxton called from behind me.

Seeing him point to our left, I followed his finger. The bouncing gallop of the horsi-gator made it tough to focus on details, but I didn't need to. What Jaxton had spied was very obvious to see.

A block of vampire cavalry had split off and was heading toward us.

"It must be Corvis and the Nacht Bringers!" Aaron shouted.

How he could tell that, I didn't know, but it felt right. If anyone were going to come after us, it would be Corvis. I didn't relish the thought of going up against him again. He would probably be hot for retaliation after Aaron had all but shot him dead in the parking lot of the blood bank.

"We're not going to have long before they catch us!" I called.

"Then, we make the most of it," Aaron said.

Our lead was substantial, and it seemed to be growing, but the first time we encountered any resistance closer to the palace, we would be in trouble. Corvis was going to be perfectly primed to attack us from the rear while we were busy trying to smash our way into the throne room.

"Making the most of it," as Aaron had suggested, was going to be difficult, if not downright impossible. The Black Nacht was simply not going to give us that time.

"We need to delay him somehow!" I shouted.

Aaron didn't reply, but I could see by his face that he knew it, too. They were too close. Our plan wasn't going to work.

"Dammit."

The muffled curse was only audible thanks to my wolf's hearing. I turned just in time to see a giant black form catapult off the back of the horsi-gator and go racing toward the oncoming vampire cavalry.

"What the hell does he think he's doing?"

"Buying us time," I said to nobody in particular, just as another horsi-gator *croak-croaked* and whirled, charging after Fenrir's racing form. Astride the back of his mount, Drakul unsheathed his sword and went to aid the wolf.

Inside, my own wolf howled to be let out. She wanted to run free, too. Her mind spoke to me of power and speed. We could run far more comfortably on all fours than we could riding the beast.

Not yet, I urged, watching as Fenrir smashed into the side of the vamps, sowing confusion as he went. He was fast, and his presence disrupted the careful formation, drawing away many of the Nacht Bringers.

But a small group broke free of him and evaded Drakul's wild attack as well, charging after us instead.

"He'd better not get himself killed," I growled as Fenrir hauled a vamp down from the saddle. "That would be really stupid."

"We can't worry about them now," Aaron admonished. "He made his choice."

I didn't like it, but Aaron was right. Worrying about Fenrir and Drakul was pointless. Their fate was out of our hands.

Putting my head down, I urged my mount onward.

Faster. We had to go faster!

We raced over the ground until we reached the narrow crevasse that I knew would spit us out high above Madrigal. Our mounts charged down it, and the wind slowed as we galloped through twists and turns as fast as we could.

"Getting close!" Aaron remarked once we emerged from the split in the land, the city of Madrigal sprawling out below us.

Our mounts took a hard left and went down the long, long ramp. The Enkk came along behind us, looking as fresh as when we'd first set off.

I watched the vampire city grow larger as we descended, my gaze drawn toward the center of the city and the large rectangular building that I knew was the palace. That was where we would find Elenia. Where I would kill her.

If I can.

A sliver of fear pierced my stomach, lingering, the cold clamminess balling up, refusing to go. This was all up to me going forward. I had to kill her or everything, all of this, was for nothing. A waste.

Everyone else believed I could do it, that I was capable of ending this madness.

So why couldn't I find it in myself to believe? Why did I have this growing sense of doom?

Again, my eyes darted to the palace. I couldn't shake the feeling that once I entered, I wouldn't leave it alive.

But what choice do I have?

CHAPTER FORTY-THREE

We encountered the first resistance two blocks out from the palace. The sudden eruption of vampires into our midst yanked my mind from its ever-worsening spiral of depression and despair, forcing me back into the present.

I leaped from the saddle, clearing a sword that carved up the side of my mount by a finger's width, no more. The ground came up hard, and I curled into a ball, bouncing and rolling before leaping to my feet. Furious activity was all around me as the team, including our Enkk escorts and our mounts, fought back.

Dodging another strike, I grabbed the extended wrist of the vampire and hauled on it as I spun into him. My elbow made contact with the bridge of his nose, shattering it and the orbital bone. As the vamp dropped, I brought a knee up and into his jaw, ending the fight.

Then, I picked him up and tossed him at another vampire who was trying to haul Alexi from his mount. The unexpected weight took both to the ground, and the horsi-gator casually leaned down and crushed the vamp's head in its jaws.

The Enkk, with their four arms, mowed down vampires swiftly, clearing a path for us to continue forward.

"Come on!" Aaron shouted, reaching an arm down to me and hauling me onto the back of his mount.

We raced up the hill toward the palace, picking up speed.

"Jump!" I screamed in his ear, flinging myself off the horsi-gator just as we cleared the top of the hill.

A giant crossbow bolt, aimed down the center of the street, plunged through the neck of Aaron's ride and out the other side, narrowly missing Aaron's leg as he leaped free.

Two of the Enkk went down in a barrage of the tiny wrist-mounted bolts while the rest of our party crashed up the hill. Aaron's team fired their guns, and vampires dropped before they could reload their crossbows.

"Come on, no stopping now!" I shouted, getting to my feet and jogging alongside those still mounted. "The palace is right there!"

Twice more, we encountered resistance, but the vampires left behind were obviously not the cream of the crop. They fell before our wild onslaught, no match for Aaron's team or the whirling blades of the Enkk.

However, by the time we reached the palace, word had gone out. The doors were closed and barred, and the windows barricaded.

"Any suggestions?" I asked as we slowed to a halt, our mounts finally breathing hard and showing the exertion of the hard trek.

"Yep," Aaron said, pointing at Jaxton.

"You brought explosives," I said plaintively. "That's what they're using, isn't it?"

Aaron nodded an affirmative as Jaxton and Pieter ran up to the door while the rest of the team covered them. They quickly began to place black lumps at what I assumed were strategic places.

"You're prepared."

"I know the palace," Aaron said, backing away at an arm wave from Jaxton. "I never assumed we'd get in unnoticed. Plan for the worst, hope for the best, as they say."

"Mmm," I said, looking away as sharp blasts blew holes in the doors.

With a loud groan, the giant metal barriers fell inward. We left the horsi-gators to slow down any pursuit and plunged deep into the palace, heading for one place and one place only.

The throne room.

"You've got this."

I started at Aaron's whispered encouragement. Had he been reading my mind? The deeper we went into the palace, the more the ghostly voices in my head voiced their doubts, bringing my insecurities to the front.

She was stronger. I wasn't ready. There was no way I could win. I was leading everyone to their deaths. Nothing was going to change.

They circled me, pecking away ceaselessly, looking for holes in my mental armor, for places they could land, and feed off me, growing stronger until I finally caved.

Like they knew I always would.

"You're ready," Aaron said as up ahead half a dozen black- and gold-clad Nacht Bringers rounded a corner, taking up a defensive position.

Unlike the others, they waited for us to come to them instead of charging wildly at us. More noise behind us caught my attention. Another four vampires, as equally silent and foreboding, had emerged to block our exit.

"We'd better go forward," I said.

Rifles barked as the team let loose, but the Nacht Bringers swiftly darted around the corner, using it as cover. I saw one of them get hit, but he didn't slow, bending only slightly at the stomach where the bullet had entered his gut.

"We're going to have to go through them," Aaron said.

I nodded, then flagged down one of the Enkk. "We'll keep them under cover while you approach. You take them down."

The Enkk simply turned and strode down the hallway, two more following. Aaron's team scrambled to keep up a scattered covering fire, driving the Nacht back around the corner while we jogged forward.

Blade met blade as the Nacht were finally forced to show themselves, and the Enkk drove them back mercilessly. They worked their four arms, slowly spinning the Nacht around.

"I feel like a coward," Jaxton growled, but his rifle barked, dropping a Nacht as he shot it in the back.

"Remember, this is *her* fault," Aaron snapped. "Elenia is responsible for all this. Everything we do is worth it if we can bring her down and prevent others from suffering like this in the future!"

With the Enkk on our side, they didn't stand a chance. Our path was clear now, the throne room doors in view.

I strode forward, wrapping myself in a cocoon of what I hoped was courage and conviction.

I was doing this for all the innocent vampires fighting on the plains above, fighting and dying for a queen they likely didn't even know. A bitch who would order their deaths a thousand times over if it gave her another day on the throne.

They deserve better from their queen, I told myself as the last of the explosive charges were planted on one of the doors. Apparently, we didn't have enough to blow both in.

"Okay, this is it," Aaron said as we backed up.

Farther up the hall, two of the Enkk were still battling the Nacht that had blocked our retreat. More shadowy figures raced in from elsewhere in the palace, but for the moment, we were alone.

"Once we go through here," Aaron said, "it's no mercy. You shoot to kill. Unleash hell. We only get one shot at this. For the future."

I nodded along, eyes closed, though I was mostly lost in my own thoughts.

For you, Mom.

Aaron looked at me. I felt his concern waver through our link, but I brushed it off. I couldn't be concerned right now. Not for the team, not for him. Not even for myself.

Everything had to be put on the line to stop Elenia.

"Blow it," I snapped, snapping my eyes open.

It was time.

CHAPTER FORTY-FOUR

The bombs never went off.

Before Jaxton could plunge his thumb down on the detonator, the doors were flung open outward, one of them ripped completely from its hinges, forcing us to dive out of the way as it crashed down the hallway, taking out both the Enkk guarding our rear and the Nacht they were fighting.

I gaped as bodies and limbs were squished and separated by the flying chunk of metal before facing forward.

"How *dare* you!" Elenia screamed, her voice reverberating off the walls as she stalked toward us, her hair electric and wild, power crackling between the strands. "This is my *home*. How dare you defile it like this!"

Jaxton lifted his rifle to fire, but the queen

blurred with movement, and her backhand tossed him clear up and over our little group. He slid along the tiled hallway until he bounced limply off the door—now wedged between the walls at a precarious angle—and came to a stop with a wheezing sigh.

One of the Enkk advanced on the queen, four arms at the ready. She waited for it to approach, the tall demon walking on its bird-like legs. Elenia studied it as it came, its lower arms holding the shorter blades while its upper ones whirled the swords in slow circles.

"Shoot her, dammit," Aaron hissed.

The rest of the team snapped out of their daze and brought their guns up to fire. Elenia chose that moment to make her attack, slipping in close before the Enkk could attack. She battered its arms aside, snapping one of them in the process, before hauling it down to the floor in a crash to shield her body with its torso from the hail of bullets.

The guns fell silent, and Elenia flung herself free of the demon's corpse and scattered our team with blows. She left me for last. I evaded her first strike through sheer luck, but after that, she picked me up, shook me around like a rag doll until I saw nothing but stars, and then tossed me into the throne room.

Never had I been so casually cast about like I was a leaf in a storm. Aaron had told me she was strong, had warned me that she was more than he could take, and I thought I'd heeded his message.

I was wrong. Absolutely and completely wrong.

We couldn't defeat *that*. She was no longer a person, but a thing, a force of nature. By the time I landed, came to a halt, gasped, wheezed, and gotten into a sitting position, perhaps three or four seconds had passed.

In that time, the queen had quite literally ripped another Enkk's limbs from its body, used those same limbs to batter another demon to a pulp, slam Alexi through a wall into whatever lay beyond and disarm everyone else.

Now she stood face to face with Aaron, and the bitch wasn't even breathing hard. It just wasn't fair! How were we supposed to face that? To stand before her power?

"This was a mistake," I muttered, coughing through the pain as I pulled myself to my knees, groaning at the pain. "Definitely a mistake. We should have just nuked the bitch. That would have been the better move."

While the queen and Aaron argued about something—they weren't yelling, and my ears were still ringing—I tried to gather my senses. I was in the throne room. True, I hadn't made a bold entrance but instead had been unceremoniously dumped at the foot of Elenia's throne, but I was here, nonetheless.

Too bad it wasn't going to matter.

Have to try, though. You've got to try.

Shaking it off as best I could, I got to my feet. Out of the corner of my eye, I saw movement. My eyes darted to the lounge area Elenia kept at the far right of the room. Comfortable couches and piles of cushions were mostly hidden behind thick, plush purple curtains. Yet within their shadows, I saw people moving.

Worried that they might be more troops waiting to ambush, I staggered in that direction. At least I could take on some regular vamps. Maybe. I was pretty shaken.

Yet, they recoiled from my advance. Not warriors, then, but what? Flinging back the curtain, I look at the cowering forms. All of them were naked, three-quarters male, but all exquisite specimens of the human form. Any other time, my eyes would have been more than happy to take in the sight of Elenia's blood slaves.

There was no doubt in my mind that's what they were. The evidence was trailed down their throats and chests, the trails of dried blood from fresh holes. She had been feeding before we arrived.

Over a dozen faces looked up at me. Their eyes were glazed with fear. Thick chains kept them bound to one another. There was no escape for them.

A pained cry from outside the doors forced me to spin around, just in time to watch Aaron hurtle through the entrance. He hit the base of the steps that led up to the actual throne itself, and his head snapped back, cracking hard on the stone.

In that instant, I knew what I had to do. Even as the pain flooded over our link and blood started to pour from his head, I realized I had no choice. There was only one way out of this mess.

Snarling, I reached for the nearest blood slave. The shadow in my mind surged forward as it recognized what we were about to do, my fangs sliding easily into place.

If you kill one of them, you're never coming out again, I admonished, but the entity wouldn't understand. It didn't care. All it wanted, all it knew, was how to feed.

And feed we did. The fresh blood filled me like pure energy. I inhaled sharply as the lingering wooziness fled my skull. My skin stretched taut, muscles swelling as I drained the slave. He fell to his knees without a word.

More pain battered at my link. I couldn't bear to turn around, to see what was happening to Aaron. I just had to hope Elenia wanted to toy with him long enough for it to matter.

Enough! I screamed as the pale skin under my

teeth turned white. With a mighty mental howl, I tore myself away—only to latch on to the next nearest on the chain of slaves.

I hated the way the power made me feel. The glorious energy that burned away my fatigue and the minor aches and pains I hadn't realized were there. I was growing, my clothing becoming tight. I quickly slipped out of it, barely able to restrain the Hunger inside me long enough. I would be naked soon enough anyway. No sense in delaying.

Slave after slave fell before my fangs, their blood powering me, leaving them on the edge of death, but still alive. I drank deep and greedily. There was no time to be polite. My face and the front of my body were streaked read from mouth to navel, and it ran down my legs as well. I was a demon born of hunger, and I wasn't stopping.

This was Elenia's fault. She had done this to me, turned me into this, this *thing*. I had become the monster I always feared, and I had done it so I could stop the one everyone *else* feared.

Brilliant lancing pain flooded my mind. I staggered, just in time to see Elenia stomp down on Aaron's leg, snapping the femur.

"Fuck you. I hope you rot in hell!"

Elenia laughed, grinding her foot down into the shattered bone, making Aaron scream again.

"I will rot in nothing. I am the *queen*."

Snarling in anger at her arrogance, I grabbed the last blood slave in line and hauled him with me to the edge of the curtained area. Chains rattled as the others were dragged along.

"Hey, Queen *Bitch*," I shouted.

I wanted her to see this. To know that she was in deep shit.

Elenia's head whipped around to stare at me, her eyes widening in surprise and then anger.

"Why don't you pick on someone your own size?" I snarled and sunk my fangs deep into the last of her blood slaves, while over his neck, I stared down the queen, making my challenge clear.

CHAPTER FORTY-FIVE

Elenia howled in fury as I dropped the last of the blood slaves, his chest still rising and falling. The sheer hatred I felt for the tall woman in front of me had allowed me to focus with crystal clarity. I'd used that clarity to overpower my Hunger and pull myself free before killing any of them.

There would be damage to my psyche from what I'd done, but that would pale in comparison to the wounds I'd just inflicted on the slaves themselves. My only consolation was that they still lived, and if their gift allowed me to defeat the queen, then they would be able to go *free*. Something Elenia would never grant them.

"Those are *mine!*" the ruler of all of vampire kind shrieked, coming at me like a miniature tornado.

I flung myself at her, and we slammed to-gether with a tremendous *crack* that echoed throughout the throne room, slamming to the floor in a flurry of blows. Her momentum gave Elenia the upper hand, and she got on top of me, a fist flashing toward my face. I yanked my head aside at the last moment, just as her fist pulver-ized the stone tile, shattering it.

Angrily, I pulled both hands into my chest and then slammed my palms out at her with all the crackling energy I could muster. Elenia flew off me, launched ten feet in the air from my blow. Using that time, I rolled to the side as she flailed uselessly on her way down.

My scything kick caught her just before she hit the floor. A mighty *oof* announced the depart-ure of air from her lungs as she slid across the ground and into the steps of her raised throne, hitting hard.

For a moment, she was stunned, and I took advantage of it. Reaching deep into my mind, I threw off the chains, releasing the shackles that had held my other half down for so long. I didn't fight her this time, didn't try to hold her back for fear of what she might do. This time I welcomed her in and embraced her.

My wolf surged through me, howling at the power that infused us as we shifted. Our bones cracked and reformed while mottled gray and black fur covered my entire body. Paws bigger than my hand sprouted claws while my snout jutted forward, filling with teeth eager to clamp around Elenia's neck.

Seeing what was happening, the vampire queen hauled herself up and came at us in a blur. We didn't have time to get fully to our feet, and she wisely stayed out of range of our bite before slugging us hard in the flank.

Yelping with pain, we slid across the floor, trying to gain purchase with our claws. This wasn't our ideal fighting ground, no soft earth beneath our feet for traction, no trees to hide among while we stalked our prey, but it didn't matter. This was a fight we *had* to fight. And on top of that, one we knew we must win.

Snarling, we got to our feet and raced back at the queen. Thanks to the blood we'd drawn, we had size, power, and speed on our side. Our body tingled with unrealized power, and we intended for our prey to feel it. Of course, she didn't wait for us. Recognizing that we were her equal, she dodged our attack and ran out the main doors.

As she disappeared, others entered, swords held at the ready. Corvis looked at us warily. He'd tangled with us before, and it hadn't gone so well for him. Baring our teeth, we crouched low. Our every desire screamed to move past him, to launch ourselves down the hallway after the fleeing queen, but we couldn't. We had someone to defend.

Glancing at Aaron, we hesitated, indecisive. He waved us off and pulled several plastic vials of blood from the inside of his suit pocket.

"I got this," he said, ripping them open. "You go."

We looked at him, then at the half-dozen figures blocking the exit, then back at him.

"If you want to take a few of them out on your way by, be my guest," he said, red streaks of blood streaming down the sides of his mouth. "But you leave him for me. He's mine. This time I'm not letting him get away."

Nostrils flaring at the scent of blood, we struggled for a moment, drawn toward him.

No! A voice cracked through our skull just as a pulsing wave of cool confidence came through a link. Our head tilted to the side, and we saw Aaron wink at us.

He had a trick to play.

Snarling at him, we let him feel our emotions. *You had better be here when we get back.*

"I will," he said, speaking aloud. "Now go!"

We didn't hesitate any longer. Muscles twitched, and we surged across the throne room.

Corvis had been ready for our charge and easily dove out of our way, but three of his followers were much too slow. We bodied aside two of them, the impact of our powerful body slamming them back into the wall hard enough that they weren't ever going to move again. The third lifted its sword, but our jaws darted past it and tore his head from his body.

We did it all without slowing, hurtling out of the door into the main hallway, sniffing deep as we picked up the scent of the queen, eager to take up the pursuit and bring the battle to a cl—

A shriek from above alerted us, but it was far too late.

The queen hadn't fled as we'd assumed. She'd climbed the walls and waited for us. Something sharp pierced our side as she landed on our back. It withdrew, and more pain blossomed at a different site.

Immediately, we went down and rolled, trying to crush her. But Elenia had been ready. She flung herself free like a cowboy jumping off a falling horse. The blade she'd been holding flickered out of her hand, and we howled as it cut a long gash down our face.

"I will rip you to pieces," Elenia hissed, delivering a quick kick to our jaws as we tried to get to our feet. The blow rocked our head back, and we saw stars for a moment until our fury at the vampire burned it all away.

She danced backward as we narrowly missed snapping our jaws on her shoulder, the sudden reverse of our movement catching her by surprise. Fast as we were, however, she was faster. Still, the momentum was on our side now, and we kept at it, leaping after her.

The queen was forced to turn and run, fleeing for real this time. We followed as she ducked down one hallway, then another, heading deeper into the palace, to places we hadn't been before. She was fast, but her scent betrayed her, and every time she gained a lead, we closed it on a straightaway.

There would be no losing us. This was going to end in one way and one way only. When one of us was dead.

We nearly caught up to her on a long straightaway that seemed to have been a mistake, but she narrowly avoided our reaching jaws, turning at the last second with a radius we couldn't match. So intent had we been on sinking our teeth into her, we missed the upcoming turn. Trying to stop frantically, we couldn't and resigned ourselves to hitting the wall.

Except we went *through* the wall and tumbled down a set of circular stairs. Elenia came after us, cackling with laughter as we descended floor after floor, bouncing and flopping, unable to stop our momentum until we hit bottom amid a pile of debris.

The queen appeared at the hole in the wall far above and didn't hesitate to pick up a large chunk of stone and fling it at us. We barked at the pain, the sting enough to open a small cut.

She came on, using her strength to fling several more projectiles at us. One caught us in the eye, swelling it closed immediately. A longer, thinner projectile dug deep into our right leg.

On she came, picking up more debris, her mighty strength inflicting wound after wound on us as we struggled to get to our feet from the fall. Another spinning projectile took out our front leg, dropping us down to the ground again.

"You could *never* defeat me!" Elenia howled. "I am the rightful queen, and you are nothing but a disgusting half-breed, unfit to exist!"

Pulling a wicked-looking knife from her waist, she leaped the last half-dozen stairs, heading for our flank, aiming to plunge her blade in deep. We didn't let her. Rolling, we let ourselves fall farther down the stairs.

Elenia landed amid the rubble, but it didn't slow her. She came on in a rush.

Just like we wanted her to.

Our initial goal had been to overpower her and kill her. But during our game of cat and mouse, we'd realized that the queen was quite crazy. So, we used that to our advantage. Goading her along. Pretending to be weaker than we were. Slower. So that she, in her arrogance, would assume she could kill us with ease.

She was wrong.

Our "roll" took us down and over—and also let us reorient ourselves to face her. Elenia suddenly hesitated as our muscles tensed and our jaw opened wide, the sole good eye focusing on her.

"Oh, f—"

Vampire-wolf fangs crunched down around her body, and we shook her like a ragdoll, whipping our head back and forth with abandon until we released her, letting her hit the wall with a sickening impact. She slid to the floor, breathing hard, barely alive.

It was time to end this.

CHAPTER
FORTY-SIX

"Here," I said, tossing the half-alive body of Elenia back into the throne room as I walked in, back in my human form.

The queen slid across the tile, leaving a bloody streak behind her as she came to a halt halfway between Aaron and me, wheezing for breath, her eyes barely focused.

I took in the other bodies in the room with my working eye. Aaron sported some new wounds on his side, including a deep stab, but he otherwise looked fine.

The same couldn't be said for Corvis and the two other Nacht Bringers I'd left behind when I went after the queen. Their bodies were riddled with bullet holes. Far more than could have come from one gun.

I arched an eyebrow at Dave, who was sitting on the steps. The rest of the team was there in various states of hurt. But they were all alive. I breathed a sigh of relief at that.

"Told you I had a plan," Aaron said.

"You should have let us kill Corvis, too," Dave said. "He stabbed you in the gut."

I eyed the corpse of the Black Nacht, his head sporting a gaping wound where his face should have been. There was also a smaller entry hole under his jaw. I could only picture what had happened. Aaron must have suckered him in close, then stuck his holdout pistol into the bottom of his jaw and pulled the trigger.

"Gutsy move," I said.

Aaron looked down at the hole in his stomach, then back at me, then at the hole in him again. "I think that joke hurt more than the sword going in."

"Not as bad as laughing at it will hurt."

Aaron started to laugh, then clutched his side in pain. "Dammit. That's not fair."

I smiled, but the humor faded as the queen coughed up blood.

"What's this for?" he asked, pointing at the remains of the vampire.

"In case you wanted to say any last words. Or anything else."

Aaron looked up sharply at my last sentence.

Everyone knew what I meant by "anything else." I was giving him the chance to kill her. To be the one to end her reign. He held a lot of guilt over what she'd done, thinking that he could have stopped her so long ago. Perhaps this would relinquish some of it and let him sleep a little better at night.

"Last words," he said, mulling the idea over while I watched on, as did the rest of the team.

"I ... am ..." Elenia started to croak out, "the q —"

Aaron's arm blurred, the pistol emerging from his back holster and firing. The *crack* echoed around the throne room while a small hole appeared in Elenia's forehead.

For a moment, there was nothing but silence as we all watched. Then, Aaron emptied the rest of his ammunition into her. When he was done, he tossed the gun away and stomped over to me.

"Fuck her," he growled, pulling off his tattered and bloody jacket and giving it to me.

I frowned, wondering why he was doing that until I remembered that I wasn't wearing any clothing. Clutching the jacket tight around me, I covered up as best I could.

"Thank you," I said, doing up the buttons.

"You're welcome," he whispered, carefully leaning down to kiss the top of my head, doing his best to avoid aggravating his stomach.

"Next time, just shoot them all from the start, okay? I don't like seeing you hurt."

"Me hurt?" he said. "You're the one with an eye the size of an apple, not to mention the giant gash on your face and the limp because of a crater the size of my fist in your leg!"

"I'll live," I stated bluntly.

"And so will I," he returned with equal blandness. "What's your point?"

"I don't know."

He had no response to that.

"There's something else I need to do," I said, patting him gently on the arm before easing free of his grip.

Limping heavily—much as I said I would live, I *did* hurt all over—I headed toward the dais, upon which sat the throne. I paused to grab Elenia's corpse and dragged it up several steps, dropping it like it was garbage so that she lay visible for any who entered to see.

Reaching the top, I turned and looked down at the room. It was only Aaron and his team, along with the slain bodies. There were no others to witness this, but it didn't matter. All that mattered was it was over. Or, at least, it *would* be over once I sat down. That was all I had to do. Sit on the throne and claim it. Take up that responsibility for myself.

"What are you waiting for?" Aaron asked from

the base of the throne as I hesitated.

"I'm no queen," I told him. "No ruler. I don't want this power. I wanted her gone, but there must be someone more qualified than me."

Dave snorted. "There's quite literally *nobody* more qualified than you. Only a woman can sit on the throne, and you're the only known female vampire in existence. That basically means either you sit your butt down or nobody rules and we devolve into chaos as everyone tries to turn a ton of women and put their candidate on the throne."

"Oh." I mulled that over.

Could I risk another Elenia assuming the throne just because I didn't want the responsibility? Was that fair to all the vampires who would suffer because of it?

Footsteps clattered down the hallway.

"My Queen!" a voice shouted before it was in sight. "My Queen, they are retreating. The demons, they return to their own realm."

The owner of the voice, and half a dozen other warriors with it, came to a screeching halt as they entered the throne room and saw the scene before them. I wasn't sure what they had expected to see based on the devastation in the hallway, but their faith that Elenia would win was supreme.

I suppose it's time to put that to rest.

Sitting gingerly, I rested my arms on the sides of the throne, looking down at the newcomers like I felt a queen should.

"Good," I said, trying to sound like a ruler and hoping it didn't sound as stupid to everyone else as it did to me. "Let them go. There is no further need for violence today. Too many have suffered already."

The head vampire stammered in shock, looking around as he worked to puzzle out what had happened. I watched the understanding come to him when his eyes finally settled on Elenia's corpse lying at my feet.

"Well, what are you waiting for?" Aaron snarled. "This is your queen. Kneel before her!"

Putting action to word, Aaron took a knee. Those members of his team who were able did so. The others clasped their fists to their chests.

Slowly, still unsure, the newcomers did the same.

"Go," I commanded. "Spread the word. The fighting is done. The city is to return to normal. That is the command of your queen."

"Queen Joanna!" Aaron shouted, a cry taken up by the others and repeated eventually by the newcomers as their shock wore off.

Once they were gone, I sagged back into the seat. This was too much already.

"Someone free those blood slaves already," I

said. "Make sure they're taken care of."

"Of course," Aaron said. "Then what?"

"Then," I said, taking a slow breath, sitting up straighter. "Then, it's time for some change."

CHAPTER
FORTY-SEVEN

"I hope we're not too late," I said nervously.

"We're fine," Aaron murmured under his breath, jogging alongside me as we hurried toward the doors at the end of the hallway.

A full dozen warriors bedecked in their finest outfits lined the corridor, standing stiffly at attention as I passed by. I had to check myself not to prepare for an attack. It had been two days, and the vampires of Madrigal had adapted with ease to me as their new queen.

I, on the other hand, was having a hard time with it. It was second nature to assume they all wanted me dead. But to them, whoever sat on the throne was the queen, and that was that. I had killed the last queen and taken her place, and the power was now rightfully mine to command.

Aaron said it was also because many of them had hated Elenia, and though I had doubted him, I was starting to see the truth. Many vampires had left when they'd gotten word, and I knew we would have to go after them and force them back into the fold, but for now, I had to focus on uniting those who remained in Madrigal.

Peace might have come between the realms with my ascension, but there were lingering tempers everywhere, not to mention the sudden, abrupt surge to find female vampires. Already some of the more eager ones had journeyed to Earth and brought back several newly turned vampires. All women.

Jaxton and the rest of the team were currently working on stomping out *that* idea. Anyone who did something like that would be found guilty of breaking the law. It had only taken four public killings to get the point home. There would be no purposeful killing of humans just to bring women to Madrigal. It would happen naturally, over time.

I still wasn't quite sure how *that* would work. The idea of converting humans didn't sit well with me, but Aaron assured me it wouldn't matter. We could never eliminate all the vampires who refused to submit to proper rule, and they would go on converting new humans, many of whom would come to Madrigal to live.

The only difference would be that now many

of the women would come with, instead of being killed on the spot. I didn't like the idea of rogue vampires wandering around freely, but apparently, that was a fact of life I had to accept. Once things were calmed down within Madrigal and its various power factions, I intended to send Jaxton and the team to Earth, with the mission to bring down every vampire they could who converted a human against their will.

Right now, though, politics were the farthest thing from my mind. I was focused on one thing, and one thing only.

My mother.

As we approached the doors, the nearest guards reached out and pulled them open for us, revealing the misty grayness of a dimensional portal.

"After you," Aaron gestured with gracious chivalry, "My Queen."

"Thank you," I said with a fierce eye roll. "My *Consort.*"

Aaron shuddered. "I hate that term."

I just glared at him.

"Yours is real, though!" he protested. "You are the queen. It's my duty to call you that."

"And as the queen, I created the office of the Consort. Which means it's real now, too. And therefore *my duty* to call you that. At all times. In front of as many people as possible."

At least one of the guards lining the hallway snickered.

Aaron's head whipped around, but they were all staring straight ahead, still as statues.

"Oh, knock it off, My Consort," I repeated in a loud voice. "You're the one acting like you've got a stick up your bum. It's a nice butt, though."

Multiple audible chuckles were heard this time.

"You undermine my authority," Aaron complained.

I looked him straight in the eyes. "I *am* the auth-or-i-tay," I mimicked, drawing laughter from everyone, including Aaron. "Now, come on, we've got places to be."

Joining hands, we stepped into the gray mist. Behind us, the guards waited for our return, their weapons ready if something else came through the open portal.

Aaron and I stepped out onto the plains of the Direen. Looking around, we oriented ourselves with the giant gates in the distance and began jogging toward them while we waited for Vir to come and transport us to his safe house somewhere under the ground.

"It's going to be fine," Aaron assured me. "Trust me."

"I do trust you," I said, grabbing his hand again and squeezing it hard. "But you can't know that.

None of us can. This is all new. Nobody has ever spent two decades on these pills. Since we never found out what Elenia did to the maker of them either, we can't slowly wean her off. She's going to come off her high in the next few hours and be faced with reality. A reality she won't recognize."

"Your mother is strong," Aaron said. "To do what she did for so long, to protect you. That takes strength. Don't sell her short."

He had a valid point there.

Eventually, Vir appeared in front of us. We exchanged pleasantries, but the god could see that my mind was elsewhere, and he wasted no time taking us down to his shelter, where he'd kept my mom since bringing her there for safety.

As usual, we appeared in the middle of the underground chamber on a circular platform with three bridges leading over a stream that circled the arrival platform. Vir pointed to the bridge leading to the sleeping quarters.

"I put her in the bed," he explained. "Dani and I have been staying in Shuldar and traveling back."

"Thanks," I said, hurrying over the arched walkway and around the edge of the stone wall to where the bed was sheltered from view.

Vir hung back and went elsewhere while Aaron paused to give me some time and space. He was within view, so if I needed him, he could see it and be there. But otherwise, he gave my father and me some privacy.

"How is she?" I asked, observing her form.

"She's fine," my dad assured me. "Her next dosage was due thirty minutes ago. I would assume that in the next few hours, she'll start to come around. In whatever manner that means."

"Yeah," I said, crouching next to the bed, watching my mother stare aimlessly at the ceiling.

She didn't respond, but I was used to that. It was the normal.

"I'm here, Mom," I whispered. "I don't know if you can hear me in there or not, or what it's like, but I'm here. Dad's here. We're ready. And it's safe now, Mom. You did it. You kept me safe long enough. Now, I can do the same for you. You can come out."

There was no reaction to my words. I hadn't expected there to be. Sitting back on my haunches, I waited patiently. Five minutes went by, then half an hour. At the two-hour mark, I got up to work my leg muscles, but I never left the room. My dad stayed seated the entire time.

At the three-hour mark, she started to stir, but there was still no more recognition in her face than before.

"Come on, Mom," I urged. "You can do this. I know you can."

Her eyes blinked at the sound of my voice, and

with aching slowness, she turned her head to look at me.

"J—Joanna," she whispered. "My sweet Jo."

I trembled, shaking at hearing her words. All my life, I'd waited for that. The outburst that had started all this didn't count. This, *this* was my mother. My mom. She was still in there after all.

"Marie," my dad said, coming to the side of the bed. "Here, take a sip of this."

I stayed silent while he took the bottle of water and tilted a tiny trickle into her mouth, giving her time to swallow it. With each passing minute, she became more alert.

"Why am I awake?" she asked when she was ready to speak again. "Ron, where are my pills?"

"They stopped coming," he said, stroking her face.

I blinked tears from my eyes as I watched their love rekindle before my very eyes. It was as if no time at all had passed between them.

"It's okay, Mom," I said, trying to stop her panic. "You don't need them anymore."

"Yes, I do," she said, her voice still hoarse. "I have to take them."

"Mom," I said forcefully. "You do not have to take them. The rule is gone, lifted. You don't have anything to worry about. She won't send anyone after you. And I'll be here to help you. I've gone through what you will. I know how to harness it, and," I said, looking at my father, "I know just the way to help you focus."

If my confused feelings for Aaron had helped me learn how to harness *my* inner demon, then the love my mom had for my father should make the task trivial.

"What? How?" my mom asked.

"Your daughter is strong-willed," Aaron said, interjecting at last. "She decided that change was necessary, so she went out and made that change."

"Change?" my mom repeated, confused. "What do you mean?"

"Your daughter now sits upon the throne of Madrigal," Aaron explained. "As queen of all vampires."

My mom's face turned to me, her mouth hanging open. "My dearest Jo," she whispered. "What happened?"

"Uh, well," I said, feeling sheepish and suddenly all of my not quite twenty-two years. "That's a long story, Mom. But I did it for you. For us. So we can be a family again."

My mom shook her head. "I've got a lot to get caught up on, it seems."

"And you will," I whispered, letting my father take both my and her hands into his own. "And now we can do just that. Together. As a family."

Tears glistened in her eyes. "A family," she

agreed.

CHAPTER FORTY-EIGHT

"Time for a little truth," I said, watching a shirtless, sweating Aaron lift another block of stone.

"What's that?" Dani replied from where she stood next to me, though her eyes were focused on an equally shirtless and sweaty Vir, who was carrying *two* blocks.

Show-off.

"A year ago, on the night of your Soulshift, did you *ever* in a million years picture us being where we are now? You, goddess of shifters, and me, queen of the vampires? Be honest."

Dani snorted violently. "Yeah, *right*. How could I ever have imagined that? Neither of us knew that either of those things existed!"

"You always thought there was some truth to the legends of the shifter gods. Fitting that you and your father brought that knowledge back."

"I guess," Dani said. "But can I be honest with you?"

"You'd better. If you think you can stop being my best friend now, I'll clock you one, goddess or no goddess."

"I'd pay to see that," Vir said immediately.

"I'll match his wager," Aaron chimed in.

We both turned from looking at one another to glare at both men.

"In your dreams," we said in unison.

The men moaned and groaned good-naturedly before going back to work, lifting the stones and hauling them out of the ground and back up the hill. Jaxton and Alexi continued to dig out more of the worked stone chunks, while farther up the hill, Dave and Pieter were busy working on assembling them.

"Now, what were you going to say?" I asked, impressed with the progress that had already been made rebuilding Drakul's castle, despite it lying in ruins for centuries.

"Just that, although I know what I am, I really don't *feel* like that's me," Dani confessed. "I'm just me, Dani, twenty-two and a half. I'm so young. Part of me feels like my life was robbed from me by giving me this power and responsibility."

"Me, *too*," I gushed, glad to be able to talk to freely in a way I couldn't when I was in my palace.

Although Aaron, his team, and I had made good progress instituting changes to the vampire realm and its inhabitants, many resisted. They *liked* the systems Elenia had put in place, mainly because they'd been able to game them to their advantage.

I was so sick and tired of it. Thankfully, as queen, I could undo much of the damage with a simple command. That created enemies, of course, and I had to watch what I said. The palace had ears.

"Like, sometimes I just want to get drunk and party all night," Dani said, caressing her stomach as she said it. I knew my friend well enough to know she was simply daydreaming.

"Can we?" I asked, brightening. "After the baby comes. We'll just dress up, go out in Kellar somewhere. Dance the night away. We can drink all we want and not have to worry about getting too drunk to get home. It'll be so much fun!"

"We totally should," Dani agreed. "I definitely don't want to lose my pulse on humanity. I don't intend to be some sort of recluse, only emerging once a century or something."

"Me neither. I've actually been trying to figure out some way to better integrate with humans. I was thinking of opening a club in Kellar, to be honest," I said. "Vampire-themed and the like, so we could move around in it freely, interact with humans, and just retain some of ourselves. Living entirely in a different realm is bad for our mental well-being."

"That sounds fun. I'd go there," Dani said. "We could wear some tight little outfits—"

"Some booby tops!" I added excitedly, watching the boys for their reaction. Well, *one* boy in particular.

"Rude," Dani said, sticking out her tongue while indicating her own less than filled-out shirt.

"You know what I mean," I said. "A push-up bra does wonders."

"Sounds just grand," my friend agreed.

"And we'll do it all without the nasty boys," I said. "Girls' night!"

"Girls' night!"

We laughed, and for the first time in months, I felt like our relationship was in the right place again. We'd been best friends since we were kids. I wasn't about to let myself lose Dani. Not now. Things had been so wild since her Soulshift and then mine. Our lives had changed drastically, and they would never return to normal.

But this new world didn't mean we couldn't be friends. If anything, I thought it would be better for us to stay close. Perhaps we could help bridge the gap between shifters and vampires. Build some sort of community out of it. Who knew?

Footsteps through the undergrowth announced someone's arrival. I glanced over my shoulder to see Fenrir emerge from the cave that led deep into Drakul's castle.

"How goes it in there?" I asked.

The two of them had been working on cleaning it from the inside while the others helped rebuild the structure so that the castle walls were slowly rising from the ground once more. It would be a long project, taking quite a while to complete. Most of the time, it would just be Fenrir and Drakul working on it, but we had come to visit, and Aaron didn't believe in not pitching in, and his team followed his lead. So, for today at least, there was help.

"Good," Fenrir said. "Slow, but good. It gives us something to do."

I looked at him, wondering if I should open my mouth and ask if my hunch was correct about what was going on with them.

No. Let them have this.

"I'm glad to hear it," I said, hoping he would get my full meaning.

If he did, he didn't even react to it. His eyes were focused up the slope, where a slow but steady stream of ancient, pre-cut rock was being unearthed and hauled up the hilltop to form the basis of the new castle.

"I'm going to stay here," Fenrir said at last.

"With Drakul. Where nobody will bother us."

"Sounds good," I said. I'd been wondering what he would do, given that he was still a hunted man. Erebus, and possibly even Odin, would want to see him back behind the bars of Mordathu's prison walls. I wasn't so sure that was the right option anymore, and I was determined to do my best to grant him this freedom.

"Is that your formal permission to stay, My Queen?"

I looked at Dani. "Is he talking to you or me?"

"I'm not the ruler of shifters," Dani said. "Just a goddess, apparently. So, he's most definitely talking to *you*."

"Well, in that case, yes, it is my permission and blessing," I said. "I will tell no one about where you've gone, and I hope that you can find some measure of the peace you seek."

"Thank you," Fenrir said, nodding his head respectfully. "I have found something I sought, though I wasn't aware of it at the time. But it's here, and this is where I'll stay."

"I understand," I said, my eyes searching the hill to where Aaron was making his way back down. "Better than you might think."

"Maybe you do," Fenrir agreed. "Maybe you do."

"I hope you—" I stopped, realizing he was gone, disappearing back into the castle.

"Hey, you, construction worker," I said as

Aaron came near. "Come over here."

"Can't, ma'am. Not on a union mandated break just yet," he said with a wink.

"I'll make sure your boss doesn't give you a hard time," I said, grinning as he approached.

"Good luck with that," he muttered slyly. "Real harsh taskmaster, that one."

"I'll show *you* harsh," I growled, leaping at him.

I'd forgotten he'd been working hard.

"Gotcha!" he crowed, his slippery, sweaty arms wrapping around my waist.

"Ew! No! Ack! Gross! Get off me. Ew. No, no more, I give. I yield! Ahhhhh!" I yelped, trying to squirm my way free.

It was no use. He had me firmly and tightly and was making the most of it.

"Now get over here," he growled, hauling me up a little higher on his waist so that he could kiss me.

I took it because I liked it, and I pouted when he broke away. "Not fair."

"You came at *me*," he pointed out. "This is all your fault."

"You're just doing this because you can get away with it."

"And?" he joked. "This is what you get for making me your *consort*. You do know that's the male version of a concubine, right?"

"Maybe," I said cryptically. "Your point?"

"That I've been slacking on my job duties," he murmured flirtatiously. "And I intend to rectify that very, *very* soon."

Dani snickered and moved away to give us some privacy.

"Is that a threat?" I whispered huskily.

Aaron shook his head. "A promise. Now meet me around the bend in the river in ten minutes."

"I can manage that," I said, biting my lip.

"Oh, and one last thing," he said as he pulled away from me.

"What's that?"

"Go for a dip first," he said straight-faced. "You're covered in sweat."

***

***

Thank you for reading Queen of Darkness. If you enjoyed it, please consider leaving a review so that others might enjoy the adventure as well.

Next Book: *A Throne of Skulls*

>>>*Click me to get a free scene with Dani's Soulshift*<<<

ARC Team Signup: *Riley@HighHousePress.com*

OTHER BOOKS
BY RILEY STORM

Thanks for checking out my other books!

Below you can find all my novels, divided up by series. The brackets indicate which of my worlds the series is written in. So dig in!

Soulbound Shifters (Soulbound Shifters #1)

The Wild Moon

As Darkness Falls

Fate Unbound

Blood & Fangs (Soulbound Shifters #2)

Soulbitten

Blood Letter

Queen of Darkness

Dragons of Mount Aterna (Five Peaks #1)

The Complete Box Set - Link

Includes:

A Mate to Treasure
A Mate to Believe In
A Mate to Protect
A Mate to Embrace

Dragons of Mount Teres (Five Peaks #2)

The Complete Box Set - Link

Includes:

In a Dragon's Mind

In a Dragon's Heart
In a Dragon's Dream
In a Dragon's Soul

Dragons of Mount Valen (Five Peaks #3)

Her Dragon Guardian
Her Dragon Lord
Her Dragon Soulmate
Her Dragon Outcast

Dragons of Mount Atrox (Five Peaks #4)

Dragon's True Mate
Dragons' Second Chance Romance
Dragon's Fake Wedding Date
Dragon's Devotion

Dragons of Mount Rixa (Five Peaks #5)

Dragon Claimed
Dragon Loved
Dragon Bound
Dragon Savior

Storm Dragons (Winterspell Academy)

The Complete Box Set - Link

Includes:

Stolen by the Dragon
Trapped by the Dragon
Dragon's Chosen Mate

High House Ursa (Plymouth Falls #1)

*Get the Complete Shifters of Plymouth
Falls 15-Book Box Set*

OR

Get the Five Book Bundle (Click Here)

Includes:

Bearing Secrets
Furever Loyal
Mated to the Enemy
Shifting Alliances
Blood Bearon

High House Canis (Plymouth Falls #2)

Get the Complete Shifters of Plymouth

Falls 15-Book Box Set

OR

Get the Five Book Bundle (Click Here)

Includes:

Savage Love

Blood Mate

Moonlight Bride

Shadow's Howl

Royal Alpha

High House Draconis (Plymouth Falls #3)

*Get the Complete Shifters of Plymouth
Falls 15-Book Box Set*

OR

Get the Five Book Bundle (Click Here)

Includes:

Fire Dragons Bride

Mated to the Water Dragon

Ice Dragon's Caress

Earth Dragon's Kiss

Claimed by the Dragon King

ABOUT THE AUTHOR

Riley Storm

Riley is one of those early morning people you love to hate, because she swears she doesn't need caffeine, even though the coffee-maker is connected to her smartphone. She lives in a three-story townhouse by the good graces of a tabby cat who rules the house, the couch, the table, well, basically everywhere. When she's not groveling for forgiveness for neglecting to pet her kitty enough, Riley is strapped into her writing chair coming up with crazy worlds where she can make her own decisions of when feeding time is and how much coffee can be drunk without her friends—of which she has three—holding yet another intervention that they threaten to post on the internet.

Find her on:

Riley Storm's Website
Riley Storm's Amazon Page
Riley Storm's Facebook Page